RUNNING WILD NOVELLA ANTHOLOGY
VOLUME 5, BOOK 1

EDITED BY PETER WRIGHT

CONTENTS

OTHER PEOPLE'S CHILDREN
By Riva Riley

Other People's Children	5
About the Author	73

CREVICES OF FROST
By Gabrielle Rupert

Manik	79
Magnetism	92
Cryomythology	101
Driveshaft	107
Broadcast	112
The Breaking of Ice	119
Ice Carvings	125
Spark	130
Gone; By(e)	141
Browbeat	147
Slip	153
Cold Case	160
Reject	165
Theodor & Michael	170
Family Gathering	175
Rumble	181
Still Life	187
Watercolor	192
Crisis	199
How These Things Go	204
Reclamation of Stone	209
About the Author	211

UNDERWATER EYES
By Brian Philip Katz

Underwater Eyes	215
About the Author	295
About Running Wild Press	297

Running Wild Novella Anthology, Volume 5, Book 1

Text Copyright © 2022 Held by each novella's author

All rights reserved.

Published in North America and Europe by Running Wild Press. Visit Running Wild Press at www.runningwildpress.com Educators, librarians, book clubs (as well as the eternally curious), go to www.runningwildpress.com for teaching tools.

ISBN (pbk) 978-1-955062-05-3

ISBN (ebook) 978-1-955062-49-7

OTHER PEOPLE'S CHILDREN
BY RIVA RILEY

To Rick Stanley and Gabby Salazar, who first introduced me to the Smoky mountains

It was a curious phenomenon that everyone in Batterby, the town nearest to Waukasee State Park, was obsessed with BMX; other than that, Jacob Adelman liked it well enough. He didn't love the biker boys racing through the woods all the time, and he didn't get much out of the sport itself, not to mention that the local competitions brought undesirable traffic and riffraff into town. Despite the occasional commotion, it was a charming enough place, small enough to have a soda fountain and a general store, but within a couple hours of a major airport. He had poured so much money into conservation efforts for the Smoky Mountains, and Waukasee was his greatest triumph; his efforts had saved over 200 species of native plants and at least five songbirds. He wanted to build his estate as close to the park as possible as a refuge from the murky bustle of his business in DC. Batterby was his best option, and Adelman was pleased to establish a small estate there.

Once he was living in the Smoky Mountains, Adelman could feel more ownership over Waukasee's beauty. Every morning he woke up to a symphony of birdsong, their songs swooping through the steep forests and down to the valley, where the Batterby's town center was clustered. The wildlife was truly a marvel and the birdwatching was top notch, almost tropical, but it was the profusion of plant life that really filled Adelman's lungs and had compelled him to cordon off as much as the Smoky Mountains as he could. Waukasee had four different growing zones, so many different habitats for plants in every color imaginable, little gemstones glittering in an emerald ocean. Waukasee's conservation area encompassed the ringed ridge of mountain surrounding the town and spread several mountains in all directions. The terrain was so steep that it was relatively safe from intruders, and there were no crowds of campers or hikers to accommodate. The sheer brutality of the mountains helped keep thousands of species safe, and Adelman admired that. Adelman wanted to fashion his little estate in the image of the nature that surrounded it, but his knowledge of the place was intellectual more than practical, perhaps, and he was surprised that there were no established landscapers who used native plants. This seemed liked a perfect opportunity to engage the locals, and Adelman figured that this would be the perfect opportunity to engage impressionable youngsters with the stunning, sacred nature that surrounded them.

    He contacted the school district and asked his housekeeper to post signs at the BMX park and arcade offering small sums of money for local plants with their roots intact for his garden. Adelman wanted to plant patches of local vegetation to show off to the donors who might visit and emphasized that only common plants should be taken. To his initial disappointment, no one seemed to take him up on it, and he increased the bounty on each plant for another couple months. Finally, in the hazy heat of early June, he looked up from his morning coffee just in time to see a kid on a bike bloom into his backyard from the steep embankment falling off the forest, soaring a short way before landing in an elegant twirl on the back wheel that looked, frankly, physically impossible. He could only barely tell it was a girl, as she wore boys' clothes and her hair tied back, but the softness of her face gave her away, even as she commanded her bike with as much swagger as any cowboy on a bucking bronco. The bike finally completed its improbable rotation and it occurred to Adelman to wonder: Where on earth had she come from? There were no mountain bike trails on this part of his land. She finally hopped off her bike and started to saunter around to the front yard. She saw him watching her and froze.

    "Well, hello there," Adelman said from his front porch. She shrank down, clearly frightened. He stood up and gestured at the steep embankment that led up from his back yard. "Don't worry, I won't tell on you."

"I'm sorry, sir. Mr. Adelman? I've just, I've brought you some plants, and that was the quickest way here, and, I'm, just, sorry," she said.

"Well, that's okay! What have you brought me?" Adelman asked, striving to keep his voice warm and jolly so this poor child wouldn't look so scared of him.

"I've got three ramps," she said, showing him the wild leeks settlers coveted centuries ago. "I've also got two showy orchids, these were my favorite," she said of the white and purple fringed clamshell flowers, "and also an elephant ear bud. Here's what I have, if you'd like to check." She handed him a dirt-streaked but neatly itemized list with the number, type, and location of each plant. The root balls were all carefully encased in pieces of plastic or damp cloth and labelled clearly. She couldn't have been more than nine or ten years old, and the bags under her eyes looked incongruous on her childish face.

"Oh, my," Adelman said, his mouth arcing into a smile. "Two baby's blanket orchids? That's impressive, and very good record-keeping. I must owe you about forty dollars." He forgot the prices he had set, but that seemed about right.

"No sir, just thirty-three," she said with the same sincerity. He had no intention of turning the house upside down to find dollar bills.

"We'll call it a tip," he said, and he handed her two twenties. She stared at them.

"I've never had so much money," she said. She looked like she were worried it might burst into flames. She stowed it carefully in a wallet made, improbably, out of duct tape. She looked back up at him.

"Thank you," she said. "They should both be planted soon,

I reckon. If you know where you want them, I can get them in the ground. The orchids should go in shade."

"Do you know where these plants live?" Adelman asked her. She regarded him.

"Some of them," she said. "I wrote down where I found them all, though, so you'd know." She was sweating, beads gathering on her upper lip and trickling down her face. She looked exhausted, even though her expression was alert.

"You must be thirsty," he said. "Will you sit on the porch with me and have some lemonade while you advise me where to put these lovely plants?" The child hesitated. Adelman added, "My housekeeper Elena Beaker makes such delicious lemonade."

"Oh, Mrs. Beaker is here?" The child knew the housekeeper, and only when Elena popped out to say hello did she seem comfortable joining Adelman on one of the rocking chairs on the porch. She was right to be wary of a stranger, and Adelman approved her caution. It was so hard to teach those sorts of things to children – Adelman hadn't managed to teach his own son such practicalities. She introduced herself as Lisa Lowry, nine years old, and said please and thank you and gratefully drank a couple glasses of fresh lemonade.

"This is so much better than the powder. Thank you again," she said when they finished their run-through of all the plants. Adelman would have liked to invite her to stay and help him do the planting, but he had a conference call just before lunch.

"Go get some rest," he told her. "I could use some help in the garden, so if you'd like to earn some extra money, and your parents don't mind, why don't you come by tomorrow and help me?" He intended to hire a full-time gardener but hadn't gotten around to it yet. Something had compelled this child to work herself to exhaustion to make some money, and whatever it was, it was touching. Adelman's son had never had to work and would never have considered trading sweat for money.

"Yes sir, Mr. Adelman. I'd like that a lot," she said. Solemnly, she put out her hand. The gesture moved him, and Adelman shook her hand with a great deal of care.

"Very good, I'll see you tomorrow," he said.

That night he got a call on his landline (which Adelman hadn't realized was connected) from the local mechanic. He must have been a big, gruff man, from the sounds of him, and Adelman made pleasant chit-chat about the town while he enjoyed wondering what caused him to call.

"I'm glad you're settling in," the mechanic said. "We've all been mighty curious about your big house and whatnot. Anyway, I'm calling because my daughter, little scamp named Lisa, claims you gave her forty dollars for some plants?"

"Oh, yes, that," Adelman said. "I put up some fliers, did you see them?" The mechanic grunted that he had. "And little Lisa came to my house today with gorgeous specimens of my favorite plants. Ramps and orchids; it was astounding she found them. I had hoped to get the local kids interested in botany, but Lisa was the only one who brought me anything."

"Some of the others tried, but they couldn't tell one type from another," the mechanic said. "Lisa is real good in school, and she's got a good head on her shoulders, I just wanted to make sure... forty bucks is a lot of money for some plants."

"She brought me beautiful specimens," Adelman assured him. "I don't know how she found them. Maybe she's saving up for a Nintendo or something."

"Lisa doesn't play video games much," the mechanic said. "She said also that you'd be paying her to help garden?"

"Yes, I'm really keen on encouraging her interest in

botany," Adelman said patiently. "I won't have her if you're not comfortable, of course, I just thought it might be nice for her to get more experience with plant life."

"You'll be teaching her?" the mechanic said.

"Well, I hope so," Adelman said, more ruefully than he had planned.

"That's kind of you," the mechanic said. "She's smart and knows how to follow instructions and fix anything that moves, so you can put her to work in the garden."

"Okay then. I'm excited to hear what she has to say," Adelman said. It amazed him how easily the mechanic trusted him, and he suddenly saw the possibility in teaching a local child about the wonderment all around her. Not that you could trust any kid to listen, but maybe this would be different. He knew a lot more now than he did before. He knew which mistakes to avoid. And more, probably, than either of these things, he felt instinctively that Lisa deserved care and education. He hadn't ever had the chance to do right by a child, and he wasn't going to let this one go.

Adelman took his breakfast in the front room, and he realized he hadn't given Lisa a time to come. He figured he'd call the mechanic back after he finished with the paper, but just as he was getting up from his armchair, she burst out of the thick vegetation on her muddy bike. He could see the wild joy on her face as she flew, easing herself back down to earth as though she weren't subject to gravity like normal people. She handled the rusty old thing well, but god knows how she managed the terrain. It was only a matter of time before she took a tumble and broke her neck; the thought made Adelman's stomach swish his coffee most unpleasantly.

"Perfect timing!" he said, striving to keep his voice calm as he opened the door to let her in. This would never work if he lectured her right off the bat. She parked her bike carefully under the porch, which softened him a little. The last time his son had a bike, he threw it behind him heedlessly when he got bored of it.

"Ms. Beaker told my mom you finish your breakfast at 9:30," she said. "Thank you for having me."

"My pleasure! I thought we'd start with the orchids," he said, feeling a little uplifted that news of him was spreading through the town so quickly. He refocused on Lisa, wanting to figure out what she already knew, and her eyes opened and shone a little as she studied the plant he was holding. She told him that showy orchids preferred shade and recounted exactly where she found them. She followed him around to the backyard and immediately suggested a handsome stand of sycamore trees as appropriate shade. He grinned at her.

"You've got a good eye for design, too!" he said. She smiled shyly, and they went to the shed to grab the brand-new spades and trowels Adelman had ordered and never used. To his surprise, Lisa sunk a spade into dirt with a swift kick and hefted up to leave a tidy depression.

"You're really strong!" he said approvingly. She unwrapped the plant and covered its root ball in dirt. "Do you know why this orchid prefers shade?" He pressed, leaning on his spade. She hesitated, and he urged her to guess. She muttered that her guess was probably stupid, but he encouraged her and praised her patiently when she finally ventured an explanation. It was wrong, but well-reasoned, and he made sure to detail how clever it was. She was reticent and seemed a little suspicious at first, but by lunch he got her chatting fluently. She even smiled a couple of times. By the following week they were laughing through lunch and she had brought him a lovely, delicate sketch of an elm tree. He thought about posting it on the fridge, as was traditional, but it was so well done, and given so self-consciously, that he had Elena get it framed in town.

In mid-July, she brought a spray of Elf Hair, a stylish little wispy plant, and a map of where she had found a pink Lady Slipper, an orchid too rare to risk transplanting. She had spent a lot of time wandering the woods, and he was delighted when she told him about a stand of Pawpaws on his land. She described leaving her bike at the lip of a ravine and shimmying down to a little stream, in which she swam and waded half a mile before she arrived. It sounded wondrous, but he also gripped his pen so hard that his hand hurt when she recounted how she climbed up to her bike and rode three miles down the mountain through thick foliage back to town.

"My tires only hit the ground a few times," she told him with relish.

"I'll tell you what, that sounds like the most insane, amazing fun I've ever heard of," he said. "Add the pawpaws to your map of where you've found the plants, okay? But can I ask you to do something next time?"

"Of course, sir," she said easily. His pulse was beating through his temples. Once, he had told his son to wear his seatbelt when he borrowed his car, and his son literally spat in his face. He had wiped the string of spittle out of his eyebrows and lashed his son's leery teenage face three times. Obviously, that made things worse, and Adelman regretted it, but he hadn't been able to contain the rage that spiked inside him. He had a chance to do this right, and Lisa was a totally different kid: so much younger, so much kinder, and so much more like he had hoped.

"The way you pop out of my forest is just crazy cool," he said. 'Crazy cool' was a phrase she liked to use, and her dimples showed when he said it. "But, you know how adults worry, and I'm a little nervous about you riding around without a proper mountain bike helmet, and protective gear." He cleared his throat, studying her face, which was calm. "Before you go out again, could I please get you some? It would make me feel better as you go exploring."

"Oh, protective gear is a great idea," she said. "That's why I'm trying to earn money, so I can finally stop hiding the trail riding from my parents." He almost burst with her candor. She hadn't told her parents, but he had known for weeks, and more than that, she agreed with him! He was emboldened, but he berated himself to be calm and moderate, and not inspire the ugliness he had brought out in his son.

"We've got a good collaboration going," he told her. Her head tilted, and he explained what collaboration meant. She dutifully used it in a sentence, as she always did when he taught her a new word, and he proceeded, "Let me get you the gear, whatever kind you want, and you know, we should get you a proper mountain bike. Some ancient tree is going to snap yours eventually." Her eyes looked like gumballs. She almost tried to protest, although it was clear that she wanted it desperately, and he chuckled, so profoundly relieved he might have wilted in the summer heat if he stayed outdoors. He led her inside to the kitchen table and brought in his laptop so they could look at safety gear and mountain bikes online.

"If I have a mountain bike, I can fully rig this one for BMX," she told him. "I... I mean, I'm pretty good, but I'd be 10 times better if I could ratchet it up and tilt the seat and...." She went on a little. When they went to look at gear, she pointed immediately at whatever was the cheapest.

"Don't worry about the price," he told her. She looked at him like he had three heads. It snapped into his head that her family was obviously not well off if she was puttering around the forest on that ramshackle two-wheeler. "Think of this as indirect sponsorship for your BMX," he said. "And to make sure you can fill in as much of the map as possible. Now, pick the *best* gear, all right?" She pointed out that she was still growing and it didn't make sense to get the splashy stuff, which startled him – he had never known such a forward-thinking, smart child. They settled on reliable, high-safety rated equipment in the mid-range of price. He was able to convince her to get a higher-end mountain bike by pointing out that she could give it to a younger rider when she outgrew it. He found it very touching that appealing to her ability to be generous was what convinced her. Adelman put in the order, which would arrive in late the next week, and Lisa could barely contain her giddiness. He had the sense that she felt she was breaking the rules, and he went out of his way to assure her before he had to head to work. She mounted her bike on the porch and glided down the road to town. Adelman had thought it was a rickety old jalopy of a bike, but it always rode silently, all its mechanisms turning smoothly. He watched her disappear down his drive for a moment. She must be about his grandsons' age, if he was remembering correctly.

"That was a very kind thing to do, Mr. Adelman," Elena said from behind him. He started, surprised to hear her. She spoke so seldom, although her presence was not retiring. She was a tall, striking woman who always seemed to wear a focused expression. She didn't look intimidating, exactly, but Adelman had gleaned that she had some grown children and she looked like she could protect them.

"She deserves it, I reckon," Adelman said. Elena nodded.

"That child deserves the world, you know?" she said. By then, Adelman was determined to give it to her.

He started with that bike, a fine mountain bike for kids Lisa's height, but when the bike and safety gear arrived the following week, she sank to her knees, running her hands along the frame. She was murmuring, and Adelman only understood snippets. "Good tires," was one. "Suspension system," was the other, and "soup up the shocks" was the last. He peered over her, suddenly nervous; her assessment was so expert and obviously critical. She evaluated every part of it, every sprocket and seam, and finally she got to her feet. She looked solemn.

"It's the best thing I've ever had," she told him, and before his brain could adjust she threw her arms around him. He realized in retrospect that her tone all along had been reverent.

"Oh! Oh, I'm glad," he said. She was so small but there was real strength in her arms. It felt so unlike the smarmy, unctuous embraces his son used to put on when he wanted something, even though, whatever it was, it was never enough. Adelman hugged her back, staggered, and when she pulled away she was smiling, all impish dimples and shining eyes.

"I'm going to explore this entire ridge, I promise," she told him. "And I'm going to take my old bike down to my dad's shop and rig it up properly. Gosh, it's going to be amazing, I'm going to just kill it at the park tonight." She thanked him about a dozen times and, to Adelman's continued amazement, immediately got out the safety gear. She adjusted the new helmet and kitted herself happily in all the protective adornments. Adelman never saw her ride the trails without them again.

Her infectious joy lasted over a week, but something had changed when she brought him the first draft of their map along with a few rhododendron cuttings. The map was surprisingly extensive, not to mention pretty accurate, and Adelman put on his reading glasses to manage her tiny, neat labels. She had redrawn it from the dirt-streaked notes she usually carried. She looked tired again, and like she might even be a little sick.

Adelman had been away for a long weekend and felt dismayed at the change. Her forearms were crisscrossed with scratches from branches and the shadow on her face was a bruise.

"Did you spend all night in the woods," Adelman asked her. She turned away from him a little, looking at him sidelong.

"Not all night," she said. "I just needed to get out of the house for a while."

"Oh yeah? Why?" Adelman asked, striving to be gentle even though he had a strong innate negative feeling about a child roaming around in wild forest by herself at night. His son had been so senselessly angry all the time; Lisa, he could understand, and all he needed to do was show he understood her for her to listen to him.

"Well, it gives me some time to think and be by myself. I have to make sure my brother is okay most of the time," she said.

"How come?" he said. She shrugged.

"He's got muscular dystrophy. Anyway, I take care of him a lot, and I don't mind. He doesn't deserve to suffer like that."

"No, of course he doesn't," Adelman said in a hushed voice. "I'm sorry to hear that." This must have something to do with the way Elena spoke about her.

"It's okay," she said. She and Adelman set the cuttings up to root while Adelman explained how they spread themselves. She listened avidly, as usual, and asked questions and learned everything he had to teach her. Soon all the plants were anchored, and they turned in for lunch. His anxiety was still rankling over her roaming the woods by herself at night, and she could obviously tell.

"Are you mad that I worked on the map at night?" she asked as she nibbled nervously on a pickle. "I always bring a flashlight and I swear, nothing bad has ever happened, and..."

"I'm not mad, just a little nervous!" Adelman said. "I just

really don't want anything to happen to you. I know that sometimes, we just have to do something, get out of a situation, get time to yourself, and you deserve that. Just, you know you can always come here. We could even set up a room with botany stuff and a computer so you can work here." She stuttered over the idea of a computer; again, his world was shining too bright for her.

Determined to make good on his generosity, she turned his yard into something out of a fairytale, all fueled by a nine-year-old's gratitude. It was so lush and green it looked like a painting. She drew him a sweet, touching drawing of a mouse under a leaf amongst dewdrops and continued to absorb everything he told her. And, one August weekday simply too hot to be outside in daylight, she asked him shyly if he might like to come see her at a practice BMX exhibition in town that week. Her invitation was somewhere between an honor to him and a favor to her, and his obvious, immediate delight made her stand a little straighter as an earnest smile bloomed over her face. He immediately blocked the date out on his teleworking calendar. Infuriatingly, that was the day his conference call went late, and so he had to jump into his car and rush into town. He clicked in his dress shoes through the town square, which seemed unfathomably quaint, at least until he got to the bike park. He was just in time to see Lisa pop over the rim of a big dip on her dubious-looking bike, twirling as elegantly as any ballerina. Adelman's ex-wife had dragged him to more than his fair share of ballets, so he was in an authoritative position to admire this new kind of grace. He ran into the bike park just in time to see her glide back to the ground, transitioning from air to earth seamlessly as she coasted forward to the next jump. People were clapping for her, and Adelman applauded too. She launched up again, this time stretching herself out into open space and twirling her bike in some different kind of dance, and she landed that too. She alighted back onto flat ground just a few yards away, joining one of the groups of teenage boys hovering on the edge of the bike park. They were slapping her gently on the back. One of them handed her a water bottle that she heartily chugged from.

"Nice! I didn't land such a solid flare until I was 13, and with the double tailwhip!" one of the older boys said. Lisa was not only the only girl in the group, but she was the youngest and smallest.

"Lisa, that was astounding!" Adelman said. The boys froze. Lisa looked timid but pleased he had showed up after all. "You're not just good, you're amazing!"

"I didn't think you would make it," she said. "Mr. Adelman, this is my BMX crew." How absurd, but Adelman kept his face impassive.

"I'll bet you don't know too much about BMX," said the largest, greasiest boy, a really scraggly-looking punk, with a well-worn teenage sneer. Adelman felt his pulse quicken; funny how a triggered memory could kick at his heart. The punk was clearly their leader, but Lisa yanked on his sleeve angrily after he spoke in such a tone of voice. He looked a little chastened. Adelman's son would never have listened to reason like that.

"You're certainly right," Adelman said. He took a deep breath, reminding himself that their similar appearance was only a fluke, and this boy could be nothing like his son if Lisa were able to calm him down. "Would you explain those tricks to me?" The biker punk looked a little surprised. As another rider took their turn Adelman listened attentively, nodding and asking ingratiating questions. Lisa had taught him well, he realized with a wry smile, and the punk warmed to Adelman quickly. Adelman felt a surge of satisfaction that he knew how to relate to young people – if he could make friends with this motley assemblage, surely he was a natural. He realized he hadn't spoken to a teenage boy since his son left home for good, but he didn't have time to dwell on that because everyone started chiming in and Lisa was fielding their answers, proud, Adelman realized, that he had come there for her. The park lights came on, illuminating the bike park in stark light. A megaphone cried for Lisa to take her last turn – she leapt onto her bike and poised on the edge for a moment, looking back to make sure Adelman was watching. Then, he got to see her do a full run, blazing up and down walls and twirling and flipping and leaping on that scrappy bike.

"Show off!" Another 'crew' shouted at her, good-naturedly, it seemed, as she stood to the side with the exhibition staff, waiting for her score.

"Lisa's a BMX prodigy," the biker punk told him matter-of-factly.

"Sure seems like it," Adelman said. "What's the story with her bike?"

"Basically built it herself," the punk said. "She's a whiz mechanic too. Her parents couldn't afford a BMX bike in a million years but she managed that out of spare parts. It's held up all right, and she's won a few of the local youth tournaments. If her dad lets her, she's eligible to compete in qualifiers for the top division in this fall's competition."

"Why wouldn't he let her?" Adelman asked. The punk shifted.

"Well, her family can't afford regulation BMX safety gear, but we'd chip in and cover her whether she likes it or not. Really, the issue is that her dad doesn't really like BMX, thinks she's going to get hurt, and they have enough medical expenses as it is." Adelman winced – he could have added BMX safety gear to the order of her mountain biking stuff – but he smoothed his expression out as Lisa flew out of the arena and landed silently beside him.

"Well sir, what do you think?" she said.

"I think it's marvelous," Adelman said. "It must feel like flying." She smiled again, and Adelman spotted the gap in her smile where an adult tooth hadn't come in yet. He smiled back at her involuntarily.

"How long is the exhibition? Do you get another run?" he asked. She shook her head.

"Once Jared's run is done, we're through for the night," she said. Jared was the crew leader, the biker punk Adelman had been talking to. "The 18-25s get the park at eight-thirty."

"Gosh, watching you guys ride is crazy cool," he said, watching her eyes light up again, and he listened carefully to her commentary as Jared thrashed through the park. He had a much rougher style, but never fell. When he was done, and rejoined them, Adelman said to Lisa, "That was wonderful. Do you think I could take you and your crew for ice cream?"

"Well sir, I reckon we'd like that a lot," she said, actually laughing now. "Jared, what do you think?"

"My treat," Adelman said, to make it clear, and everyone seemed willing enough.

"So, what's it like being the new rich guy in town?" a younger punk said.

"I'm still trying to get my feet on the pedals, but I do like it here," said Adelman, and to his satisfaction, his stark honesty and attempt to reference BMX made them like him more. They led him to the soda fountain, parking their bikes in one of the town's ubiquitous bike racks, and he encouraged them to get extravagant sundaes or huge milkshakes. He got himself a root beer float, something he hadn't had since he couldn't remember when, and they cooled down in the air conditioning and gorged on ice cream. They told him about the town and gave him pointers about where to eat and which gas station's slushie machine was always broken, kid stuff like that. He also learned the terrifying fact that some of these hellions' bikes didn't have brakes, and by design. As far he could tell, Lisa was the only kid here who had ever used her bike for something other than BMX.

"Thank you so much for the ice cream, and for coming," Lisa said to Adelman in a private moment amongst the loud bantering of the others. "I'm going to have to go in about five minutes."

"Can your brother have ice cream? Would he like anything?" Adelman said. Lisa stared.

"You remembered Evan?" she said, and soon Adelman was slipping out of his seat for a moment to make a to-go order. He handed it to Lisa surreptitiously. Lisa looked at him gratefully as she got up. Her thankfulness lit him up from the inside out.

"Okay, team," Lisa said, interrupting the merriment and causing everyone else to groan loudly. "I have to go."

"You need to negotiate a later curfew, kid," one of the smallest punks said.

"I'm nine, so that'll be tough," Lisa said. Jared laughed at that. "Thanks so much, Mr. Adelman. See you all tomorrow night." They shouted good-bye far more loudly than was necessary. Adelman assumed he'd end up leaving soon himself, but the boys ended up drawing him in. He didn't understand everything they were talking about, but they relished the chance to show off their knowledge with lengthy explanations. He ended up sipping his float and basking in the youthful ambiance until the soda fountain closed at ten p.m.. When the owner came to shoo them away, they trooped out together, the boys shouting their thank-yous and looking over their shoulders at him curiously as he headed back to his car. He had to pass back through the square, and as he glanced into the bike park, he saw that the older kids didn't ride as deftly as Lisa. Whatever adjustments she had made to her bike must have propelled her to a different orbit.

It was easy to take an interest in BMX after that, and between botany, BMX, and the range of topics they found themselves discussing, Adelman's lessons with Lisa became the highlights of his weeks. He cleared with her parents and set up a savings account at the local bank for her, and she was dedicated to the map of his estate and kept making improvements and additions. By the time summer ended, they had a legitimate botanical map with a key and an index with photos and descriptions of soil, light, and water conditions in each locality. It was a marvel, and Adelman submitted it to his foundation and celebrated by throwing a little party at his estate for Lisa, her family, her BMX crew, and their families. Adelman lavished the best food and drink he could find in the area and it was beyond wonderful, all those people having a good time with him, and Lisa smiling and laughing and turning to him to readily to ask questions or tell stories about the map to others.

"She's a different kid. She's never been this confident before," the mechanic told him, a glass of champagne gripped awkwardly in his hand as he looked at his son, Lisa's handicapped brother, slumped in his wheelchair on the porch with Lisa's mother. His body was subtly and strangely misshapen but his eyes looked alert, like Lisa's. Adelman had tried to conceal his shock to learn that Evan was Lisa's older brother; he was Jared's age and half his size.

"She's a great kid," Adelman said. They sipped in silence for a while. Adelman could tell the mechanic didn't want to owe this debt, his daughter's happiness, but he loved his daughter too much to prioritize his pride. Still, the mechanic could deny Adelman his only spark of joy in a long while, and perhaps that bolt of desperate fear led him to confide, "You know, I never forgave myself when I lost my son." He saw the look of piteous grief on the mechanic's face, and he startled him further. "Oh, my boy isn't dead, at least as far as I know. I've got two grandsons I've only ever met twice. They live with their mother, or I hope they do, anyway. I don't know where any of them are."

"Oh," the mechanic said. He wasn't one for words, something Lisa had unknowingly let on, but he at looked stricken.

"So Lisa has helped fill that void, and she's the only thing that ever has," Adelman said. The mechanic grunted. A silence ensued; the mechanic would receive his confession, but there was nothing more to say.

"I wish I could stop her wasting her time with that BMX bullshit," he growled, glaring at his daughter chatting and laughing with the teenage boys. Adelman wished he could convey how, despite their looks, they took care of her like a little sister, but he knew the mechanic's futile frustration.

"One thing I learned from my son was that I was never able to stop him doing anything he put his mind to," Adelman said. "He almost died half a dozen times teaching me that, and over stupider bullshit than BMX. I reckon, let her participate in a few competitions, and she'll lose interest eventually." In Lisa's case, 'eventually' might mean in her seventies, but Adelman didn't stress the details. The mechanic grunted again. Adelman was starting to see why Lisa was drawn to him if all she heard from her dad was that guttural ineffectuality.

"You're right, and I hate it," he said with a surprising smirk, and caught off guard, Adelman laughed.

Just a couple of days later Adelman had worked out the details and gotten Lisa some proper BMX gear, and he went out to the garden to give her all the good news. He found her dutifully tending the Black-eyed Susans, pretty flowers with yellow petals that looked like miniature sunflowers. The school year was going to start the following week, and Adelman told her to take a break and come in for lemonade and cookies. He had some very exciting news – Adelman had talked her dad into submitting her for entrance into Batterby's annual BMX competition in October, and she shrieked and hugged him, promising Adelman that she would win for him. He glowed a little, recognizing how much he had come to legitimately enjoy watching her perform. After she calmed down, he continued,

"School starts soon, huh?" he asked her. She kicked her legs under her chair, one of her charming little quirks. He continued, "Do you still want to do botany then?"

"Oh, yes!" she said. "I haven't even shown you the pawpaws yet!"

"Well, good," Adelman said, his heart swelling. "But, I think we should get a full-time gardener when you go to school, the garden has gotten so big, and you put so much time into taking care of it. Do you have any thoughts?"

"Well, sir," she said, suddenly serious again. She was bolt upright in her chair, her legs no longer dangling. "I do have one idea. Jared's older brother Billy would be a great gardener – they have the biggest, prettiest garden in the city, and Billy manages the whole thing. He's the one that first taught me to identify plants."

"That sounds splendid!" Adelman said. Lisa hesitated.

"Well, the only thing is," Lisa said, "Billy is autistic. That's why he can't hold down a job, he can't stand being inside too long, and he's almost nonverbal, like he's not very good at talking to people. But he's really sweet, and works really well outside, and follows instructions and can read and write." Adelman felt it then, too – the chance to do something meaningful. The chance to be better than whatever he had been before. He seized it.

"It sounds like he'll do a great job," Adelman said, and Lisa emphatically agreed. She gave him the number to Jared's family home. Within a week, he had it set up. Jared's parents, who he had met at the party, were falling over themselves with appreciation, and Jared's brother did everything he was asked to do. He was bigger and stronger than little Lisa, and he kept her garden impeccable.

Of Lisa's BMX crew, which was now Adelman's sponsored crew, only the oldest and youngest, Jared and Lisa, qualified for the final rounds of the surprisingly prominent Batterby competition in October. Four other members crashed out early in the preliminary elimination rounds and came to watch with personal disappointment but admirable excitement for Lisa and Jared. Adelman had booked seats throughout the tournament in the Batterby BMX arena for Lisa and Jared's families, and himself, of course – he had all this money, he might as well use it – and both kids made good on it. Both Jared and Lisa snagged a place in the Park and Vert finals, and Lisa had a spot in the Street and Dirt finals as well, which meant she would be appearing in all four events. This itself caused a stir – there was no women's event at this competition, but Lisa was so good they simply had to let her compete in the top division, which consisted entirely of teenage and adult men. The Dirt competition was Adelman's favorite to watch. Dirt took place on an actual dirt surface, and he suspected that Lisa's relentless mountain biking habit might give her an edge. Vert was a long half pipe where riders ride back and forth, popping over the rims to do elaborate tricks, and Park took place in Batterby's own skate park, which Lisa had been riding every night that weather would allow since she was four years old. Street was similar to Park, but on a course without any quarter pipes or bowls; it was more technical, Adelman gathered. Ten players made it through to the finals of each competition, and Lisa was the youngest by several years. Now her name was booming around a packed open-air arena as she skimmed by on that crazy bike. Everyone was marveling at her and wondering what she was riding. Adelman's heart was bursting with pride, and the finals hadn't even started yet.

The Dirt competition really was another thing entirely, and The Dirt course finals were first. Lisa looked like an eagle as she twisted and flipped and soared over the course. Adelman cheered himself hoarse until the Dirt course competition's last round – a hush had descended in the stands. Lisa was the seventh player in the sequence and was ranked second, her first place score just bested by the rider before her. Adelman could see her determination all the way from the stands, even though she looked so small all the way at the end of the course. She tipped her bike forward down the long entry ramp, and then leapt it over the edge. 720 front flip handlebar spin; perfect landing, skimmed to the next jump, took off into the air, full flare rotation hands off the handlebars, and then the final ramp, a vertical take-off, spinning with a flip tail-whip and then the smoothest landing that Adelman had seen all day. The crowd, a surprising twenty-five hundred people all gathered in this tiny town for this obscure sport, were on their feet, thundering their admiration. She deserved it, and took the lead by seven points, which Adelman knew was essentially unbeatable. No one even came close, and when the last scores came in, the other riders scooped her up carried her to the winner's podium. It was hectic and wonderful, and Adelman streamed down with the crowd to congratulate her and bring her back to her family. Lisa spotted him first, and he turned with just enough time to brace himself before she launched herself into his arms. He twirled them around with her momentum. Later, that was the picture that would appear in the local paper, him beaming and Lisa smiling so wide her dimples were deep and her stub of a new tooth was visible.

It wasn't all rosy, of course. Nothing ever was. Lisa won silver in Vert (Jared managed bronze) and bronze in Park, which were disappointing after her big win, and she crashed out for all three runs in Street. He absolutely loathed watching her wipe out: she was so small and the force of the falls seemed so punishing, like the ground was hitting her harder than the other riders. Every time she vaulted back to her feet, but she was barely holding back tears when she found him, and he crouched in the stadium and tenderly took her hands.

"I can't let my parents see me cry," she told him. He had a carefully prepared pep talk that emphasized how hard she had worked and how amazing it was to rank so highly in a competition meant for accomplished adults. He didn't emphasize how incredible it was that she had bested so many full-grown men, as she didn't seem to be fazed that she was the only girl competing, and Adelman wanted her to be nonchalant for as long as possible. She was starting to calm down, and Adelman noticed the blooming bruises on her arms as his pep talk wound down. She was composed by then; she believed him, he realized.

"Win some, lose some," her dad greeted her when they came up into the stands to greet her family. "You gave it a shot."

"I sure did," she said almost airily. Adelman was fascinated and a little troubled to see this difference in demeanor. "Next time I'll get it."

"You okay, sis?" Evan asked, reaching his feeble hands toward her hurts. He was wearing all the medals she had won.

"Yup," she said. "Next time I'll get you the fourth, I promise." They started the arduous process of mobilizing her brother's wheelchair and heading to the accessible exit. She was limping; she must be aching all over, Adelman realized.

She was right, though – she did get it the next time. She cleaned up on the local circuit all autumn, all while bringing home straight As and roaming the woods like a wild thing. She often hung around Adelman's house, sometimes with Jared, who had turned sixteen and promptly gotten a driver's license so he could drop off and pick up his brother. Adelman was skeptical, but Jared was a fastidiously careful driver. To Adelman's delight, he found that Jared had hundreds of car questions and listened carefully to Adelman's answers; one day he even took the boy to the local racetrack to take his sportscar for a spin. He had never let his son drive the racer, a fact his son never stopped hounding on, but Adelman could see the crazed look in his son's eyes whenever he tried to wheedle his way behind the wheel. He had totaled three cars by the time he left home. Looking at Jared, though, Adelman wasn't worried at all. He tossed him the keys and got into the passenger seat with a sort of liberated, fatherly pride.

Jared was almost delirious with excitement, although he drove so cautiously that Adelman had to urge him to give the racecar its head and really zoom. After, Adelman took him to dinner, their conversation easy and avid, and Jared hung around even more after that.

Adelman even managed to have a serious, man-to-man about Jared's grades and plans for college one evening. Jared was a mediocre student, but Adelman promised him a trip to a big BMX competition in Florida if he did well. He was making a real difference in Batterby, he realized one day. Lisa was in her room typing an essay on the computer and Jared was helping one of the younger BMXers build a model of a dam for a school assignment. Adelman focused on his work in the periphery, sorting through some old spreadsheets until Lisa asked for his help with math. She had been promoted to the year above for math, something Adelman was particularly pleased about, and he put out a bowl of M&Ms for the kids before sitting down to explain the simple equations to her.

Adelman didn't realize how late it had gotten until his doorbell rang – he ignored it at first but remembered that Elena had already gone home. He hurried to the door to find Lisa's mother smiling wanly at him.

"Just come to fetch our girl," she said. "She was supposed to be home for dinner, I hope she wasn't an imposition?"

"Oh, no! I'm sorry, I didn't know," Adelman said. "She's just been reading, come in, won't you?" She shuffled in. They could hear the boys bantering in the kitchen.

"Evan feels bad that she's here so much," Mrs. Lowry said. For a moment, Adelman thought she was trying to make him feel guilty. Really, though, she just looked tired. "I know it's hard for her to constantly be on call for him. We're applying for Medicaid for a caretaker, but he doesn't want one. He wants his sister. He knows... we know it's not fair, and it's not Lisa's fault for pulling away. She just never says anything! I just wish she'd say something."

"I'm sorry," Adelman said, softly and humbly, and for the first time in a while, with genuine empathy. He rarely thought of himself as a parent, even though his son haunted his thoughts and his house was full of laughing children.

"It's not your fault. She's lucky as anything you came here and took a shine to her. God knows, we can never give her the time she deserves. And, and if I'd have known how much that BMX meant to her, I'd have talked to my husband about letting her compete, but every time he said no she just went blank and walked away. I didn't know how little we knew her. It seemed so insane, that we could raise her and she'd live in our house and we would know nothing about her inner life."

"All parents feel that way, please, trust me," Adelman said.

"I do," Lisa's mom said, finally looking at him.

Christmas came and went. Adelman spent the holiday alone, although the Lowrys and Jared's family came over for New Year's. Lisa had brought him five drawings of ferns, their current plant of interest, and indulged in a brief, furious rant about how much she hated visiting her relatives. Her cousins never wanted to do activities that Evan could participate in, and so her mom was either mad at her for not spending enough time with Evan or for ignoring her cousins. After a couple of minutes, she calmed herself, although Adelman assured her that everyone is cursed with family in some sense. That made her smile – after her fight with her mom, she wasn't allowed to complain about her cousins to her parents anymore – and she returned to her family, as serene as they had ever seen her. By the end of winter, though, she was feeling so cooped up she told Adelman one afternoon she felt like she could crawl out of her skin if she had to spend another evening stuck at home. Adelman brought her to the indoor BMX park a half hour away so she could practice as much as possible, and she was massively excited to start competing again in the spring. She won so many events a couple of websites requested interviews, and in June, after school ended, Adelman took Lisa, Jared, and Lisa's mom to a major competition in Orlando. He had wanted to bring the whole Lowry family and take them to Disney World after, but Evan wasn't able to travel, and his caretaker only worked the day shift.

Lisa did Batterby proud, winning both the Dirt and Park competitions, and while Jared ranked in the top five for one of his events, no one came to take his picture. Adelman noticed that, curiously, Jared never got jealous of Lisa's success. He finally asked him, and Jared shrugged.

"I taught her how to ride, you know," he said with a grin. "How could I be mad that she's so good?" Adelman clapped him on the shoulder, unable to express how much he respected that sentiment. Jared didn't know it, but Adelman set aside a trust for his college education that evening. Adelman knew he had to be careful – these were proud people, after all – but there was no reason to let his life's work go to waste.

They returned from Orlando tan and bearing a full suitcase of gifts and souvenirs for the BMX crew and Lisa's and Jared's brothers. Lisa had never left the Smoky Mountains before, and she described the ocean to everyone she ran into. Elena chucked about it to Adelman over his breakfast; Adelman's heart was melting but he managed to contain himself to a small smile.

Summer rolled out for them all like a dream. Lisa spent every morning Adelman had free working with him in the garden; he started giving her little math problems and puzzles to do while they worked to keep her sharp. She spent her evenings on BMX, flipping and twisting and flipping into the sunset. She also stepped up, Adelman noticed with a pang of pride, to help with the kiddie clinics.

"You have to be 10 to help with the little kids," she told Adelman importantly.

"You're so good, do you know that?" he told her. Adelman would never admit how pleased he was about this, but in July, the Lowry's air conditioning broke, and Lisa and her brother spent most days at his place while it was fixed. Jared would drive Lisa, her brother, and his own brother up in the mornings before heading off to his summer job at a local theme park. Adelman had put a lot of thought into Jared's summer and developed more formalized math homework for him. Jared made a face when Adelman handed him a textbook, but he said cheerfully enough,

"It's annoying, but you're right – I appreciate it." He and Adelman had figured out that he needed to improve his unimpressive math grade to qualify for admission to the state university, and he did every assignment on time, without fail. On the first of August, the local high school, which Adelman could see was really trying its best, let him re-take the math final. He got a 97% and bumped his grade up from a B- to an A.

"Now we're talking!" Adelman told him, giving him a hearty handshake, and to his surprise, Jared threw his other arm around Adelman's shoulders.

"I *am* going to get into State U," he said. Adelman started thinking about helping prepare his college application; it was going to be a much more intricate process for Lisa, who would be applying to loads of competitive places, but even Jared's would require some time and planning. Adelman peeked on the university website to see if he might have contacts who could make a difference. He had been doing some light scheming all summer, while whooping and cheering through BMX tournaments, including a pretty major one in Tennessee, and had a plan in place for Jared by the time school started. Meanwhile, Lisa was doing a little botany experiment in the backyard for fun, and Jared's brother had found a trio of orphaned kittens and was painstakingly rearing them in the shed. When their eyes opened and they could toddle around, Jared brought them inside to show Adelman and, Adelman realized, mutely plead for their asylum. It was the first time Billy had ever stepped foot inside Adelman's house, and he cradled the tiny kittens in his arms with the most poignantly beseeching expression Adelman had ever seen. He was a handsome kid, Billy, and Adelman had never noticed before. Adelman had never kept cats, but there could be no question that these would live with him.

The kittens became a part of Adelman's ever-growing brood and Lisa loved them, of course, giggling so sweetly when she dangled a ribbon for the boisterous tom kitten on the porch. Billy came in every so often to visit them and Jared was touched at this development, almost as happy as he had been to learn that Adelman was arranging a future for him. Adelman sat in the rocking chair with some spreadsheets on his laptop one afternoon, Lisa and a few of the BMX boys letting the kittens climb all over them while Jared worked through algebra in the chair beside him. This was not how he had imagined his sixties; he had never thought he would achieve a life like this.

In September's last week of summer heat, when the house was quiet with all the kids at school, he had his feet up in luxurious air conditioning and was reading a book with a gangly gray cat snoozing on his lap. Elena was also reading in the room with him. Adelman thought about getting a dog. Lisa and the other kids would be ecstatic, and it would be lovely to have a good-natured retriever or spaniel keeping him company alongside the cats as he worked. He was about to ask Elena what she thought when the phone rang. He and Elena shared a puzzled look – the only other time they could remember the landline ringing was when Lisa's dad called for the first time over a year ago.

"Hello," Adelman asked with genuine curiosity.

"Hello, this is the New Mexico Department of Child Protective Services. I'm looking for Jacob Adelman."

"Speaking," Adelman said, his heart pounding; it seemed to realize what was happening before his brain did.

"Sir, your name and information were given in relation to your grandsons, Chad and Benjamin Adelman. Can you confirm their relation to them?" Now his head was pounding, too.

"Yes," he managed to say. "I can confirm." He had no idea how the woman speaking could be so calm and even while describing how the children had been found locked inside a small apartment; their mother arrested on drug charges. Adelman assumed that his daughter-in-law had been desperate to keep the children out of foster care, as she had given child services Adelman's name and everything she knew about him. It had taken them a couple days to find him, but he could hear relief creeping into the woman's voice as he confirmed that he could take the children in, that he could provide for them, and that he could come pick them up as soon as possible.

"Outcomes for children tend to be much better when they can be placed with a relative, so this is great news," she said. She said a lot more things, including something about a child psychologist, and Adelman wrote it all down because his mind was spinning too fast to remember it. This was it, his last chance, perhaps, to redeem his own bloodline. He was stunned into answering the social worker honesty – he had only met the boys twice, and doubted if they would remember him, especially the younger one, Benjamin.

"Where is my son? The boys' father?" he asked the social worker when she was getting ready to the end the call.

"I'm afraid I don't know, exactly. The boys' mother said he's in prison," the social worker said. Adelman had no more questions, and the call ended. He looked up at Elena, who had been following the conversation.

"I need plane tickets," he said hoarsely. "And everything

necessary to care for two traumatized boys ages eight and eleven."

Retrieving the boys was a grueling, painful nightmare. The younger one, Benjamin, burst into tears at the sight of him and wept for his mother the whole plane ride home, except for the couple hours he fell into a fitful doze. The other one looked him right in the face and snarled,

"My dad told me all about you, and you can't make me do anything."

"I'm sure you're right. You know, I couldn't make your father do anything, either," Adelman replied. Unlike the Batterby boys, his honesty did not disarm this child. He had had extensive consultations with a child psychologist and fretted over sending the boys to school or offering them a home tutor for the first few months; he had a tutor on their way to his house for the boys and had mobilized everyone he knew in town. He had gathered up his whole BMX crew and divulged this personal, devastating thing to them, imploring them to help his grandsons, and thinking of how they would help him was his only comfort as he had to coax his furious older grandson off the plane. The flight attendant was starting to dial for the air marshal before Chad got sullenly to his feet. Benjamin started wailing as they stepped off the plane.

"Shut up, okay! Just shut up!" Chad shouted at his little brother. Halfway through the jet bridge, Chad grabbed Benjamin by the back of the neck and hit him three times as hard as he could right on the chest. It was almost shocking in its sudden violence.

"Hey! Don't you ever do that again!" Adelman shouted, and before he could stop himself, he had grabbed Chad by the elbow and pulled him away from his brother with a hard jerk.

"My dad always said you'd hit us," Chad sneered.

"I'd rather shake you than let you hit him," Adelman said, knowing it must be the wrong thing to say but unable to hold his temper. "He's your little brother, you're supposed to protect him!"

"I never asked for him," Chad said. Adelman took a deep breath. The child psychologist had warned him about this sort of anger and horribleness; he couldn't take the bait and start to hate him. He turned away from Chad, denying him attention, as the child psychologist had prescribed, and knelt in front of Benjamin, who was crying silently now.

"I'm so sorry," Adelman said. "I'm so sorry about all of this. You don't deserve it. You don't deserve to leave your friends and your mom, and you sure deserve better than me and better than your brother." Adelman turned to look at Chad for a moment, and then back to Benjamin. "But I'll do everything I can to take care of you both, okay? You can cry all you need. Now, we're going to go to my car and drive to my house. It'll be a long car ride, but when we get there, you and your brother will have your own bedrooms and new bicycles. I have an ice cream cake for you in the freezer, how about that?" The social worker had tipped him off that the boys loved ice-cream cake.

"What flavor?" Chad asked.

"Half is mint chocolate-chip, and half is chocolate and strawberry," Adelman said, still looking at Benjamin.

"I need to go to the bathroom," Benjamin sniffed. He seemed to have recovered from his brother's assault pretty well. Adelman stopped by the men's room and brought them to a kiosk to pick out snacks for the drive home.

Adelman peeked into his rear-view mirror midway through the drive to see that both boys had fallen asleep. That was a blessing. They stirred as the terrain got more rugged and were wide awake by the time they pulled into Adelman's driveway.

"*This* is your house?" Benjamin asked in an awed voice.

"Dad told me you were rich," Chad snarled.

"Well, he was right," Adelman said. "Now, come on, let's get your things and go in." The boys only had one backpack each – Adelman found it shocking they were allowed to take so few things. He showed the boys upstairs to their rooms. Chad claimed the bigger one right away, but Benjamin was in fresh awe over the mountain view from his room. Adelman had gotten each boy a stuffed animal, listening to Lisa's counsel that too many toys might overwhelm them, and Benjamin cuddled his otter as he gazed into the forest.

"Here, you can have this," Chad said, wandering into the room. "I don't want it." He tossed his plush tiger on Benjamin's bed.

"Really? Cool!" Benjamin said. Adelman took them back downstairs and introduced them to Elena. When Benjamin saw her, he immediately burst into fresh tears. Adelman was dismayed at the backslide, but within minutes Elena was sitting on a chair rocking the younger boy while he blubbered. He had instinctively recognized a mother, apparently. Chad was standing coolly back.

"Having the chance to spend time with you boys is a special occasion, so how about a soda pop?" Adelman said. That got Chad's attention, and soon Chad was sitting at the kitchen table slurping down a Coke. Adelman would have to speak to him about table manners, but that could come later.

"You boys have been through a lot," Elena said, still cradling Benjamin. "Let me cook you some dinner. What would you like?"

"Mac and cheese," Chad said.

"Coming right up," Elena said, making him betray a glimmer of surprise. "And you, little man?"

"I like mac and cheese," Benjamin sniffled. "Can I have some ice cream cake?"

"After dinner, you can have a great big piece, does that sound good?" she said. Benjamin nodded. Adelman looked at Elena with the gratitude she deserved; she had agreed to come in for the evening, and Adelman knew what a lucky thing that was.

After dinner, Adelman showed them where the television was and introduced them to one of the cats, the brave tom who had finally come out of hiding. Benjamin was immediately delighted. He sat on the floor and scooched as close to the cat as it would allow.

"What's its name?" he asked.

"Lisa named him Luke," Adelman said.

"Luke is a good name," Benjamin said, and at hearing the name, Luke came purring into Benjamin's lap. He giggled, reminding Adelman of Lisa with a sharp twinge of affection.

"Who's Lisa?" Chad said, making an innocuous question seem aggressive.

"Lisa is about your age, she lives in town. She's interested in botany and studies some of the plants around here," Adelman said. "She's also the best BMX rider around."

"BMX? That's cool. But that's not for girls," Chad said.

"No reason it's not for girls," Adelman said as mildly as he could. "Lisa is better than all the men. Are you interested in trying it out?"

"I guess," Chad said at the same time Benjamin piped up that he wanted to try.

"Well, I got you both bikes. I'll take you to the BMX park in town tomorrow and Lisa and Jared, the BMX crew leader, will show you around, how does that sound?" Chad shrugged while Benjamin chirped his assent, carefully petting the cat, trying to figure out the cat's favorite spots. After the cat wandered off,

Benjamin went to bed willingly, at least once Adelman showed him where the master bedroom was in case he had a bad dream. He changed into the new pajamas Adelman had bought and even hugged Adelman good night. Chad, on the other hand, steadfastly refused to go to bed when Adelman came back down. He was angling for another fight, but Adelman said,

"I understand; it can be hard to sleep after a big change. Here's the remote to the TV, there's a Netflix account for you set up." Jared had warned him about parental controls and had set the TV up so that nothing inappropriate could be accessed. Chad was already rifling through the Netflix offerings. Adelman continued, "There are snacks in the kitchen, and pajamas for you upstairs. Is there anything else you need to be comfortable?"

"You could leave," Chad said, staring at the screen.

"Well, this is my house," Adelman said. "So, I will certainly not leave. I do have work to do in the study; you can find me there if you need anything." He left him then. God, this kid was making it easy to despise him. He went immediately to a video conference with the child psychologist he had on call. She listened sympathetically to him – he told her everything, even yanking Chad on the jet bridge– and told him he was doing well. She gave him some tips for Chad's behavior, which essentially boiled down to the original advice: Don't take the bait.

The next day Lisa and Jared came over after school, as planned. Adelman had already warned them about Chad, and he didn't disappoint. He jeered at them as they spoke gently to Benjamin about Batterby and BMX and he mocked their accents. When he called Lisa a hillbilly, Benjamin told him reproachfully not to be a bully. Chad growled, literally growled, and slapped at him wildly. He moved to hit him harder, but Jared moved between them before Adelman could react.

"Hey, hey, cool it!" Jared said.

"Don't tell me what to do!" Chad shrieked.

"Hey, hey, listen, you're a free man, but you should *never* hit someone weaker than you, let alone your own brother," Jared said in a soothing voice.

"What about you?" Chad said, and Jared caught his wrists before they could land.

"Well, you can try," Jared said. He kicked Chad's legs out from under him and let him smack the floor with his full weight. "But it might not end well for you."

"Chad is so mean," Benjamin said. "Can I go see the bikes?"

"What do you care? You can't even ride a bike, you stupid sissy," Chad said. He hadn't gotten up. His insult, more than the slap, brought Benjamin to the verge of tears.

"There's nothing wrong with that," Lisa said. "We can teach you how to ride a bike, if you want. Can we go down to town, sir?" She was a year older than Benjamin, but they were the same height, and his eyes lit up when he looked at her. Adelman felt so relieved.

"Of course. Come on boys, want to see your new bikes?" Adelman asked. Chad got to his feet and following them, grumbling ominously. Benjamin was too nervous to bring his bike down to the park, but he went to watch them, and he was borderline reverent when he saw Lisa take a turn on the course. The rest of the BMX crew had joined them, and they described the tricks everyone was trying to him and were generally making Benjamin feel included and even special. He was starting to laugh and ask questions, and he clapped when Lisa landed after a run. Chad, who had brought his bike, scoffed at her.

"You're still just a girl," he said.

"I don't think that was ever in question," she said without missing a beat. Adelman could have cried, she was so unaffected; she was doing him proud. She met his eye and he gave her a grateful nod.

"I'll bet I could do better on my first time ever," Chad boasted. Lisa was finally moved out of her calm.

"No! Wait, I don't think you're ready for this course yet. It's not for beginners!" She said, seizing his handlebars.

"Shut up," he told her, shoving her away as he pushed his bike over the rim into a steep curve. Adelman rushed to the edge. Somehow, Chad managed to stay on the bike through the sharp drop, but the ground then curved up steeply and he didn't adjust. His front tire jammed and he launched over the handlebars, catching the fall on the concrete slope headfirst. His body folded over and he flopped a couple of rotations back to the flat before thumping into stillness. Jared was on his bike and hurried over to him, riding the electric current of fear from the bystanders. Chad wasn't wearing a helmet and was a motionless heap on the concrete. Adelman hurried around the outside of the course, praying he was okay.

In some sense, he was. He got to his feet, cursing.

"You okay," Jared asked him. He glared and hobbled away, trying to find a way out of the basin. Jared rode alongside him, his jaw working. Adelman recognized the motion of someone struggling not to yell.

"Listen, park rules are strict – no one rides without a helmet, and it's stupid not to wear one." Jared said. "If it happens again, you'll be banned. You're lucky you're walking away from that crash – many don't after going headfirst."

"Also, if you ever disrespect anyone in the crew again, I won't be able to bring you back," Adelman said. "You owe Lisa an apology."

"Make me," he said. Adelman shrugged.

"I can't," Adelman said. "But I can't let you mistreat people I care about. Come on, let's go home."

"Aw, please, let us stay, I want to watch some more!" Benjamin pleaded.

"That's okay, you can stay as long as you like. Jared?" Adelman asked. Jared nodded.

"Of course, little buddy. I can bring you back to your grandpa's in an hour or so." Adelman mouthed his thank you as he met Chad at the ladder out of the course. He tried to offer his hand, but the boy jerked away. Jared carried his bike up but Chad refused to take it. Adelman had to slouch down to wheel the boy's bike back to his car.

That was how it went over the next couple of weeks. Benjamin had a couple of weeks with the tutor during the day and the BMX crew in the evening before he was clamoring to go to school. He would be in the same building as Lisa, and after discussing with the school and receiving reassurances from Lisa, Adelman had him enrolled so he could socialize (other than with his brother, which was a lot more abuse than socialization, in Adelman's estimation) but kept him working with the tutor as well. He was a little behind in school, understandably, given all the upheavals in his life, but he was young enough that it shouldn't hurt him in the long term. Lisa made his transition so smooth and pleasant, coordinating constantly with Adelman. She sat with him at lunch and spoke to the younger kids she knew, and soon he was sitting with his classmates and making friends with kids in his grade. He talked about Lisa all the time and became determined to learn to ride his bike. He went to the BMX park, safely under the wing of the BMX crew, and they took turns holding him upright and jogging alongside him as he got the hang of it. After the first few weeks, Adelman finally got Chad to go back to the park, and he spent the whole evening with his arms crossed over his chest. Benjamin barely looked at him, he was so focused on learning how to ride his bike. After an hour and half's solid effort, Jared let go of the handlebars and Benjamin started to ride on his own. The whole crew whooped and cheered as he rode the length of the park. When he successfully used the brakes and stopped his bike, shaken but proud, Jared scooped him up and they carried him around the park, cheering and chanting "Ben-ji! Ben-ji!". Lisa gave him a huge hug, which made him grin and blush.

"They'd do that for you, too, if you were respectful," Adelman said to Chad, hoping he sounded mild and not reproachful.

"I don't need them, I already know how to ride a bike," Chad said.

"You know what I mean," Adelman said. "You could enjoy your time here a lot more if you chose to, and I'm sure you're smart enough to realize that."

"I don't even know how long I'm going to spend here," Chad said. "No one will tell me anything! I mean, I'm betting it's going to be for a long time, until I'm old enough to leave on my own. Mom got caught dealing way too many times, and she can't always sleep her way out of it. I told her that." Chad spat bitterly onto the sidewalk. Adelman's head was spinning.

"That is a hard, horrible thing for you to go through. I'm sorry," Adelman said. Chad spat again.

"I never let Benjamin see. I don't think he knows," Chad said. "Dad always hated you so much, I don't know why Mom would send us here. I guess because you're rich."

"To be honest, I don't know," Adelman said. "I only met your mom once, and I never understood your dad. I'm sure he told you all the reasons he hates me so badly, and I could tell you all the reasons I should have hated him. But I never did – he was my son – even though he behaved in ways that make you look like a little angel."

Chad snorted.

"Yeah, not surprised," he said. Adelman took the whole crew to the soda fountain again to celebrate Benjamin's victory, and Chad went sullenly. At least he didn't say anything horrible, Adelman thought. As usual, he bought Evan's favorite sundae to go, and Lisa hugged him to say thank you and hugged Benjamin again in congratulations before she had to head home.

For two and half months everything teetered on, Benjamin blossoming and Chad limping moodily along. Lisa did wonders for Benjamin and took time away from her own training to help him at the BMX park, but she avoided Chad whenever possible. Adelman asked her to make more of an effort, but she hesitated and said frankly that the older boy's flights of violence scared her. He was only a year older but almost a foot taller and so much heavier that Adelman realized she was right to be nervous. Adelman could never ask her to feel unsafe, so he said he understood and made sure she wouldn't feel too guilty. Jared was willing to engage him politely, but once Chad's hackles raised for no apparent reason, he moved on. That left Adelman stuck with Chad and apart from Lisa, Jared, and his BMX crew. He felt awful for neglecting his protégés and, more than guilt, simply missed their affection and buoyant company.

So, although Chad resisted, he brought both of the boys to see Lisa ride in autumn's last competition and show her that he was rooting for her, and that he still cared as much as he had before. He whooped as she won in three out of four events and adorned her brother with all of her medals, as usual. Chad was staring at Evan, and a couple of times Adelman had to remind him that it was rude to stare. Evan was having a good day, and his arms were more mobile than usual and his voice was clear and strong. He and Lisa took a few pictures together and with their parents and the whole crew was in high spirits, with some of the other members winning medals in the youth events. Adelman had a pizza party planned at his place afterward, and his house was boisterous with the youngsters and their pleased parents. Benjamin was right at home, having adopted the nickname 'Benji' and gotten to know the BMX crew. Adelman had also invited a couple of his new friends from school, for good measure, so he had kids his own age to play with while he enjoyed being the favorite of the older kids.

All in all, it was still an idyllic evening, and the party went late because the parents were having so much fun mingling while the kids played. Lisa and her family left last, making sure to hug Benji and wave uncertainly at Chad as they went. Benji was tired and a little overexcited after, but he brushed his teeth and went to bed with his otter and tiger. Chad, on the other hand, was angry and argumentative again. He wouldn't go to bed and followed Adelman around as he did a little clean-up to make Elena's life easier the following day. He refused to help but called Lisa an 'arrogant bitch' trying to get a rise out of Adelman. Adelman gritted his teeth so many times his jaw started to hurt. At least Chad had an explanation for all this rage. He had so much rage and trauma all bottled up but was refusing to talk to the therapist Adelman took him to.

"You know I'm very fond of Lisa," Adelman said. "Why are you so upset about her?"

"Because she's a stupid, ugly... whore!" Chad's eyes were flinty and glinting from the cruelty. "She thinks she's so good because she can ride a fucking bike."

"Chad, what's this really about? The only reason you would speak this way is if something is bothering you because no kind, rational person would talk about Lisa like that, and I believe you're capable of understanding that," Adelman said.

"You know, you could get rid of me. Get me sent away somewhere else," Chad said. "Why don't you?"

"You have a home here for as long as this house stands," Adelman said. "I will do everything I can to make your life excellent. I wish I knew how to help you deal with these toxic feelings instead of you taking them out on others."

"You're a pussy," Chad said. Just then, Luke the tomcat wound around Adelman's ankles. Adelman picked him up.

"No, this is a pussy," Adelman said, feeling outrageously pleased with the cat's timing. Even Chad laughed in spite of himself.

"She's not better than me," Chad said. Adelman sighed.

"I mean, she's way better than you, but Chad, she's been riding a bike since before she could walk, there's no reason to..."

"No, I don't care about stupid BMX. I mean, she's not a better person than me. I've done more for my brother than she's ever done for hers," Chad said. Adelman considered him. Chad was being insufferable, but he actually cared about what he was saying.

"You've been a big brother in impossibly difficult circumstances," Adelman said. "I see what you're saying. The reason Benji is doing so well is because of the sacrifices you made, right?"

"Yeah, exactly!" Chad said.

"And you succeeded – he's going to be okay," Adelman said. "But we're both worried about you. I hope you kept enough of yourself left for you to be okay. Do you understand what I mean?"

"Kind of," he said.

"It's understandable that you feel so much anger and pain. But you don't need to be defined by it," Adelman said. "It'll take work, but you can move past this, if you choose to."

"I'm not ready to go to school," Chad said starkly. "I'm terrible in every subject. I haven't slept a full night since, well, maybe ever."

"You don't have to go to school yet," Adelman said. "I'll keep the tutor fulltime; you can learn here until you're ready. Are you ready to talk to the therapist? They can help you process experiences that no one your age should ever have gone through."

"Yeah. Maybe," Chad qualified. He hesitated. In a rush, he said, "I want a bearded dragon. They're easy lizards to take care of and Mom said I could have one if we got an apartment where it was allowed."

"You can get a bearded dragon," Adelman said. "You could get a Komodo dragon, if it would make you happy."

"I'm serious," Chad said.

"So am I!" Adelman said. "Well, okay, I guess we can't break the law. But if things calm down and you feel good enough to travel, I can take you to the island of Komodo where they actually live. How's that?"

"Huh," Chad said, regarding him. "Okay, deal. When can I get my bearded dragon?"

"Well, what do you need to take care of it?" he asked. Chad listed off all the equipment. Adelman was so happy to see him positively interested in anything.

"They'll have all that at the big pet shops, won't they? We can go to the one twenty minutes away tomorrow, no wait, on Tuesday, while Benji is at school. We can get all the equipment and pick one out. What do you say?"

"Yeah, all right," he said seriously, and he went upstairs to bed.

Adelman thought he had made a modicum of progress, and Chad was far less hostile than usual the following morning. It was a day off from school, and Lisa and her brother came over with Jared and his brother in the afternoon. They hadn't done that in a while, and Adelman struggled not to acknowledge how much he had hoped for their presence in his house. Billy sat on the porch, a compromise between inside and outside, and cuddled with the cats he had rescued. Adelman came out, enjoying how happy they all were to see him. Chad even came down at first; Lisa said hello, averting her eyes, and hurried past him to get into the house. Jared and Evan talked about a fantasy book series they were reading (Adelman had gotten Evan an e-reader designed for people who struggled to hold a book and turn pages) and gossiped about the kids in their year in school. Lisa and Benji worked on Lisa's botany experiment in the mudroom, which now lived fully up to its name. Chad went back up to his room for a while but must have gotten hungry. Adelman found him chugging orange juice from the carton and gnawing on a string cheese.

"There are more snacks in the great room, if you want to talk to the other kids," Adelman told him casually when he came out of his study. Adelman had asked him not to drink straight from the carton before, but he let it go.

"I don't want to hang out with those losers," Chad said.

"Suit yourself," Adelman said, and he went to check in on Lisa and Benji. They were just finishing up, and they washed their hands and entered the new data into Lisa's logbook. The teenagers and younger kids were all sprawled out on sofas, brightening the great room with their youthfulness. Chad wandered in, and Adelman saw everyone visibly tense. He wished they wouldn't do that, but he couldn't really blame them.

Chad didn't say anything at first, just came to stand strangely near their circle. He didn't sit, as they were, and didn't say anything, just generally unnerved everyone as they pretended not to notice.

"So, what's wrong with you?" he said abruptly to Evan. "I noticed the retard out there" – he jerked his thumb toward the porch where Billy was – "and you're all messed up. Is there something in the water in this place?"

"Hey!" Lisa said, suddenly on her feet, too. "Watch it!"

"Oh yeah? Or what?" Chad said. "Will he show me who's boss?" He flicked Evan on the nose.

"Chad!" Adelman cried.

"Don't you ever touch him again," Lisa said, her voice shaking. Evan was trying to smooth things over, being such a sport about things that Adelman ached for the dying boy, but the waters were impossibly choppy. It happened so fast Adelman couldn't possibly have stopped it.

"Or what?" Chase taunted again, flicking her brother on the ear. Lisa rushed forward and pushed him away from Evan, and that was all the invitation Chad needed. He punched her so hard she wiped out onto the floor. For a moment he had a wild, triumphant look on his face, but Jared and Benji had risen in simultaneous rage. Jared's punches were a lot stronger, and with a furious cry Benji kicked his fallen brother with all his strength right between the legs. Jared looked up at Adelman and for the first time since that fateful BMX exhibition over a year ago, Jared looked like his son. Veins were popping out of his head, his face was so red it glowed, and his eyes were on fire.

"I'll *kill* him if he ever touches her again," Jared said, seizing the moaning, curled-up Chad from the floor and throwing him at Adelman's feet with his young man's righteous strength. Chad bounced on the floor but didn't unfurl. He was clutching his crotch and cheek.

Evan was starting to tear up, speechless that his sister had taken a punch for him, and Adelman couldn't comfort him.

"I wish you'd have died that night!" Benji said to his brother, who twitched a little. Adelman had no idea what he was talking about. He was torn between Lisa, who still hadn't gotten up, and Chad, who was writhing below him. Jared was taking deep, protracted breaths as he knelt next to Lisa.

"I'm sorry," she groaned, holding her nose, seemingly unaware of her lip. Her blood was on his Persian rug. "I'm sorry, sir, you said not to take the bait, you said..."

"Don't be sorry," Jared said. "Don't be sorry. Come on, are you okay? Can you move your hands and feet?"

"Yeah, I don't think I'm that badly hurt," Lisa said wryly enough that Jared exhaled mightily with relief. Adelman felt like a vein of rot was growing in his gut. Lisa's nose was bleeding so much he couldn't see the rest of her face. "Come on, guys, we should go," Lisa said, starting to get to her feet. Jared steadied her and urged her to sit back on the ground. He wrapped his arms around her protectively, smoothing the blood-soaked bits of her hair out of her face.

"Honey, your lip is split pretty seriously," he said. Elena was there, crouching in front of her. "Your nose should be looked at, too," Elena said gently.

"Ugh! I'm sorry," Lisa said, gurgling through the blood. "I'm sorry, I just... he..."

"Don't, don't worry, sweetie. Come on, I'll take you to the clinic, okay?" Elena said. "Mr. Adelman? Is that...?"

"Yes, perfect. Thank you," Adelman said. He had thought he would take her, but of course. "Jared, can you take Benji with you, and stay with..."

"Yeah, yeah," Jared said, calming back to his usual self. He rubbed Lisa's back and started to help her to her feet.

"Come on, Benji, you'll stay with me, right?" Evan said through his tears, so kindly that Benji gave him a watery smile. Evan spoke just like Lisa did, Adelman realized, or maybe it was the other way around. Lisa probably learned to speak from Evan. Chad flailed against his feet and Adelman had to resist the urge to kick him. How could anyone be capable of such cruelty? Elena was gently pressing a cloth to Lisa's face, and the pressure was making her eyes water, the tears diluting the blood.

"I'm sorry," she said again as Elena took her from Jared and hugged her as they made their slow way out.

Adelman stood rooted to the spot, trying to spread himself over everything that was happening and succeeding only in maintaining his stillness. Jared wheeled out Evan and called gently to Billy as he got to the porch. Adelman had had a wheelchair ramp installed, and he heard it creak as the wheelchair passed over it. Then there was the thick vroom of Jared's car coughing to life, and finally the fading hum as it left.

"Chad," Adelman finally said. That was where he was, with Chad. With greater effort than he had ever exerted on his son, he said, "Can you talk now? Are you okay?"

"I'll kill him," Chad said, crying a little, though he didn't sound sad, exactly. "Just wait, I'm going to kill him."

"Chad, I can't let violence under my roof," Adelman said. He was straining as hard as he could to keep his voice neutral. Even so, it shook a little.

"Well, it's *Lisa* you should be mad at," Chad said, squirming a little as he tried to stand. Adelman stepped away from him. "She pushed me first! She started it. This is her fault!"

"Chad, you bullied her crippled brother. You must have some sense of personal responsibility," Adelman said. "You've suffered a great deal, but you are responsible for your actions. I'm disgusted with you." He saw Chad bare his teeth, but he whined in pain before he could retort. Adelman couldn't believe all his hard work in this town was going to flush away because of this despicable scene. More than that, he felt the full weight of failure. He could not help Chad; it was too much for him. He didn't know what he was doing, and his ineptitude had spilled Lisa's blood. He got his cell phone out and called the police.

"What are you doing?" Chad wheezed as Adelman dispassionately described what had happened to the police department. He was trying to get to his feet now; Adelman wondered if he should retreat to his study and lock the door. He stepped further away and requested a paramedic to make sure Chad was okay.

"I'm fine! Tell them I'm fine, tell them not to come!" Chad said, doing his best to scream. Adelman had met most of the local police force at BMX competitions, and they knew him and his relationship to the town well. They sounded calm and sympathetic and told Adelman they were on the way.

"You were right; I can't help you," Adelman said with great difficulty. Chad had his son's look on his face, even though he looked nothing like him. Benji had the same cowlick and stormy gray eyes, but Chad must have looked like his mother. Adelman couldn't quite remember her.

"This is not my fault!" Chad said. He bleated the same story to the two police officers who came to investigate. They weren't cruel to him, but their stony dislike was evident. Adelman recognized the older officer, Officer Johnson. He was a big, imposing man with stern features but kind eyes. The gossip around town was that he was next in line to become Sheriff. Adelman asked him for a private word and they stepped into his study. In a rush Adelman told the officer everything, the ongoing bad behavior, the advice from the psychologist, the trauma, trying to absolve himself with evidence of his effort and care.

"Little Lisa is asking not to press charges," Officer Johnson said to Adelman in a low voice. "But we can certainly talk her parents into it. It might do him good to spend some time in juvenile detention, let him see what's in store for him if he continues like this." Adelman had read some wrenching things about juvenile detention centers and had used every favor available to him to keep his son out of one. Maybe he shouldn't have – maybe some real cruelty would have scared his son into line – but Adelman didn't think that was how cruelty worked. For some reason, Adelman thought of his own father, such a patient, calm man. His father had counseled him to find tranquility in himself when things started to get bad with his boy. Adelman never thought his anger was that bad but he had tamed his temper anyhow and here he was with a monster of a grandson.

"What if I sent him to a special school, or treatment center for adolescents, something like that?" Adelman said. Chad was in the next room shrieking at the second police officer. Adelman's son used to scream bloody murder with a smug look on his face just to torture Adelman and his ex-wife when they wouldn't give him what he wanted. At least Chad a reason now, Adelman reminded himself, trying not to wish he could send Chad back to New Mexico. He had frequently wished he and his ex-wife had had kids earlier, gotten a better egg and a nicer sperm, but those thoughts never comforted him. "Like, a ward for troubled kids, kids who have trauma, that sort of thing? Do you have any recommendations?"

"Well sir, the people around here don't generally have enough money to consider that option. But I'll tell you what, the child psychologist you've been talking to should have some ideas, right?" Officer Johnson said. Adelman was grateful again for Lisa; she had introduced them at a competition last May, and the officer's leniency had almost certainly grown from their repeated interactions at BMX events where Adelman was playing the part of patron.

"Right," Adelman said, relief flooding over him. "Maybe just a few months, some intensive therapy and care. I just, I don't know how to help him. I just don't know what to do." He hadn't had the heart to send his son away at all, but he knew better than to try the same thing twice. The world would be a better place if he hadn't let his son rampage through it; there would be no traumatized, violent preteen terrorizing this little town. Adelman couldn't escape cosmic responsibility for the trouble Chad had caused, but he had tried so hard and had planted the seeds of some real redemption here. Whatever he did, he couldn't let his life in Batterby wither.

"Don't worry, sir. You've done the best anyone could with a losing hand," the officer said. "Little Benji is thriving, and that's a credit to you. I'll go talk to Chad again. I'll warn you, if he tries to strike either of us, I will have to bring him in."

"I understand," Adelman said. He followed the officer in.

"Listen, son. I said, listen!" The second police officer was saying as the first joined. They loomed over Chad, who was cowering in an armchair like a cornered cat and hissing in much the same way.

"You're in a lot of trouble," Officer Johnson said. "We're going to let your grandfather decide what to do with you, and you should be grateful he can do that. The next time we see you, you better be tipping your hat and saying 'Howdy.' Do you understand?" Chad made a face but didn't respond.

"You call us if he gives you any trouble," Officer Johnson said to Adelman, and then they left. Adelman sent a quick message to the child psychologist's urgent mailbox. He then went back to spend some reluctant time with Chad.

"I'm not scared of juvey," Chad said. "Go ahead, send me off."

"You're not going to juvey," Adelman said. "But you are going somewhere."

There it was. The crack in Chad's composure. He had merely been taunting him previously.

"What? You said I could always live with you!" Chad said, jumping to accusatory.

"Well, it was juvey or a treatment center of some kind. Juvey will just harden you further. We need to get you help, Chad, do you understand? You need to behave in ways that are appropriate and kind. Clearly, I wasn't capable of teaching you that. Hopefully, someone else will be. You'll come back, of course, after you've had some time to recover and think about everything."

"You're the *worst*," Chad said, and then darted off the armchair and up the stairs. Predictably, he slammed his door as hard as he could.

"Right back 'atcha," Adelman muttered, thinking about how to break the news to Benji and how he could ever ask Lisa to forgive him. Lisa deserved the world, like Adelman, Elena, and so many others in town had said. He had never felt fulfillment like he had since he met Lisa and Lisa deserved his help, even if he didn't deserve to ever feel peace. Chad was his son's responsibility and whatever mistakes he made, he did not turn his son into whatever it was he became. He would not let his son hurt Lisa, too.

. . .

That night, Jared's cheeks were ashen and his face clean but sweat-coated when he brought Benji home. Jared's eyes looked half-wild and half terribly resigned. He had slicked back his longish hair. He smiled at Benji, who looked just as haggard, and sent him to find Luke. Once the child left, Jared immediately spoke.

"Sir, I need to apologize. I shouldn't have punched your nephew. I understand if you can't associate with me anymore, but I hope this won't affect your sponsorship of the rest of the crew. All those kids depend on you, sir, and I promise, I won't ever..."

"Jared," Adelman said. His heart was breaking even more, though he had thought the pieces couldn't be ground down any finer. "Jared, of course I'm not upset with you, and gosh, I hope *you'll* associate with *me* again!"

"I've never lost my cool like that," Jared said. "Not when he pushed Lisa at the BMX park, not ever, with anyone. I don't know what came over me."

"Him punching Lisa was probably the kicker," Adelman said. "Listen, I'm sending him to a treatment facility. He's been having such a hard time and I just can't get through to him. I don't think being around his brother is helpful, I had thought it was, but, obviously..." Adelman sighed. Jared looked honored but overwhelmed at his admission, and Adelman stopped professing and just clapped Jared on the shoulder.

"I'll make this up to you all, I promise," Adelman said. The righteousness of his choice began to materialize. He couldn't subject his crew to such a malicious, violent force. Jared lightly grasped his hand, and after that small moment of affection, Adelman dismissed Jared and went in to deal with Benji. Benji had found Luke the tomcat and was coaxing him to play with one of his many toys. Luke was batting at the dangling feather, half-interested, as he watched Adelman come into the room.

"How are you, son?" Adelman asked Benji. Benji twitched. Adelman was used to using that endearment with the BMX boys, but hadn't yet with his grandsons.

"Fine," Benji said without looking him in the eye. "Jared promised me that Lisa would still be my friend. Do you think she will?"

"Yes," Adelman said heavily. "I'm sure she will. Benji, I have to ask. What happened that night? The night Chad almost died?"

"Nothing! I don't want to talk about it." Benji had gotten so stiff so suddenly that Luke bolted.

"Okay, that's okay. I'm, just worried about him. I..." Adelman couldn't backtrack fast enough.

"They almost killed him and I didn't help, I didn't do anything, I just stayed hidden under the bed like he said!" Benji cried, and with a crazed, high-pitched shriek, he punched himself in the forehead. Adelman grabbed his hands as quickly as he could and, for a crazed moment, had to restrain the frantic child. Their grappling pitched them both to the floor, and finally Benji went limp. His eyes looked glassy.

"Those gangsters came looking for dad," he said like every syllable caused him pain. "Chad threw the phone at me and told me to call the police and stay hidden, he told me he'd break my leg if I didn't. Mom told them Dad wasn't there, and then they must have hit her. She screamed, and Chad ran out and then he screamed, and then he was begging, and they kept hitting him. When the police came he wasn't screaming anymore. I didn't recognize him at the hospital. He didn't wake up for a whole week."

"Oh, son," Adelman whispered. Why on earth hadn't the social worker told him that? An angry bump was blooming on the boy's forehead, and Adelman pulled him into a hug. Benji pressed his face into Adelman's chest.

"I don't wish he had died," Benji cried into Adelman's shirt. "It's not his fault he's mean to me. He had to be. I didn't know any better."

"Oh, son," Adelman said again. "Oh, son. I'm so sorry. You poor boys. I'm sorry."

"I... I didn't want... I didn't know what to do," Benji sobbed.

"There was nothing you could have done," Adelman said. "Benji, son, there was nothing. You did the only thing you could have, do you understand?"

"Chad shouldn't have... but they would have found us, I heard them say my name," Benji choked. Adelman clutched him harder.

"Benji, please," was all Adelman could think to say at first. "Please, we're going to do everything we can, okay? The police were mad at Chad, but I convinced them not to send him to jail. He just has to spend some time at a special school, somewhere that will help him, all right?" Adelman smoothed the boy's hair and cupped his cheek. He looked so much like his father.

"How could he ever not be angry at me?" Benji whispered.

"So you're shipping me off, huh? Let those hillbilly losers gang up on me and then just ship me off?" Chad was in Adelman's face as much as he could be. He was going to be tall, like his father, and like Adelman himself, but he was only eleven.

"One of those 'hillbilly losers' was your own brother," Adelman said.

Chad sneered, showing all his teeth.

Adelman sighed. "You were right all along. You've suffered such terrible things, and I couldn't help you. I want to get you the help you need so you can learn to be happy. You're going to an inpatient facility for children who have suffered trauma."

"That's bullshit!" Chad said.

"Your psychologist and social worker have recommended a treatment center nearby," Adelman said. "Benji and I will visit as much as we can."

"We're supposed to go get my bearded dragon today. I want to bring my bearded dragon!" Chad slammed his fist on the table.

"I'm sorry, but you can't have pets there. We'll get your bearded dragon when you come home," Adelman said. Chad hurled the salt shaker at the wall, where it shattered. "We'll get you two bearded dragons, and a snake if you want one," he added.

"I don't want a fucking snake!" Chad said.

"Language, please," Adelman said.

"You faggot asshole piece of shit!" Chad screamed.

"Very mature," Adelman said before he could stop himself. He sighed again. "We're leaving tomorrow morning. Do you want Benji to come?" Chad's teeth were out again but his eyes were shining.

"I don't care that I'm grounded, I'm leaving!" Chad ran to the door. He stopped with his hand on the handle and turned to stare at Adelman.

"Maybe a walk will clear your head," Adelman said, and Chad screeched more curse words and slammed the door as hard as he could.

"It's not your fault," Elena said from behind him. Adelman felt his eyes prickling.

"I don't know what went wrong with his father," Adelman said. "My son, I don't know... I wasn't a perfect dad, I know that. I made mistakes, but I don't know why he turned out like he did. But I know what happened to Chad. This is all my son's fault."

"It's not *your* fault," Elena repeated. She made him a cup of tea and they sat in the kitchen together until Adelman was calmer. Only then did he rise to finish the paperwork for Chad's treatment plan. He tried to think of how he could make the night special, how he could show such a rage-blinded child how much he cared and how badly he felt. Perhaps his son's worst act was this reenacted history, the horrible brutality of it for Chad and Adelman alike. He brooded over that all morning, half-obsessing as he did his best to get his work in order (he was taking two days off to get Chad settled in the facility and comfort Benji) and wonder what else he could do for the Lowrys. He had paid Lisa's clinic bill and sent flowers. He had had a wrenching talk with Evan on the phone that still made him ache.

"It's not supposed to be like this," Evan had choked, through tears or his own failing muscles, Adelman couldn't tell. "It's not supposed to... older brothers aren't supposed to be like this." It was enough to make his anger at Chad surface, and he did his best to let it pass. The world was a messy, heart-shattering affair, and Adelman should have known that.

So, it should have been no surprise at what happened next, everything he loved and feared, the scene playing out of earshot in distorted colors. He meandered to the great room to gaze at his garden only to see Chad was whipping rocks at Billy. He didn't know why everything was in slow motion, but it was, and even though he was running, time was oozing. Billy was trying to shield his face and as Adelman burst into the yard, he could hear the strange, donkey-like "Haw!" as his cry for help. Billy was so much bigger and stronger than

Chad, but he didn't defend himself, not even when a shard slipped past his hand and left a gash on his cheek, a spurt of blood spraying in its wake. Chad was screaming something, but it was unintelligible at this distance. Adelman rushed off the porch, his legs dragging through the air as time slowed even further. There was a second scream, higher and clearer, and a clod of earth burst against Chad's head. Lisa, with her nose bandaged and her lip stitched, was standing on the side of the embankment, upright like a mountain-goat, and Adelman was drawing nearer, and he could hear her furious shout,

"You asshole piece of shit, don't you dare touch him! Come on, try to hit *me* again, I dare you!" Adelman had never heard Lisa curse before, but before he could recover, he realized that Chad was roaring as he grabbed his bike and surged up the embankment. Adelman hadn't realized Chad had paid any attention to his bike, but he had it on hand, as if he had planned to ride it. Maybe he had, and now Lisa muscled to the top with a strong kick, turned back one more time to shout at him, and launched into the forest the moment before his hand would have grabbed over her ponytail. Chad hesitated for a fraction of a second and then disappeared as he took off after her. Adelman was screaming too, but he couldn't tell what.

"Get in your car and get to the bottom of the mountain. Go! Now!" Elena was there with his keys. He lurched to his driveway and threw himself into his town car. He tore down the long, winding, sloped road from his house down into town, blasting the horn to warn other cars he was coming. Just as he rounded the last bend, he saw Lisa explode out of the canopy. Her face and body were tensed as she landed, her back-wheel crumpling from the impact, and she yanked the bike into a wide, sweeping arc, sparks screeching against the asphalt. An inch more and she would have hurtled off the side of the road into the river that snaked through town. Adelman jammed on his hazards and leapt out of the car.

"Lisa! Lisa, are you okay? Oh my god," he said as he careened toward where she had managed to stop herself. She had another deep cut on her left calf – it was dripping blood into her sock. She tried to step toward him, but both her legs buckled and she sank to her knees.

"I tried to keep him on the shallow slopes, the easy parts," she said, gasping through her words. "I tried, but he must have been practicing all this time and he was about to catch me so I had to leave the ridge and dive down the slope, and I think he followed me but I lost him there, the slope is brutal coming down..."

"Lisa Lowry, why on earth would you pull a stunt like that? You've trashed your nice mountain bike!" a stout older woman scolded. Adelman blinked. They had an audience – the general store was at the bend and everyone had come out to the porch.

"Lisa, that ridge is crazy goddamn dangerous, you know better than that!" The shopkeeper was starting to come down the steps to the road, along with one of Elena's relatives, Adelman believed. Lisa tried to get up, and in a fresh new emotional wound, Adelman realized she couldn't. Adelman scooped her up and carried her to the porch. She was trembling in his arms as he deposited her carefully onto one of the rocking chairs. People were murmuring and gathering around them. Elena's relative realized that Lisa was bleeding and applied pressure to the wound. Lisa squeaked in pain and grabbed blindly at her leg. Adelman winced, clutching his chest and hoping desperately that her legs weren't broken. They must have taken so many rough jolts on her way down the mountain.

"Chad followed me into the forest and was chasing me," she said, wheezing as she tried to catch her breath and speak at the same time.. "He was bullying Billy bad, really bad, like he was throwing rocks at him hard enough to really hurt. I provoked him so he would chase me instead, but he was faster than I thought and the only way to lose him was to come down the flank of the ridge. I don't know how I stayed on the bike, I was grinding over logs and any pile of mud should have thrown me off, but..." The sunlit green flashed by in streaks as she desperately piloted her bike and rode out the tidal wave of foliage. She ricocheted her tires off of trees to keep steady and at one point broke through the treetops, completely airborne, having no idea what launched her so high or how she was going to land in the tangled undergrowth. A couple of men fishing on the river saw her soar into the sky and arc back into the forest and thought they must be losing their minds. She managed to keep her fall parallel to the severe slope and the impact of the flight went mostly into punishing the moss.

"It was stupid lucky," was all she said right after, too shaken to appreciate her feat. "We need to send a search and rescue up the mountain, he must have fallen, I think I heard him scream but I couldn't stop, I was going too fast." People were already mobilizing. The shopkeeper was on the phone with emergency services and the fitter patrons were preparing for a long, arduous hike.

"We're going to find your boy," the shopkeeper said when he had finished the call. "And after that, I don't ever want to see him again."

"Oh, why," Adelman whispered. "Why was he attacking Billy? Why would he do that?"

"I don't know," Lisa said. "I just, I couldn't defend my brother but I had to defend Jared's, and I knew I could lose him on a bike, and I just, I had to." Her nose was bleeding again, and in a horrified rush Adelman realized that she hadn't had to defend Billy at all. She could have flown past both Billy and Chad on her bike and been at the house before Chad could stop her. But how could he blame her? She was just a kid watching her vulnerable, defenseless friend get cut up.

"Come on, I'm taking you back to the clinic," Elena's relative said. Adelman tried to move to do it himself, but he was rebuffed. "You have to get back to yours and be ready for whatever they find. That ridge is dangerous to hike down, let alone bike – they might find him in bits, you know." The shopkeeper lifted Lisa up and followed Elena's relative. Lisa looked back at Adelman, so clearly distraught, and Adelman called,

"Don't worry, I'll see you soon!" It was all he could think to say.

"Where's Chad?" Benji asked immediately when Jared dropped him off. Adelman had briefed Jared over text about what had happened, and it was a miracle of composure that Jared managed to calmly interrupt BMX to return Benji and seek out his own cowering, bleeding brother in the garden shed. Elena had been unable to coax him inside.

"We don't know," Adelman said heavily. "He... had an accident, we think." For an uplifting moment, it occurred to Adelman that Chad may have given up the chase and just decided to run away. But the hope sank as quickly as it arrived. Lisa remembered his scream. It had required supernatural skill for her to navigate such treacherous terrain, but Adelman wished she had been supernatural enough to stop her bike and check his damned grandson. Of course, Chad was a violent lunatic, so even if she could have stopped, she shouldn't have.

"I want to look for him!" Benji pleaded, but Adelman had to gently shut that down. Adelman himself wasn't allowed to join the search party, despite his relative strength and stamina for a man of his age. Lisa could roam these hills like some kind of elf, but she was still in the clinic having her legs x-rayed and fresh stitches put into her lip and calf. Adelman was so relieved to hear her legs were merely sprained. She was calm enough to convey that probably the reason she had been able to stay in the saddle was the modifications she had made to the shock absorbers on her bike, but she was too overwrought to appreciate her own cleverness and remained completely dissolved in guilt and fear. Adelman had forgotten that she modified the bike – she did it at her father's mechanic shop – and had to stifle his spark of curiosity over what she had done to it. She just kept crying into the phone that she was sorry. Adelman could tell from her tone of voice that she thought Chad must be dead. That scared him more than any other fact, although he still did his best to comfort her. The core of his being was in agony but still he managed to say, tenderly and with genuine care,

"Oh, sweetie, please, don't cry. It'll be okay, it'll be okay, I promise. Think about which new mountain bike you want now, how's about that?"

"I don't deserve a new bike," she wept in response.

"You deserve a new bike more than anyone," Adelman said. "And you know what? You were getting too tall for that one anyway." She broke down into fresh sobs, but they sounded less anguished. He told her how proud he was of her and how well she had done to get down the mountain. When the call ended he stared at his phone for a moment, his heart so heavy he felt like he might implode, before going to comfort Benji, who was increasingly hysterical.

Adelman got a call about 20 minutes before the helicopter arrived. They had found Chad. He was unresponsive and barely breathing, and they didn't have direct access to his head, which was jammed between a sapling and a fallen log.

"His neck is probably broken," the paramedic told him after they had stabilized him and were waiting for the emergency helicopter. "His arm is definitely broken in at least two places, and his knee was dislocated. It's not clear the extent of the spinal cord damage." The paramedic told him these things dispassionately, too distracted to hoist a veneer of sympathy over their brutal competence. They relayed that he had made it a quarter of the way down the slope before wiping out. His bike had tumbled a half a mile down the mountain from where the forest had snared and mangled him. He was unconscious, which was a mercy.

"We're going to chopper him to the nearest trauma center," the paramedic said. "Can you meet us there?"

"Yes, of course," Adelman said through the solid lump in his throat. It was an hour's drive away. Benji was bawling and insisting he come, and Adelman knew he had to take him. He wished he could take Lisa to soothe Benji, but how could he ask anything of her? He wanted to ask Jared to come, but how could he ask anything of him? How had he come to rely so much on these vulnerable children? Jared was still putting ointment on Billy's lacerations as Adelman mobilized.

"Sir? What's happened?" Jared said, leaving his brother on the porch with a grape Popsicle, Billy's favorite; Adelman kept the grape ones in the garage freezer, where Billy didn't mind going so much.

"Benji, go pack some of Chad's pajamas, okay?" Adelman said.

"I'm not allowed in Chad's room, he'll kill me if I touch his stuff," Benji said.

"Don't worry about that, just go on, he'll need some pajamas in the hospital," Adelman said. Benji looked worried but seemed to understand, and he disappeared upstairs.

"They found him unconscious," Adelman told Jared. "Broken, dislocated limbs, but his neck... they think it's broken." Adelman's voice went high and hoarse on the last word.

"Jeez," Jared said, visibly struggling. "Sir, I'm so sorry, I'm so... I don't know why he'd ever think he could catch Lisa on a bike, even though he'd been practicing. Hell, I wouldn't bet I could catch her."

"I'm so sorry about Billy," Adelman said. "I don't know what possessed Chad to do that, I..."

"It was the girl cat," Jared said grimly. Adelman knew that Jared could communicate with his brother with shocking fluency, and Jared reported, "He takes her out and she follows him around when he works. She scratched Chad when he was storming around and he kicked her. Billy pushed him away and Chad went nuts. The cat probably needs to see a vet, she's crying and seems sluggish; that's why my brother didn't want to leave the shed. Is it okay if I take her?"

"Yes, of course," Adelman said. His faint hope for Jared's company fizzled out. "And Lisa, will you..."

"Already there," Jared said. "I hope the little man is okay." Adelman realized he meant Benji, who was shuffling down the stairs with a duffel bag full of Chad's stuff.

"Me too," Adelman said. Jared hugged him, finding the generosity from some deep-seated source of goodness within him, and when he and Adelman parted Adelman didn't feel like he was leaving a boy behind. There was nothing Adelman could give him or Lisa that would measure up to what they meant to him, and he wondered if, on the whole, he had brought positive things to them. He hoped so as much as he had ever hoped for anything, and that desperate hope matched his seething dread that he was taking Benji to a fresh new trauma. He realized he had barely even thought about Chad, and that guilt was an added misery.

. . .

Chad's face was busted and bloated and his chest barely moved as he breathed. Benji couldn't look at him without splintering apart.

"In addition to the spinal cord injury, he's got some pretty serious head trauma – wasn't wearing a helmet. We don't know if he'll ever wake up from the coma," the doctor told him in a low voice over Benji's sobs. Benji was clutching Adelman so hard that it hurt, and Adelman crouched down so he could wrap Benji in a full embrace. The doctor continued, "If he does, we're not sure how bad the spinal damage is. We'll know more when his records from New Mexico arrive." They arrived a few days later, but little changed. Chad's face had deflated and started to heal, looking more serene than Adelman had ever seen it before. Maybe this was for the best, Adelman thought, desperately and with self-loathing for letting such a thought cross his mind.

A fortnight passed – the BMX crew visited the trauma center, bringing Benji's bike so he could practice riding in a nearby park. Jared and Lisa, poor, black-eyed bloodied-up Lisa, sat with Adelman. How those kids did it, how they forced themselves to visit. Adelman could see Lisa's soul twisting whenever her eyes drifted over to the comatose boy.

"It's not your fault, I promise, I promise more than anything, I'd promise my life," Adelman told her when she finally had to leave the room. He followed her into the hall. He sank to his knees, grasping her shoulders, and repeated himself. Her eyes were wet and hollow and her jaw was twitching, her wrists slapping her hands at thin air. Adelman told her again how proud he was of her and she finally broke, and when she wept, he held her too. When it was time for Jared to bring her home, Adelman told her to inspect the new orchids and inventory the garden plants. She needed some purpose, something to do to distract her from all the trauma Chad had inflicted. She had another three weeks before she was cleared for BMX again, and Adelman knew those three weeks would drip by miserably for everyone involved in this awful mess. Life had to resume, so Adelman relaxed his vigil and came and went, bringing Benji to visit his brother after school every evening, and finally, one night, the sleeping face scowled.

"Chad? Chad?" Adelman asked, leaping out of his chair so fast it toppled over. Chad's eyes were moving beneath the lids. Adelman jabbed the button to call a nurse and continued to call Chad's name. The lids peered open, and then Chad screamed. It was a weak scream, but a scream nonetheless, eerie because his body was so still. His lips were moving, distorting the noise, but no words ever formed.

Chad came home in a wheelchair. Adelman and Benji chattered to him with shared, forced cheerfulness. He still didn't seem able to speak, although Adelman half-hoped he was just being stubborn. Adelman had tortured himself in a hundred different ways as Chad's recovery hit such disappointing dead-ends. What if he hadn't let the kids come over and had gotten Chad his lizard right away – would he still have punched Lisa? Would he have ever been in a position to chase her down the mountain? Hell, what if he had let the cops arrest him? Would he have ruined himself in jail?

"Here, I told you she would forgive you!" Benji said, carrying the girl cat to Chad's lap. The cat had needed surgery and had almost died from his vicious kick. Chad curled his lip and the cat leapt away. "Never mind, you can give her treats when you can walk again, she'll love you then," Benji said. He wheeled his brother back to the porch. Chad still didn't speak.

. . .

As the weeks bled to months, it became clear to Adelman that Chad simply couldn't speak. His face showed expressions – he was always sneering – but no sounds ever came out except for screams and squawks. Adelman showed him a binder of bearded dragons from a local breeder, and his eyes widened as his hand twitched to point at the one he wanted. He and Adelman shared a look of excitement, but Chad's eyes soon shaded over again. Adelman hoped the lizard would help, and he drove two hours to pick it up and immediately showed it to Chad, who actually smiled. The lizard would sit sedately on Chad's lap, which was nice, because none of the cats would have anything to do with him. Chad spent most of his days on the porch with his lizard. Adelman thought he must have named it, and the tenor and sound of his groans changed when he stroked it with his trembling hands, but Adelman couldn't make out the name.

The wheelchair ramp on his house got a lot of use that year. Adelman hosted a Christmas party for the BMX crew, and although it was more subdued than past parties, everyone came and seemed to have a good time. Lisa, Jared, Evan, and Billy stayed late, lounging around and laughing together with Adelman like old times. Chad sat silently amongst them; Adelman wondered if he imagined his lizard like a little dragon protecting him from everything he had lost, symbolized so vividly right in front of him. Evan told a joke and everyone laughed, Lisa and Benji literally rolling on the floor as Evan grinned, looking pleased with himself.

There it was, a guttural sound from the other wheelchair. Chad had tried to say something and startled his lizard – Benji lunged to catch it, missed, and chased it to the other room, yelping in fear that it would get away. The mean look on

Chad's face said it all, even if he couldn't access the words anymore. He snarled and gurgled at them, his hand flopping up and down off his lap.

"Huh," said Evan, craning his neck. "Cat got your tongue?" Jared laughed again, meanly, although he quickly stifled it. Evan gave Chad a long obvious look-over and sneered right back at him. "God, it must suck to lose yourself as badly as you, huh? I feel sorry for you. You're more broken than I've ever been, and I'd rather die young than live like you."

"Evan!" Adelman said, his exclamation knee-jerk. He had no admonishment ready, and Evan's expression was hard.

"What?" he said. "This is all his fault, and somewhere in his mushed-up brain he must know that. He must know that this is what he deserves." Lisa straightened and her mouth opened, but she stopped herself. She looked at her brother and said nothing. Jared was still.

"Well," Adelman said, his breath catching. He cleared his throat as hard as he could. He could not cry in front of these children; he could not blame them. He would deal with this later. He had to think, even though he wished desperately for some peace. "Well, kids. I think we better call it a night."

"Sir!" Lisa was on her feet. "Sir, we're sorry, we..."

"You can show yourselves out," Adelman said, his voice hitching, and he fled to his study.

These kids – his utterly wonderful kids – they couldn't tolerate his devastation. Jared and Lisa came the next day with earnest, heart-wrenching apologies. Adelman couldn't help it: his throat throbbed and his eyes spilled over. He covered his face in his hands and they hugged him as he gruffly apologized until he finally composed himself.

"I just, I just don't know what a good life even looks like for him now," Adelman said. "I think he understands me, but he hates me just as much as he ever did. The rehab specialists say he might improve, but it gets less and less likely as time goes on. I just... this is no one's fault, except for my nightmare of a son, but here I am, stuck."

"You're not stuck," Lisa said. "Benji needs you so much and he's a prince of a boy. And we need you too."

"You're our guy," Jared said. "You're the only reason we're anybody. You put us on the map. You taught me math, for Christ's sake. Did I tell you they're moving me to honors for senior year if I catch up over the summer?"

"Ah, well, we'll have a lot of work to do," Adelman said. With a pang, he found he was honestly looking forward to it.

So, Adelman retained his BMX crew, and as Chad relearned how to say (or more accurately, shout) "NO" and "I DON'T WANT TO," the crew flourished. Benji even started participated in some kiddie competitions, and Adelman took Benji to his third tournament and cheered himself hoarse. Lisa and Jared were competing in the main events, and Benji watched those with the avid fascination of a budding BMX rider. As usual, Adelman got seats for everyone, and Lisa's parents were still pretty chilly to him – he couldn't blame them – but Lisa came to him for her usual pep talk and waved to them all from the arena. She zoomed and twirled and all but flew to glorious victories. Watching her left Adelman in such awe, and he felt this huge swell of pride. He wondered if he deserved it. Whatever he had done for her, she had already known how to ride a bike.

END

ABOUT THE AUTHOR

Riva Riley is a biologist whose real-world experiences enliven this tale. Originally from the Chicago area, her research focuses on South American aquatic life which strangely brought her to England to study Zoology. This is her first novella.

CREVICES OF FROST
BY GABRIELLE RUPERT

To my mother, who told me to write happier endings.

MANIK

David Watson scanned the desolate cold wilderness, searching for bystanders within the trees along the northern shore. Even though he was in the middle of the thawed Sea of Mortla, which was, at its widest point, calculated to be about three hundred miles, he couldn't be too careful. Not that he thought what he was doing as wrong, but he knew he could get in trouble for it.

It was summer, but more importantly, these were the only two months of the year that the sea wasn't frozen. The sun only set for an hour or so at night, and time didn't seem to exist. Except it did. Soon, citizens of both Sinaaq and Itcha Navak would leave work and come out onto the water to relax. He was closer to Itcha Navak, his home, so he would see less of the stuck-up indigenous peoples of the other town. Still, no one must catch him.

With the kayak paddle tucked in the bungee cord behind him, David had a small tackle box open on the sprayskirt that covered his lap. Bobbers and lures were organized by color, and he picked up the top shelf of the container to reveal a small glass jar. Inside the jar was a reddish powder, similar in appearance to paprika or cayenne pepper.

The worm daggered on David's hook thrashed around in the illegal powder, attempting to bury itself in the spice-colored dirt but unable to hide underground. All the worm found was hard glass at the bottom, unable to escape.

Once the worm was sufficiently coated with the powder, David closed the tackle box and tucked it into the dry box by his knees. Two common salmon twice the size of his hand were tied loosely to the cord by the dry box. Speckled with green and grey, they gleaned wet in the sun overhead, laying against the hard plastic of the kayak. He secured the fishing pole at the front end of the kayak and dropped the dusty wiggling invertebrate into the cold, clear saltwater. And waited.

Paddle in gloved hands, David brushed the black teardrop-shaped blade against the surface of the sea. Just a little so his vessel glided. His eyes shifted from the dragging fishing line to the area around him to his paddle blades. They reminded him of whale fins and he imagined how much bigger the fins of marine mammals would be.

As David began to wonder if he was foolish to buy the crushed plant, and thought maybe it *was* just paprika and cayenne pepper, the fishing line became taut, drawing a straight line to the water's surface. David felt himself choke on the brisk air in his lungs, and he set his paddle on his lap. He reached for the pole, but before his fingers grazed the stick, there was a strong tug on the line from the side of the boat.

David had either shifted his weight with excitement, or the catch was simply strong enough, but the kayak tilted, tilted, flipped, splash!

Fighting the urge to open his mouth, David squinted through the freezing water. His earlier two catches hadn't been tied tightly, and now slipped off the cord on the kayak and drifted gradually down from the light blue to the darker mesopelagic. The gradient of brightness unnerved David as his eyes stung, the unknown black below playing with his imagination, wondering what hid beyond the light. He felt much like the worm in the powder.

Regaining sense, David positioned his arms and torso to the side of the kayak, close to the surface. He grabbed his paddle and set it perpendicular to his kayak. Bracing his body, he pushed the paddle's blade down against the water, forcing his hips into the seat of his kayak. As the vessel snapped up and the water poured from his face, he sucked in the fresh air.

His tackle box was still secure with his drybag, and surprisingly, the fishing pole was still held in place in the notch at the front. His short hair was wet, as well as his shirt and jacket, but he had spares in his drybag. *Damn, it's cold*, David thought as he reached for the pole. The line was still dangling in the water.

Hands placed on the hard, plastic string, David pulled the line toward him. He felt resistance, and couldn't help smiling. The muscles in his shoulders and back strained as he fought against the strength of the catch. Reeling the line back in as slow as his eagerness allowed, he looked around to see if he was still alone. Of course, he was.

The surface of the water was broken by a variety of colors in the shape of a fish. It was half a yard in length, from head to tail, with an oblong round shape. The scales were green, red, and yellow, all vibrant and glistening against the sunlight. A beacon to show the world what David had done.

Grabbing a bag from his dry box, David wrapped the fish up so none of the colors showed. Unfastening the front of his sprayskirt, he tucked the bag between his legs. He could feel the blood pumping in his arms, his breath exhaling in shallow spurts. Fixing his sprayskirt and grabbing his paddle, he felt the sea breeze on his shirt as he set his eyes on the horizon. The town of Itcha Navak could barely be made out above the end of the sea. The sun was warm on his head and back, but he shivered from the cold water.

He did not observe the still surface of the water, which reflected the pine trees of the north and the clear blue sky. He didn't care for the otters floating along the bank, smashing clamshells against rocks. Even when a singular, grey bird with a twenty-four foot wingspan crested above him, temporarily blocking out the sun, David did not notice. All he could think about was the rare jewel at the bottom of the kayak, dead. His legs could feel the rustle of the bag as he shifted his feet against the plastic, and he felt giddy. Was the meat exactly how fishers described it? Or would it taste just like tuna or salmon? A sickening ache dropped in David's stomach as he thought about the possibility of disappointment. All this struggle, the money he spent on the powder, the risk of getting caught and sent back to the city, the possibility of paying a fine he couldn't afford, just to catch a fish that only appeared special. The thought disappeared from his mind as he reminded himself that the main thing he cared about, the one thing that kept him going, was the chase.

Attract the fish. Nibble. Lick. Bite. Catch... and onto the next big prey on his list.

Back at the shoreline, David shoved the bag further inside toward the front of the boat. Once he packed all the equipment in his truck, he placed the bag under a pile of tarp in the truck bed. Empty, the dripping kayak was set in the bed, as well.

The car heater blasted against David's cold hands on the steering wheel. The cracked paved roads were empty as he made his way back home. Weeds grew on every opening in the roads and sidewalks. The people who lived in Itcha Navak wore baggy blue jeans and thermal shirts, maybe a vest to protect against the light summer breeze. They'd all ended the work day, coming from warehouses or offices, going home or to the bar. No one walked alone, even in the daylight.

David's little house sat in the second lane over from Main street, and he hoped his neighbors wouldn't ask how his trip was.

As David pulled into the front of his house, he noticed one neighbor wasn't home and the other had one car in front. The car was red, which meant the woman currently home was too busy drinking to come out and ask questions.

Through the rusty wire fence, David carried his equipment to the tiny shed . The shed resembled a much smaller version of his house, both made of grey wood that could use new roofing and paint. Hanging the kayak up, David could smell the faint sweet odor coming from the bag. He hurried to unpack his fishing equipment and lock the shed, and went into his house, carrying his prize.

The fish rested in the yellow fridge as David changed into dry clothes. With sleeves rolled up, he set the fish up on a cutting board near his kitchen sink. He held his carving knife with a shaky hand and set the blade behind the head of the fish. He could feel the skull end in line with the pectoral fin, and he sliced down. The head came off with a tug, the scales sparkling from the dim light above the sink. The window in front of David was covered with a short cream-colored curtain, patterned with repetitive red barns and buckskin horses.

David inserted the blade an inch into the dorsal side of the fish, and cut along the back toward the tail. The dorsal fin fell away from the flesh, flopping onto the cutting board. Just past the dorsal fin, David pushed the knife through the body and applied pressure as he sliced the rest of the fish all the way to the end of the tail. After the finishing cuts on both sides, the fillets were separated and set to the side to rinse before cooking.

Examining the meatless, bony body of the fish, David noticed a strange protrusion in the stomach area. At first, he assumed it was a greyish-green organ encased in the thin lining separating meat from guts. When he poked the protrusion, it felt rock-hard, not flexible like the rest of the anatomy.

He placed his knife against the protrusion, feeling the blade scrape against metal. Carving open the fish's stomach, he pulled the slimy object out and scrutinized it under the light. The round golden mechanism was a compass. Worn from salt water, and the screen cracked. The needle no longer moved.

Turning the compass over, David could see words inscribed in the metal: A. LOCKLEAR. It was a name, though not familiar with David. Not many names were familiar with David, though, as he tried his best to keep away from townsfolk.

Setting the compass to the side, David finished cleaning up the fish carcass and making sure to dispose of it discreetly. He washed and prepared the fillets, and set one in the fridge and cooked the other up for dinner. As the steam rose from the pan, he reached over to the phonebook on the table by the phone and found the 'L' section.

"Locklear, Locklear, Locklear..." He read out loud, running a large index finger over each name, "Adam Locklear."

Partially listening to the crackle of butter covering the fillet, David picked up the phone and dialed the number next to the name. It rang twice before received.

"Oh, 'ello?" said a gruff voice on the other end.

"Hello, is this Adam Locklear?" David glanced at the stove.

"What you want?" the man said with a tone not grumpy but cautious.

"My name is David Watson, and I found a compass in the sea. I believe it may be yours."

There was a long silence, but David knew the man hadn't

hung up as he could hear other voices in the background on the receiving end.

"Found it on the sea, you say?" said the man.

"Yes, are you Adam?" David said, smelling the sweet-tart aroma filling the tiny kitchen.

"Yes." There was another long silence before Adam spoke again. "I've missed the piece-of-shit metal these past few months."

"I live off of Main Street," David said, glancing out the tiny bit of window showing the late afternoon light, "If you want to swing by and pick it up."

"Sounds good," Adam said. "David, is it?"

"Yeah."

"I'll come around in about an hour," Adam said, sounding happy. "You got beer?"

Glancing at the closed fridge, David grinned. "Sure. I'm the house with the truck."

"A truck and beer?" Adam gave a dry laugh. "Just like every other jackass in town. See ya soon."

The line clicked, and David hung up the phone on the wall. He turned the stove burner off just as the fillet was turning golden brown, and he slid it off onto a blue-rimmed plate.

The fish meat was just as delicious as David had anticipated, similar to a forty-pound trout he caught in northern Saskatchewan years ago. The tales were correct. The juices mixed with the butter, re-melting in a pool of glory and euphoria in his mouth. He let out a groan, tilting his head to the side. Not fifteen seconds had passed after his plate had been cleared when he began to think of the next best creature he would capture, whatever fish it may be.

David cleaned the kitchen quickly. As he washed the grease off his hands, he saw a large pickup truck park behind his, blocking the driveway of the woman with the red car. A large figure stepped in through his fence and came up to the front door. David didn't move from the sink until he heard the knock.

Opening the door, David was surprised to see a tall, lean man with a carefully groomed dark beard, set against olive skin. David had expected to see a man with a rougher appearance and a large gut.

"David?" the man said.

"Yeah." David raised an eyebrow. "Adam Locklear?"

"Ya." Adam pulled a hand out of his coat pocket to shake David's. "Thanks for calling."

After the quick greeting, David let the stranger inside. They immediately settled into the kitchen.

"Here you go." David handed the compass out for Adam. "It's all broken and beat up."

Adam took the compass and held it in the palm of his hand like it was a snail.

"You said you found it in the sea?" Adam said.

"Yeah." David popped the tops off two beers and handed one to his guest.

"Funny." Adam took the beer bottle and sat at the table. "I dropped it into the water. Must have been miles down on the bottom. You a diver?"

"No, no." David leaned against the kitchen counter and took a sip. "Kayaker. And fisher."

Adam's nose twitched. *Oh, I hope he doesn't smell the fish.* David thought, not letting his face show any concern.

"You're from the village across the water, huh?" David said, curious but also wanting to change the subject.

"How d'you figure?" Adam said, running a hand through his shoulder-length straight hair. "The way I look?"

David shook his head. "No. I know you all have a compass like that one."

"Oh, right." Adam held the metal piece up and shook it like a bell. "It's their tradition."

"You say that like it's a bad thing." David sat down across from his guest, trying to read him. Adam seemed to be doing the same.

"It is." Adam shrugged, taking a long sip.

"And ain't it your tradition, too?" David squinted. He had no issues with the Natives, but there was a general negative attitude toward them in this town. People here said the Natives were too righteous, too uptight, and stuck up. While Adam seemed confident, he didn't seem to care about morals.

Adam's brown eyes narrowed. "No."

The room held an awkward silence and David cleared his throat.

"Well, I'm glad you got your thing--"

"You know," Adam interrupted, leaning forward and resting his elbows on the table, "The last time I smelled a meal this sweet was when I was seventeen."

David felt bumps rise on his skin. His nose had been overpowered by the cooking and the close quarters, so he couldn't pick apart the fish smell from the smell of his kitchen.

"There's a special fish in the sea," Adam said, staring right at David, "That is forbidden to catch. The people of Sinaaq declared that for hundreds of years, and it eventually became a law by the country."

Adam took another sip, quick but agonizing as David felt frozen in his chair.

"The last known person to commit such a crime," Adam continued, a small smile playing on his lips, "Was me."

Unsure of what to say, David furrowed his eyebrows and

took a moment to finish his beer. Then he set the empty glass bottle down and glanced at Adam.

"What do you want?" he said, wondering if he needed a weapon. It would only take a second to break the bottom off of the bottle.

"Oh, nothing." Adam sat back, grinning. "I'm just glad to find like-minded people in such a small town. Tell me, David, was the meat everything you dreamed it to be?"

Glancing at the empty sink, David's throat filled with fear and uncertainty.

"I'm not going to tell on you!" Adam let out a loud laugh, slapping the tabletop with an open palm. "That'd be against everything I live for, man. No, I'm proud of you for taking what you want from the world. We could use a man like you."

"We?" David felt his mind clearing.

"My friends and I." Adam shrugged and finished off his beer. "I'm meeting up with them tomorrow right mid-morning, down on the southwest side of town."

"What do you guys do?" David said, his leg restless and fidgeting against the floor. "And why would you need me?"

"We…" Adam studied something on the far wall before looking back at David, "We like to break the rules. Just like you."

The image of catching a larger fish than the one in his rubbish bin flitted through David's mind, and he felt a surge of motivation in his chest and arms.

"Hope to see you then." Adam stood up, placing his empty bottle next to the sink.

"Why did you catch the fish?" David wondered how similar he was to Adam, if their motivations lined up.

"Huh?"

"Why did you catch the fish?" David said again. "When you were seventeen?"

"Oh, well," Adam gave another shrug and a lopsided grin, "To impress a girl. A woman, really. But she was just like the rest of 'em. Set to her tradition."

He turned to the front door and opened it. "Thanks for giving back the compass, even if it's useless. It was the last part of Sinaaq I had all these years."

David watched as his new friend left the house and walked over the yard to his vehicle. Once the headlights were out of sight, David locked the front door and turned in for the night. He wasn't able to sleep well, though as the sun began its brief rest.

The next morning, David couldn't eat breakfast. He wasn't sure if he should be happy or scared at meeting "like-minded" individuals. He wondered what "like-minded" meant as he drove down Main Street.

With the new day, the few streets were busy with citizens getting mid-morning coffee or beer. Turning down a road, David steered the truck southwest. He drove for a bit, watching the houses turn into junk yards and warehouses. He noticed Adam's pickup truck in front of one warehouse and pulled into the parking lot.

The warehouse had some windows, all boarded up with plywood. The structure appeared to be decades-old, but the large front doors were newer. One of them was open, the only part of the building allowing the outside world to enter.

David walked inside and saw a massive collection of tools and equipment, many of them foreign to him. Long wooden and metal poles with blades on the end. Tractors with pulleys and ropes, tarps half-covering many of them. On the back end of the warehouse floor, there were rows of metal poles with wide girth, and a sharp blade at one end attached to a round capsule.

Three men polished and tended to the equipment. One was Adam.

"Nice of you to join us," Adam called, stepping away from one of the tractors and approaching David. "Guys, this is David."

An older man stepped away from another tractor and tossed the dirty rag he was holding over his shoulder. He reached out his hand to David and gave a grin showing only a few teeth.

"Sawyer, it is." His grip was firm and greasy, and David resisted the urge to wipe his hand on his pants. "Adam here says we can trust you."

"Huh?" David glanced at Adam, who was grinning ear to ear. "We just met -"

"And this, here, is Leo." Adam shoved a short, lanky brunette young man forward, clapping him on the shoulder. "He's good with the vehicles."

"So..." David walked over to the tractors and hesitantly placed a hand on the cool metal, "What do you guys do, really? What do these do?"

"Well," Leo shrugged, giving a high-pitched laugh, "This one here is to drill holes, you know, the big ones."

The steel spiral had the barest amount of rust.

"This one is to load the harpoons." Leo rushed over to another machine, tugging off the rest of a tarp. "The ones without explosives, of course."

"Explosives?" David felt a tingling sensation run up his arms and legs. "Wait, wait, hold on."

"Goddamnit, Adam." Sawyer turned with a stern eye towards the apparent leader of the group, "You didn't tell him, did you?"

"I wanted to see if he could figure it out himself." Adam laughed, crossing his arms over his chest. "Guess he has."

"You're poachers?" David's voice rose but doubted anyone could hear from the perfectly-planned location of the warehouse.

"Well, no. We -"

"Yes." Adam cut off Sawyer, staring down David with dark, confident irises. "We catch the biggest fish. You interested?"

David glanced from Adam to Sawyer to Leo. The three men were all at different stages in life: old, young, experienced, novice, secretive, egotistical. How was David fit into this order? All he wanted was to fish and catch exotic species. Would his simple desires match the goals of the other men? Even though their objectives were the same as his, would their individual reasons outshine his own?

On the other side of the warehouse, lining the walls, there were tons of sculptures and art designs made out of polished white and yellowish material. Bones.

At last, David straightened his posture and faced Adam straight on.

"Yes."

MAGNETISM

When they brought back the body of Kiiñak, fourteen-year-old Aguta had been walking home from school. It was a mile walk, and the roads were becoming more icy as the autumn aged. He hadn't been able to focus on language arts or mathematics while his brother was missing. Even during the outdoor education course, his favorite class, Aguta stared out the window of the classroom, his heart beating loudly as he thought about all the terrible fates his brother had met.

It wasn't until he stepped through the front door of his house that his concerns were accurate. Abe Dolson, the sheriff of Sinaaq, was standing at the kitchen table wearing his typical crisp white button up, black tie, and blue jeans. His badge, rusty but legible, rested on the front of his brown sheriff's coat. Aguta's mother sat with her face in her hands, and she was crying. The harsh light from the ceiling gave the adults a yellow tinge that made them look fake.

"Aguta, hey." Dolson faced the kid. The sheriff looked like he hadn't slept in days, with dark circles under his eyes, and

Aguta wondered if he went on every search party for Kiiñak. "We found your brother…"

Aguta's mother sat up straight and turned toward her son. Her dark hair was already thin near her scalp, but it was frizzier and unkempt than usual. She reached out, and he could see fresh tears trailing over old ones, her dark eyes lost in discovery.

"He's dead." She told him, placing her hands on his arms as if to force him to listen. "It's just you and me, now."

"How did he… where…?" Aguta felt as if he ate too fast and the food clogged painfully in his chest.

"It doesn't matter," she said, staring off at the front window. "It just… doesn't."

Taking a step back, Aguta looked up at Dolson. "Where's Kiiñak?"

"Well, son," Dolson put his hands in his coat pockets, "His body is at the doctor's office. Old Lou is picking it up soon, so he'll expect the ceremony to be before the morning."

"That soon?" Aguta said. This was the first person he knew that had died, technically, so he wasn't accustomed to the burial traditions.

"We need to put his spirit to rest." His mother told him, her voice clearer, "As soon as possible."

"Do you need a ride?" Dolson asked Aguta's mother.

"Oh, no, thank you," she said, standing up. "We'll head down in a few minutes."

Listening to Dolson's footsteps, Aguta waited until he was alone with his mother before speaking again.

"Kiiñak was going to be my patron next month."

Before his brother's disappearance, all Aguta had thought about was the compass he would receive for his fifteenth birthday. Now, he felt ashamed for still thinking about the tiny piece of brass.

"I know." His mother said, pulling on her boots. "Your

father was his patron. Kiiñak was supposed to be yours since your father's gone. Now, I guess...."

No one can be my patron, Aguta thought, and wondered if he would be less of man. Less of a person.

"Will I not receive a compass, then?" He asked.

"That's not something you should be worried about, Aguta."

It was one of two things Aguta worried about while walking to Old Lou's house. The air was warm in the falling sun, but the wind picked up the closer they got to the edge of town. Set a few meters away from the thick forest, Old Lou's house was small and wooden. It shook during harder winds and made eerie noises even when the weather was still. The owner had been born in the house and had never set foot out of Sinaaq. The elders, like Dolson, respected him and relied on him to keep their culture remembered.

The inside of the house was overpowered with a mixture of cumin and black pepper, and warm air thick with moisture. When Aguta and his mother arrived, Old Lou was slicing red and green peppers. Aguta wondered if these would be used in the burial ceremony, but the old man just left them on the kitchen counter and led Aguta and his mother to the back room.

Unlike the front room, which had a polished wooden floor, the floor of the back room was dirt. Most of the houses in the town had wooden or plastic flooring, so seeing the earthly interior made Aguta's skin itch. He imagined the dirt covering his skin and seeping into his body, and imagined the ground surrounding him and suffocating him.

A stone table in the middle of the room presented the relaxed, clothed body of Kiiñak. The six-foot-two man had been redressed in his traditional animalskin pants and coat, with his fur-lined hood pulled up over his head to only show his triangular-shaped face. There was a long jagged cut starting at his temple and ending right above his chin. His traditional long black hair was brushed, framing his face and covering his shoulders. There were strange dark bruises on the left side of his scalp, mostly hidden by the hairline. The eyes were closed, and Aguta waited for them to open. He wondered why the shape of his brother's head looked different, and why no one was telling him what happened.

"We will guide his spirit now." Old Lou said in a gruff voice. He held a stick that was burning at one end, and he walked in a circle around the stone table. "Then we will bring his body to rest with the others on the hill."

Aguta's mother knelt down in the dirt by the stone table and placed her hands on her lap. Her eyes closed, and Aguta saw how blank her expression was. He had tears pooling in his eyes, but they didn't fall. He knelt on the other side of the table, where his knees hurt from the ground.

The flames of the candles around the room made Kiiñak's body appear more lively than it should have. The glow cast on his face hid the pale of death. The light reflected from the compass in the limp hand, slightly curled.

Old Lou was speaking in the traditional tongue, forgotten or ignored by the last generation. He waved the burning stick around while stepping away and then coming closer, turning toward the wall and then facing the table again. Aguta's mother had her eyes shut, still, and he could see her lips moving in a murmur.

No one would see Aguta's actions.

Reaching up, Aguta touched his brother's hand. The skin was cold. There was no resistance as he took the compass and brought it back to his own coat. He felt the small weight of it slide to the bottom of the pocket, feeling guilty for taking his brother's right of adulthood. Aguta had no other choice, though, as he needed his own; Kiiñak owed him that much.

Aguta's hands felt sweaty, though he didn't know if it was from the heat or from nerves. He half-expected his brother's body to sit up and grab Aguta by the coat, yelling at him for stealing something so precious.

He never did. He was dead.

* * *

The stones were the size of Aguta's fist. When he set the stones on top of Kiiñak's body, they settled into place with a heavy click, . His mother set the last stone, finalizing the burial. Old Lou said a few incoherent words that relied mostly on long "U" sounds and short "T" sounds, took her hand in a comforting grasp, and then departed on the dirt trail leading through the snowy meadow back to the town.

"What do we do now?" Aguta said, searching for guidance on his mother's face.

"We go home." She didn't look at him but instead turned toward the town. "We move on."

"His spirit is free?" he said to her as she stepped onto the trail.

"His spirit is at rest." She paused, still facing the dusky sky. "You can stay with him for awhile if you want."

Aguta's mother descended the hill, and disappeared into the figurative boundaries of the town. He turned to examine the pile of stones, wondering how it would feel to be under such a heavy, sharp weight. He felt the few ounces in his pocket and took it out to see.

The compass had nicks over the outer surface from years of use. It had Kiiñak's initials on the inside cover, and the needle was still moving. It was pointing toward the forest, which loomed dark at the bottom of the hill and past the town. The thick trees grew against each other, preventing Aguta from seeing down into the woods.

That wasn't north.

Curious, Aguta headed down the trail toward the town, but at Old Lou's house, he cut through the meadow and toward the edge of the forest. His boots crunched against the ice, and he saw the top of grass blades, sticking out from under the snow. He felt lightheaded and heard his blood pump in his ears. It was getting dark and he was unsure if he still had his knife. Pressing a hand against the outside of his heavy coat, he felt the weapon was there.

The daylight was almost gone, but Aguta stayed in line with the compass's red arrow. The anticipation and wonder pushed all concern for safety out of his mind. He knew the dangers of going into the forest at night during the autumn. Anything could happen despite being prepared with a knife, a modern synthetic winter coat, calf-high boots, and a basic wilderness survival education.

He didn't care, though. Kiiñak had always taken care of his compass. The fact that it was off-balance, now, was suspicious and strange. If it hadn't been working, Kiiñak would have brought it in to be fixed.

A herd of elk passed under the pine trees to the left of Aguta. The male paused and stared at the human, then continued walking with the females further into the wilderness. There were white hares hopping around the brush, rushing out of Aguta's path. Twenty minutes passed, and all Aguta met were common animals. If only he had brought his bow and arrow, he could have caught some food.

As he walked, he could see the trees thinning. The path ended at a meadow at the bottom of a cliff. He could see the jagged top. Snow was melting off the edge, dripping down the sharp slope and making the bottom slippery. Aguta watched his step as he touched the wall, and he looked at the compass. It was spinning.

There was nothing to see. Nothing to find. Placing the broken compass back in his pocket, Aguta turned around and stepped toward the direction he came.

The clearing lit up in a green tinge, and the world fell silent. Turning back to the cliff, Aguta noticed the sky turn a greenish-purple. He had seen the northern lights before but believed it to be too late in the season for this to occur. The forest around him was brightened by the light.

At the top of the cliff, a tall dark figure stood. Aguta couldn't tell if the figure was a man or a woman, but could make out the mask covering the face. The rest of the body appeared to be wrapped in a black cloth, blending into the shadows.

The figure stepped off the cliff, and Aguta felt his heart in his throat, waiting for the impact. Just as the person was about to reach the bottom, the dark shadows transformed into the same green and purple light from the sky. The colors splashed against the ground and the rocky wall. Aguta reached out to see if he could feel the colors, but they just dispersed through him and into the woods like fog in the mornings.

As the lights disappeared and the sky returned to a dark blue, Aguta saw the mask lying on the ground by the wall. He picked it up and felt that it was made of wood, hollowed and smoothed to fit against the curves of a face. It appeared to be one of the masks that the elders used in ceremonies. He had never seen one like this before, though.

Aguta checked the compass. The arrow was pointing back toward the town. True north.

Rushing back to town, Aguta felt excited warmth instead of

the bitter cold of the early night. At Old Lou's house, he knocked hard on the front door.

"What is the matter, boy?" the old man said, his eyes wide with annoyance.

Panting, Aguta held up the mask. "I took Kiiñak's compass. I know I shouldn't have, but it led me to this."

Taking the mask in both hands, Old Lou held it up in the firelight from inside his house. He squinted, then opened his eyes wide again.

"What does the compass show now?" He said.

"True north," he said. "What does it mean?"

After a pause, Old Lou gave the mask back to Aguta.

"What happened?" Aguta said, frustrated and scared with the old man's silence.

"Kiiñak's spirit has been lost." Old Lou said, grabbing his cane and stepping outside to meet Aguta. "We need to bring his spirit back to his body."

Aguta followed him along the trail up the hill, his mind racing with thoughts.

"It's my fault." Aguta said, his head down and shoulders slumped. "I took his compass, so he couldn't find rest."

"Aguta," Old Lou said through heavy breaths that Aguta could see, "Your brother was unable to find rest in this world, so he still isn't able to in the next. The compass will help him now."

They stopped at the newest pile of stones, and Old Lou gestured at the side. Aguta picked up a few of the rocks until he reached a still hand. Staring at the bloated skin, he thought maybe he had gone to the wrong grave. He glanced up at Old Lou, who gave a small nod for him to continue. He placed the compass into the grip, and positioned the rocks back around the flesh.

"You have to give him the mask, too." Old Lou said.

Eyebrows scrunched in confusion, Aguta moved the rocks concealing his brother's face. The skin was dark from the night, but he could make out Kiiñak's narrow jaw. Placing the wooden mask over the face, he stared at the closed eyes through the holes.

The same vibrant green glow from the cliff showed on the mask, and the material melted into this glow. The energy hovered over Kiiñak's face before sinking into the skin, and then disappearing altogether.

"What happened?" Aguta whispered, his legs shaking.

"He is rested now," Old Lou said, "And he's free."

Placing the rocks back around Kiinak's head, Aguta felt warm tears in his eyes. He brushed them away, and turned to Old Lou.

"Your mother will be needing you." Old Lou grabbed Aguta's arm as they walked down the hill. "I'll see you next month."

Aguta glanced up at his elder with a surprised smile.

"I'll be receiving your compass soon." Old Lou said, a tone of humor with a hint of firmness. "And you've learned the first lesson, Aguta."

"What's that?"

"Never take away another man's direction, and never lose sight of your own path."

CRYOMYTHOLOGY

"... and thank you for your support, either through financial or material aid. Now, I shall be telling you all a local myth, a creature that once lived, or maybe still does, on the frozen ice of the sea. That's right, guys, the demon of Mortla. Let me begin..."

Face close to the radio microphone, Eirlys Wynn told the story of when she saw a monster. She spoke of the experience as if it were another folklore passed down through generations around campfires and bars. Her words were smooth and friendly, showing no sign of the terror she still felt.

It had been three days since Eirlys Wynn last stepped in the direction of the sea. She had driven her red truck out to the edge, where snow-covered soil met snow-covered ice, and walked to the fishing holes with a bag of supplies. It wasn't far, and she didn't mind the mix of sun on her layers and quiet wind against the hood of her coat.

At the fishing holes a quarter of a mile offshore, Eirlys met her older brother, Greg. He and his two friends had driven their trucks right up to the fishing holes, unafraid of the ice. Eirlys simply didn't want to risk it, even though she had never heard of a truck breaking through in December. It was at its thickest this time of year.

The weather forecast had said the wind would pick up later in the day. But, of course, Greg had forgotten to bring extra supplies. So, just in case, Eirlys brought layers for them. She also brought beer, and had one herself while sitting with the fishers. Once she caught a fish using her brother's line, she felt satisfied with social hour.

"What story you going to tell tonight, Eir?" said Ted, one of Greg's friends. Ted had had a crush on her since middle school, but was terrified of Greg's protective watch over his little sister.

"I'm not spoiling it for you." Eirlys laughed, putting her catch in a small cooler of ice. "Guess you'll have to listen."

"He'll be doing more than listening!" said Mike, the friend who always said the crudest phrases. While speaking, he made a lewd gesture near his crotch.

It only took one glance from Greg to quiet the men. His dark eyes were more dangerous than the dark cold abyss below their feet.

"I apologize, Eir." Mike's cheeks were already purple from the wind hitting the skin. He didn't look Eirlys in the eye.

She smiled, putting a gloved hand on her hip. "If you all don't bundle up, none of you will have hands to touch yourselves with. So throw on those layers I brought before it gets windy."

The men laughed, including Greg. He glanced at his sister, and nodded his appreciation and admiration in her direction. She tipped her own fur-lined hood towards him and began walking back to her truck.

As she turned away from the men, the wind picked up. Ten minutes later she found the white and grey horizon blurred into white. While she felt a little nervous, she knew she couldn't be far from the shore.

She should have seen her bright red truck on the shoreline through the squall, though. She couldn't. When glancing back towards the fishing holes, the same wall of breezy snow blocked her view of the men and their darkly colored vehicles. It was a good thing she brought them layers, she thought as she tried to stay calm. The sudden storm was weird but she hoped it would just pass quickly.

If I keep going straight, I'll reach my truck soon. Eirlys continued her path, eyes down, shielded from the cold as she stepped one foot in front of the other. This type of situation wasn't unusual, just an annoyance. She didn't have to be at the radio station for a few more hours, and the town was only a couple miles away from shore.

Eirlys started getting concerned as the squalls became constant, transforming into a blizzard. After a few more minutes, she still couldn't see her truck, or anything at all. Stopping in her tracks, she pulled out her compass.

"Shit," she said in a hushed panic. "I've been going the wrong way."

The weather forecast that morning never said anything about snow, but even on the edge of the Mortla Sea, trajectories can get unpredictable. Especially during this time of year. But this snow was too much to have gone undetected.

As Eirlys turned east, a low moan began as a vibration under her feet. The noise reached through the ice and skidded across the surface of the snow. Feet unbalanced, Eirlys stumbled and dropped her compass into the snow. The white opened up for the intricate metal piece, like quicksand. It was gone before Eirlys could pick it up.

The howl that shifted under the snow became part of the wind swirling around the surface. All Eirlys could hear was these gusts and whispers, like hearing one's inner voice shouting. She yelled out a wordless noise, hoping it would stop the chaos. Hugging herself tight, she squinted at the surroundings.

Unlike the calm before a storm, but the eye in the center, the winds swept the snow off the ice in front of Eirlys. It appeared to be a path, starting from Eirlys and ending a few meters away where the falling snow had cleared. She couldn't see past the small clearing on the surface.

The groans under the ice quieted, but not the squalls, as a male elk walked out from the wall of the blizzard toward the middle of the clearing. At first, the creature appeared healthy and not concerned with the stormy conditions. Its branches of bone held high as it made its way across the ice.

The hooves stumbled.

Clumps of snow scattered from beneath the beast as it staggered to its knees. Fuzzy lips opened, and Eirlys expected to hear a cry. Instead, the extended throat began twitching, and thick black liquid spilled out from the mouth and onto the snow.

Sick and injured elk were not a new sight for Eirlys, but she had never seen this before. After one more expulsion of dark sludge, the elk fell to its side with a thud that echoed into the surrounding storm. The winds picked up, and the volume of the whispers increased.

The dry gusts were directed toward the fallen animal, and pulling strips of fur off the body. It was slow, at first, as Eirlys squinted from the wind, her eyes watering from the fear. The disintegration was swift as the skin, muscles, sinews, and organs flew off into the abyss of the blizzard. All that made the elk soft disappeared.

As the organic pieces parted, the gleaming shine of metal appeared. The bone was not ivory or slightly yellow, but silver. Grey. Too heavy, or too unnatural, to be picked up by the storm. The winds ignored the skeleton.

Once the metal was pure, dry from blood and mucous, the gales stilled. The blizzard skipped the squall phase, and all snow in the sky was pulled to the ice.

Less frozen, Eirlys was motionless. Her eyes flickered around the metal framework, not understanding what had just occurred.

Even through the twenty-inch-thick layer of ice, a crack snapped up from the water below and ended at the metal ribcage. The ground parted with ease. The quake seemed to think about where it was going to go, sensed Eirlys, and decided to prey on her.

Never having experienced the ice crack on its own before, Eirlys thought of all the wilderness survival training in her youth. It never prepared her for when the solid surface of the Mortlan Sea split in the dead of winter. She turned and ran in the direct path away from the ice breakage, toward the shore.

She could hear the fractures behind her, as well as the snow crunching under her boots. They weren't made for running. The fur and rubber felt like coal collected in her wool stockings. She wondered if the crack would reach Greg and his friends. Their trucks would cause a massive hole, and their bodies wouldn't be recovered until the thaw in a few months. That was if their bodies weren't carried out to the ocean through intricate pathways of rivers and bays.

Suddenly, the ground was less slippery. Looking down, Eirlys let out a shout of relief. The ice had ended. She ran past the sign that read: "Sea of Mortla." Her truck was there with only a little snow on the front bumper.

Gasping for air, Eirlys turned around to see the cracked sea. She felt choked at what she saw.

Nothing. No crack in the ice.

The bright sun lit up the shoreline, much more than it did when she parked earlier in the day. The surface of the sea was still frozen. Intact. Covered with thick, smoothed snow. There were a few clouds on the horizon, which was all that was predicted by the weather forecast. There were no fissures. No sign of elk, dead or alive, nor pieces of metal except for the few trucks out by the fishing holes. The only footprints in the snow were from her boots and the two pickup trucks.

I did not just imagine that, did I? Eirlys took the few steps to her truck, opened the door, and pulled herself into the driver seat. Her gloved fingers fumbled as she started her car and turned on the heat. As the vents warmed up, she stared out at the desolate plain. She knew what she saw. Was it real, though?

Then she remembered.

Pulling off one of her gloves, she reached her hands into her coat pocket and found it empty.

DRIVESHAFT

The fact that Leo had to interact with people put him in a bad mood. He didn't want to leave his tractor, which he had been working on all morning. There was only an hour of daylight left of the four-hour day, and Leo did *not* want to be out in the dark. He wanted the comforting harsh lights of his workshop and his tools, calling to him and waiting to be used.

When Leo entered the auto mechanic's shop, though, his young eyes grew at the sight of the perfectly organized tools on the wall. The steel and iron tools were shining from cleanliness but edges rounded with use. Six pickup trucks in perfect condition sat facing the multiple garage doors. The middle-aged blonde mechanic, Citana Carver, was found halfway under a large black pickup truck. His denim-covered legs could be seen from the door leading to the front office. One leg was stretched flat on the hard concrete floor, the other bent with the knee pointed at the ceiling. One of the feet tapping to the blues song playing on the radio by the tool bench.

"Hello?" Leo called out.

The foot stopped tapping, and the legs bent, rolling the rest of the body out from under the truck. Citana sat up in his roller seat, his greying blonde hair falling over his forehead. A streak of grease-covered the right side of his cheek, but his grin could still be seen.

"Why, hello, hello!" he called, standing and coming over to the doorway. "What can I do for you?"

"I'm looking for some stuff," Leo said, surveying each vehicle, mentally visualizing the mechanics of each one. "Do you specialize just in truck parts?"

"Usually, yeah." Citana shrugged, "But I might have something that can work for you, if you have an ATV."

"I'm looking for tractor parts. I can't have a substitute." Leo's scanning eyes suddenly snapped to Citana's face. "It *needs* to be the right parts."

"Oh, well..." Citana gave a laugh, and Leo started to feel embarrassed about being so serious, "I understand. So, you know what you're looking for?"

Leo answered by handing Citana a paper list.

"I might have some of these," Citana said, his eyes on the paper. "I mean, I got some leftover parts from the old loggers before the mill closed. Tractor parts and such."

Leo watched Citana turn back into the large room of the warehouse.

"Let me see." Citana waved a hand for Leo to follow, and led him to the far side of the room where scrap materials were piled. "My organized mess, haha."

Leo did not laugh and simply waited with his hands clasped behind his back. Citana began picking through his collection of junk, pausing to survey Leo's list, and then going to the next object.

"So, what work do you do?" Citana said while scrounging.

"Freelancer." Leo answered, annoyed. He knew more would be coming.

"In Itcha Navak?" Citana said. "Or all over?"

Leo didn't answer. Didn't think he needed to. Citana didn't seem to notice. The office phone rang, but Citana let it go to voicemail. The caller was a woman, her high-pitched voice heard over the radio music.

"*Hi, Citana. It's Jess. Just wanna let you know I'll be working late tonight, so won't be over to see you. Sorry, mwah! Bye.*"

The words had gone through Leo's ears and left immediately. He didn't care for other people's personal affairs or feelings. He wasn't interested in anything other than his enjoyment of fishing.

"That's my girl, Jessica." Citana said while going through a bucket of gears, pausing to watch Leo's face.

After a sigh, Leo said, "Your daughter?"

He noticed Citana's cheeks turn red.

"No, my girlfriend." Citana set the box of metal down hard, but when he turned to Leo, he was smiling. "She works at the bar. You may have seen her."

Leo *had* in fact seen Jessica, but only remembered her because his coworker, Sawyer, was harassing the exotic dancer a few nights before. Leo and Adam, the "boss" of the three, had to pull the gross old man away from the woman. Frankly, Leo wouldn't have recognized what was happening if Adam hadn't brought the issue to his attention. Stuff like that didn't really go noticed for Leo as he didn't care.

"I know what you're thinking." Citana's pained smile turned into a straight line, and the man appeared exhausted. "I *am* old enough to be her father. But her and I... we care about each other, and we are a partnership."

Feeling awkward, Leo shoved his hands into his coat pockets and shifted his feet.

"Do you think you have everything I need?" Leo said. He wanted to leave and fix his tractor.

"Yeah." Citana came over, holding a cardboard box in his arms. "These are all of them."

"Thanks." Leo peered inside the box at the metal pieces. "How much?"

"I'll bring this up to the office and write you an invoice." Citana turned and then paused. "How will you pay, do you think?"

"Cash."

"You want a credit account?" Citana called from the office. "'Case you need something in the future."

"No." Leo stood in the doorway, feeling impatient.

"If you ever need a truck," Citana said while writing, "I got a nice inventory."

If Leo had been born with a sense of empathy, he would realize how lonely Citana was. But he didn't connect with humans well, so he simply watched the pen in the mechanic's hand swirl and spill words onto the paper.

"You have all the tools to install these?" Citana raised a finger in the air as if he forgot to ask this question earlier.

"Yes."

"Okay." Citana scribbled a signature at the bottom before sliding the paper slip across the top of the desk. "If you just want to sign there and place the cash down."

Leo pulled an envelope out of his pocket and flipped through the bills. He noticed the quick, curious glance from Citana, but the mechanic looked away. Leo wouldn't care if the man stared at the lump of cash, as the older man's awe wouldn't have made Leo feel rich nor cautious.

"Great!" Citana said after Leo placed the cash down and signed at the bottom. "Thank you, David Watson. I just realized I never asked for your name!"

Leo answered with no emotion, opposed to Citana's lively features. There was a pause before Citana spoke again, a reaction often in response to Leo's cold stare.

"Here you go." Citana patted the cardboard box of purchases. "Pleasure doing business with you, David."

Picking up the box, Leo nodded. "Thank you, sir."

Leo knew Citana must have watched him leave through the front door, but he didn't care. He now had the parts he needed to fix his tractor. Now he was able to go back out in the ice and properly fish. The only feeling in his body was the excitement to put the new pieces on his precious machine; of learning how something works, and putting it back together. And taking it apart.

BROADCAST

Eirlys ran out of things to say during her shift on the radio, so she decided to tell the county of how the ice shifted. How the thick ice, solid enough to support heavy trucks, cracked around her and swallowed the strange animal. She ended the story by telling everyone that when the theoretical character in her fictional story turned around, the ice was solid once again.

She didn't know what to expect. Perhaps a phone call or two from others confessing their own supernatural experiences on the ice. Though, when no one confided in her, Eirlys felt more lonely.

Four days passed, and Eirlys decided she needed her own confidant. Old Lou and the other elders had told younger generations to speak up when something strange happened, but Eirlys didn't want to be a pariah. No one in the village would outright make fun of her if she said the story was true, that it wasn't just an entertaining tale like all the others she told. Most would raise her to a similar pedestal as Old Lou, but she didn't want others tuning into her radio show as if she were the messenger for the words of higher beings. She wanted people to listen because she was good at her job.

Old Lou's small house by the hill appeared smaller positioned on the outskirts of woods with the tall trees. Hardened snow pushed up against the outside wood walls, threatening to break them down. Eirlys had a feeling the house would never fall.

Smoke escaped from the hole in the roof and was almost hidden by the dark sky. The grey swirled against the white snow on the trees, and Eirlys could smell the burning wood. The road was mostly dirt and rocks, now covered in snow and ice, and she parked her truck in a cleared makeshift driveway in front of the house. A shoveled path led to the front of the house. Approaching the front door, Eirlys knocked three times.

There was a long pause before the door opened, and the short old man greeted her with a smile.

"Eirlys?" Old Lou said, stepping closer and squinting, "Need to talk?"

With a nod, Eirlys smiled back. "Yes. Are you busy?"

"Always and never." Old Lou stepped back and waved a hand for her to come in. "Hungry? I have a bean soup about to boil."

"Yes, thank you." Eirlys wasn't hungry but refusing would be disrespectful. She looked quickly around the house. Her eyes quickly passed over the door that led to the back room. The only time she'd been back there was in high school, when Old Lou was preparing the body of her parents. Ten years later and Eirlys could still smell the tea flowers and peppers brushed over her mother and father's skin. After a second, Eirlys realized she was smelling the aftermath of someone else's burial preparation, not memories.

"Here you go." Old Lou set a steaming bowl of soup on the small wooden table by the window. "It's hot."

Eirlys sat at the table and took up a spoon. Mixing the bowl's contents around, she looked out the glass window. She couldn't make out the frozen sea over the rooftops of the village. Knowing it was there, though, gave her a chill along her spine.

"While that's cooling," Old Lou sat down across from her and faced her directly. "Tell me what's going on."

Eirlys took a deep breath to calm the quiver in her chest. "Do you listen to my section of the radio? The late afternoon time?"

"My radio has been broken for months." Old Lou pointed to a rusty block of metal and buttons. The machine looked like it was bought three decades ago, with dents and scratches on most of the surface.

"Okay." Eirlys began with a shaky breath. "So. I was on the ice a few days ago, and... I saw something."

"Poachers?" Old Lou said, leaning forward with angry excitement in his face.

"No, unfortunately." Eirlys placed her hands on the sides of the bowl, the warmth spreading out through her fingers. "There was a snowstorm that wasn't predicted during the weather forecast and it was a blizzard. Something that could've left the town shoveling tunnels. In the eye of the storm, a male elk walked out in front of me, and threw up oil, I think."

Her eyes flickered up to Old Lou's face. He was waiting for her to continue.

"Then the elk died, and the wind pulled the animal apart." Eirlys watched the steam rise from the soup. "But instead of a normal skeleton, it was metal."

"Hmph." Old Lou grunted, resting his chin on his fist, his elbow supported on the tabletop.

Realizing he wasn't going to say anything still, Eirlys continued. "Then the ice broke, and the crack in the ice chased me to the beach. When I turned around, everything had gone back to normal."

"What is normal?" Old Lou said.

"Oh, um..." Nervous, Eirlys contemplated his question while picking up some soup with the spoon, but then turned the spoon over to watch it spill back into the bowl. "The ice wasn't broken. Greg and his friends were safe, ice fishing, their trucks still steady on the sea. There were no signs of elk, nor storms."

Old Lou's silence made her uneasy, wondering if he was observing the darkness of the village like she had been.

"Have you heard anything like this before?" she said. "From our ancestors."

"Premonitions, yes." He nodded, his gaze catching hers. "Eat up. Let me think for a moment."

He stood and walked around the room while she focused on the cooled food. Old Lou stopped once in a while, his hand on a ritualistic object. It was a seven-inch long rectangle of carved wood, with curves and shapes that could be interpreted as animals, spirits, or wind. From Eirlys' view, she could see all three. Then he would move to a new location in the room before pausing again. After Eirlys finished the soup, he came over and sat back down.

"Have you been out on the ice since this vision?" he said.

"No, I've been terrified." She blushed, looking away from his face. "I want to, I know I should, but what if I fall through the ice?"

Old Lou nodded and placed a hand on top of hers. "The spirits are giving you a message, trusting you. You need to trust them. If you don't listen to them, there will be unrest."

"What do you think the message is?"

"I'm not sure." Old Lou said, surprising Eirlys. "Unrest from the misuse of the land and resources."

"But that's nothing new." She shrugged. "Men have been abusing this country for centuries."

"Industry has made the world darker." Old Lou pressed his hands together and set them on top of the table. "We will never fully understand the spirits. But, Eirlys, if they are trying to tell us something, we must listen."

Gazing in the direction of the sea, Eirlys placed her hands in her coat pockets. Its emptiness made her anxious, and wondered if she should confess her loss to Old Lou. Would he be disappointed?

"Oh," she forced herself to say, "I dropped my compass during the storm."

"Were you following your compass before the vision?" Old Lou said, showing no sign of anger or disapproval.

She nodded.

"Then you know what you need to do." Old Lou said. "You were guided."

"What if I get lost?" she said. "Without my compass?"

Resting the wooden stick on the table, Old Lou went to a small box on the fireplace mantle. "Some of us are lost without our compass. Some of us need to lose it to be found."

Eirlys felt satisfaction. She had been waiting for Old Lou to say some cryptic words of wisdom since she arrived. Though his words made her uneasy. She had heard myths and legends, and the humans tested in those stories. What would Eirlys's test be now that she was being rerouted onto a new road?

"Here's an extra compass," Old Lou closed the small box and held out a flimsy plastic trinket, "So if you actually get lost, you can find your way back."

Eirlys felt somewhat relieved, taking the compass and putting it in her pocket.

"I'm glad you showed up, Eirlys." Old Lou said, sitting back down at the table. "I've had an idea for some months now and didn't know how to go about it."

"Sure."

"As you know, growing up in this village," Old Lou said. He flattened his palms against the tabletop, squinting at them, "There's been an increase in depression, unemployment, and suicide, especially among the younger generations."

"Yes." Eirlys imagined the list of names she had to report to the public every few months. The most recent name, Kiiñak, had left her feeling more restless than the others. She never knew he had been so sad.

"I have been stubborn." Old Lou said with a low tone as if he was having a hard time admitting it to himself. "I was raised that our culture, our traditions, are everything. It is a bit easier for me as my job is clear. My father was the shaman, and his father before, and so on. Other men in the village haven't had such a clear purpose. With all the jobs in Itcha Navak or farther, our village is fading. Our culture is dying."

Old Lou looked up at Eirlys, and a weird sensation bloomed in her stomach: anticipation and hope.

"You know Aguta?" He said, then continued after she nodded. "He has been very strong after Kiiñak's death, and I believe he can help our people, like you. I was wondering if you would take him on as a helper."

Eirlys took a moment to think of the idea of having a teenager working at the station. "Like an intern?"

"Yes." Old Lou smiled. "I've met with him multiple times, and he has expressed his desire for community outreach, though he doesn't know where to start."

"I wouldn't mind having a helper." She thought about the low number of staff at the station and grinned.

"Good." Old Lou stood, and Eirlys felt as if the meeting was over. "I'm happy that we have solved two problems today."

Eirlys wouldn't have said her own personal problem was "solved", but at least she had been given some insight. Old Lou opened the front door and Eirlys stepped outside into the dark. Quiet nights like these used to bring her comfort, but now they reminded her of the hidden, trapped water under the sea ice.

    "There might be a link to the poachers." Old Lou said as Eirlys turned to say goodbye. "From what you told me of the vision."

    "What do you suggest I do?" Eirlys said.

    "Go back to the sea."

THE BREAKING OF ICE

The radio station was set in the middle of the village. It was a small brick building with a slanted roof, which allowed the winter's thick layers of snow to slosh off. On one side of the station was the sheriff's station, and the other side was a two-family apartment building. As Aguta walked past the apartment, he saw classmates lingering on the front porch throwing snowballs at blackbirds. When they saw him walk by, they paused to watch.

"Hey, Aguta!" one of the boys, Jack, called out to him. "Want to go fishing?"

He glanced at the radio station building, then turned toward the main road. He could see the glistening ice of the Sea of Mortla at the end of the lane.

"I wish," he said, kicking a rock into the snow. "I'm helping out at the station."

"With the sheriff?" a girl, Clara, said. She hadn't been in class all week, though no one really reprimanded her, nor all the others who don't show up for school. Aguta wondered what she did with the free time.

"No, radio." Aguta shifted from one boot to the other, trying to look cool. "I'll see you guys later."

As he approached the front door of the station, Aguta watched the group of classmates collecting their gear from a pile on the porch. He really didn't wish to be with them but felt if he had been honest, they wouldn't have understood. He wanted to think what he was doing would help them, but he wasn't sure.

Inside the radio station was a front room with a desk. At the desk was Ms. Wright, the receptionist. Before Kiiñak's death, their mother had spent evenings with Ms. Wright, playing card games and listening to Cher and Fleetwood Mac. Now his mother only saw Ms. Wright on weekend trips to the store and bank.

Now, Ms. Wright looked up and gave a small smile when he closed the front door.

"You must be Aguta?" she said, then turned her head to the side before yelling, "Eirlys! He's here!"

Unsure of what to say or where to stand, Aguta gripped the straps of his backpack and peeped through the open door frame. There were two rooms: one was clustered with machines and appliances, and the other was quite bare.

A tall woman with long black hair came out of a door in the back and stepped through the door frame. She smiled at Aguta, which made him feel warm inside.

"Aguta, hi," she said, approaching him. "I'm Eirlys."

"Hi." He felt a ripple of nerves along his neck, and his hands were sweaty.

"I'm glad you could join me today," Eirlys said. "Let me show you around."

Aguta followed her as she led him into the back rooms.

"This is the control room," she gestured to the organized mess of computers, monitors, microphones, and mixers,

"Though Thompson usually works in here. He just stepped out for a late lunch."

"What do you guys play when there's no one working?" Aguta said.

"Music." Eirlys shrugged, stepping toward the emptier room. "Not many people listen at this time of day. Everyone's getting out of school or work."

She stepped inside the emptier room and, through a glass window, Aguta could see the control room. At a desk were a few microphones and some more electronics.

"This is where we present and talk," Eirlys said, presenting the sticky notes and calendar pad on the desk.

"Who are the presenters?" Aguta said. "Besides you?"

"So, there's Rob and Grace," Eirlys said, pointing to a weekly schedule pinned to the glass. "We each have our own shifts."

"You guys talk about different things, right?" Aguta only listened to the radio once or twice each week as his mother mainly used the machine for the CD player.

"Yes." Eirlys looked at him. "I usually tell stories. Rob talks about the news and weather. And Grace talks about... random stuff, I guess. Sports and gossip. Not my thing."

"If Rob does the news," Aguta spoke, feeling a little embarrassed to be asking, "Why do you do the obituaries?"

There was a slight pause as Eirlys's gaze rested on his face, and he looked away from the weight.

"We take turns." She nodded. "But it's just who feels more comfortable doing it. I come on for a short bit after Rob, then I come back later to do my shift."

She leaned against the desk and crossed her arms over her chest, and Aguta wondered if he shouldn't have said anything.

"I know it's a little strange." Eirlys's words were calming. "As you know, though, this town is a little weird."

All Aguta could think of was to shrug. Eirlys laugh.

"So, Aguta," Eirlys rapped the top of the desk with a knuckle. "I know we talked a little about it over the phone, but I'd like to get more of your thoughts. What type of tasks do you see yourself doing here?"

Aguta glanced at the electronics on the other side of the glass window. Most of them had red or green lights, some constant, some flashing. He hoped to learn how to use the equipment, but was worried about breaking something. His mother was always worried about money, and the last thing she needed was to pay for Aguta's mistakes.

"I don't know." He looked down at his boots and realized his backpack was still on his back and felt dumb for not taking it off. "I don't know much about work, and this place is pretty cool. That's why I wanted to start helping."

"Uh-huh." Eirlys grinned. "We all start somewhere, right? What do you like to do in your free time?"

"I help my mom," he said, thinking of his daily routine. "Sometimes I go into the woods to watch the elk."

Eirlys shifted, standing up from the desk, and then she walked over to a whiteboard on the wall.

"From books I've read," Aguta continued, "Interns get coffee and snacks. And make deliveries."

"You could do that." Eirlys grabbed a large eraser and began cleaning the left side of the whiteboard, leaving the notes on the right. Aguta could see a rough weekly schedule of the hosts, as well as possible topics for today. The word *"Obituary"* was written for Thursday mornings.

"I'm okay at writing, not great." He thought of his last report card. "I like outdoor education and survival skills. I also like learning about our culture."

"Not many people your age do." Eirlys turned to him,

gesturing with the eraser. "Let's brainstorm. But first, please take off your backpack and coat. You must be burning."

Aguta did as she asked, and set his belongings in the corner of the room. He hoped she didn't notice the sweat that made his shirt stick to his back, but she was staring at the whiteboard.

"Let's say you wanted to send a message over the radio," she said, tapping a capped black marker against her chin, "What would that message be?"

"Oh, uh..." Aguta had thought about this before, but his thought had never made sense. "I don't know if I could talk on the radio."

"You don't have to." Eirlys shrugged with one shoulder "But if you could. Don't worry, I won't make you. I'm just curious."

"Oh, okay, well," Aguta shoved his hands into the back pockets of his jeans, "Uh, I'd want to maybe, um, help my friends at school."

"Help them with what?" Eirlys wrote on the board, 'HELP FRIENDS.'

"I guess..." Aguta searched for the right words, "Make them happier."

After writing those words on the board, Eirlys nodded and leaned back from the board.

"Do you find many people at your school are unhappy?" She said.

Aguta shrugged. "I think so, I don't know."

"I think you do," she said.

"The Health teacher says our bodies are changing," Aguta felt the heat on his cheeks, thinking back to the awkward sex education course last month, "And all that stuff we have to learn at my age. And he said we have chemicals in our body that can make us sad and angry really fast."

"Uh-huh?" Eirlys waited for him to continue.

"Everyone seems sad." He thought about his mother, his

friends, Kiiñak, "Not just my classmates. People older than us and younger than us. I'm not sure why, and I don't think it has to do with hormones."

Eirlys smiled, and Aguta felt as if they had met a sad understanding.

"So, I guess if I had to talk on the radio," Aguta nodded his head at the microphone, "I would try to tell everyone how to be happy."

"Aguta," Eirlys said, capping the marker and setting it down on the desk, "I have never heard such insight from someone your age. I rarely hear such truth from adults, actually."

She grabbed a notebook from the top drawer of the desk and handed it to Aguta.

"This is yours," she said as he flipped through to find it blank. "Everything you learn here, all your thoughts, feelings, and ideas are to go in here. You don't have to show it to anyone, even me."

"What kind of stuff should I write?" Aguta felt panicked.

"Whatever you want," she said. "Make a list of ideas on how to help your friends. Or a list of songs you would play on the radio. Write about how much you hate working here."

Aguta didn't know if he should laugh, but when Eirlys let out her soft chuckle, he let himself do the same.

"If you have a great idea," Eirlys said, gesturing to the whiteboard, "Or even an okay idea, and you want to tell me, go ahead. The only way to help our friends is if we start talking about it. The reason why this has gone on for so long is that everyone ignores it."

"So, you think there's a problem, too?" Aguta had never heard an adult mention it before.

"Yes." Eirlys paused. "And I don't know how to fix it, either. But I think we can find a way."

ICE CARVINGS

Tobias Morgan rode along the frozen Sea of Mortla. He was hauling an unusually large package that had taken him fifteen minutes to tie onto the sleigh hooked to the back of the snowmobile. The sleigh's runners in the snow were made deeper from the weight. On top of the package was the usual bag of letters. Tobias did not care what he delivered as long as he got paid every Friday, the same amount, as long as every package arrived undamaged. He was the fastest messenger because he was the only one. Not many people wanted to traverse the desolate, cold permafrost twice a day, six days a week, ten months of the year, to deliver mail between two rural pop-up towns.

Tobias had left early in the morning, way before the sun would rise at noon. He reached Itcha Navak at dawn, and now, on his way back to Sinaaq, the day was bright. The wind whipped against his many layers. Snow from the ground frequently obscured his vision through his goggles. Journeying through the arctic was already cold, especially in the middle of winter.

BY GABRIELLE RUPERT

As Tobias drove on the large frozen plain, his occasional scan on the horizon furrowed when he saw a dark blur. Getting closer, he noticed that the object did not move position, but contrasted more and more with the white snow. Tobias reached the scene.

There were only two colors: red and black.

Lying on the surface of the ice was an orca. The white portions of its body blended with the snow below it. The black curves reminded Tobias of his one stark contrast in the wasteland, as he was the only black person here.

The orca was bleeding. Liberally. The large, pectoral fins had been brutally separated from the body. Blood had poured out in large quantities from the gashes, accumulating on the ice and leaking into the hole that the animal had been pulled from. There were also random irregular cuts along the abdominal section of the body, as if the poacher had been trying to bleed out the whale as fast as possible. A strap had been left wrapped around the animal's body.

The taking of the fins, but not the dorsal fins, was a sign of poachers. Gangs of foreigners would come to Sinaaq during these cold months to track pods of orcas under the Mortla ice, using high-tech satellite tracking devices, then fish for the whales. Finding the orcas had recently become easier with technology, as Mortla's ice became thicker and thicker each year. The poachers would cut the pectoral fins only; they were believed to prolong life about five years. Or so said the insincere guides of Sinaaq.

Tobias never understood how such an advanced world could still believe in myths. Once close enough, he swung his leg over the seat and stood on the snow. He walked over to the giant, stopping before the pool of blood. The whale did not move. Tobias grimaced along with his observation of the marks made by the straps.

POP! Crank. High-pitched spinning.

Tobias rushed to his vehicle to keep it on. But he could do nothing as the machine shut off, smoke seeping from the vents located by the motor. His gloved hands slammed against the seat of the vehicle. His exclamation was matched with a strange noise from behind him.

Tobias turned around. The orca made another noise, and it hurt Tobias's ears. Watching the orca, he understood that it was not dead yet. The poachers left it alive!

Forgetting about the low temperature, Tobias took off two sweaters and pressed them against the cuts of the monster. The sweaters barely covered the lacerations. Blood soaked the thick cloth quickly and ran through Tobias's fingers. Tobias gasped, then shouted incoherently because the whale's high-pitched cries vibrated in his ears. The blood was boiling compared to the air pressing against them.

As the blood poured, Tobias grabbed the strap and untied it . His cold fingers had a difficult time packing one of the wounds with the sweaters, but he was able to keep them in place with the strap. Every time Tobias put pressure on the incision, the orca cried in pain.

"I know! I am trying to save you!"

The sea creature did not stop wailing. Once the makeshift bandage was set, Tobias paused, thinking of what to do next. Then he grabbed a bucket and a rope from his sled and edged toward the large hole in the ice. If he fell in, he would most certainly die. No one would find him here.

Using the rope to lower the bucket, Tobias filled the bucket to the top and struggled to bring it to the orca. He poured the water over the orca, hoping this would keep it from drying out. The water gravitated down the soft, rubbery skin, washing the blood off the mutilated areas, diluting the blood that collected on the snow. Though the process was slowed, blood still seeped through the bandages. The other wound was still uncovered, though the contact with the ice caused a slow flow.

Perhaps, Tobias reflected, his efforts to save the orca would help it stay alive or until help came. Though he was the only one known to travel here, apart from the poachers. Tobias noticed the fading tire marks in the snow, heading in the direction of Sinaaq.

"Are you suffering?"

The orca was in a lot of pain and wanted death to arrive sooner. His hand went to the knife secured to his belt. Mentally mapping out the orca's body, he tried to guess where the brain may be. Or the heart. If he could find them, he could end the orca's pain. But if he missed, it would cause the orca more suffering.

The orca made another screech, though quieter and feebler. Tobias watched the rising of the orca's body as it inhaled. When the orca was quiet, Tobias listened to the whiny wind whistle against the flat frozen lake, picking up dustings of snow. The ice was so thick this winter that it did not creak or shift; thick enough to hold the large package he was to deliver, and thick enough to support a truck full of orca fins.

If he allowed himself to listen more closely, Tobias could hear the arduous breathing of the orca. He focused on the noise of water splashing into the orca. He tried to talk himself into leaving, knowing he shouldn't be outside at dark for long. He knew the whale would die. But could it survive? He didn't know much about whales.

Tobias stayed. He found himself talking to the orca, telling the wild animal that "It would be okay," and apologizing for "Asshole people." His muscles hurt. The bucket started slipping out of his fingers. Splashing. Wasting time. Wasting water.

The exact time was not noted mentally, but Tobias came from the ice hole to the orca for the nth time, and he noticed the orca had stopped crying and breathing. Freezing, Tobias did not know what to do. Tears brimmed his eyes but he brushed them away with the sleeve of his sweater. He poured the bucket out, put it on his snowmobile, and tried the motor out of spite.

Thundering on, there was no smoke coming out of the vents. Tobias didn't shout in joy. He realized he would see the body tomorrow. Twice a day. Six days every week. Its body would remain on the ice until the ice melted, which would be months from now.

After unhooking the sled, Tobias drove slowly over to the body, sidling up so the front of the vehicle touched the carcass. With great precision, he powered the vehicle against the body slowly, pushing the body towards the hole in the ice. He didn't want to go too fast and fall in, himself. With a plop, the orca's body slid off the edge and into the water. Tobias made a tight turn away from the hole. After the sled was attached, Tobias hesitated, turned around, and saw all the blood that stained the snow and ice. He would go around, drive on the other side of the frozen plain. After a few snowfalls, the blood wouldn't be visible.

Adjusting his seat, Tobias got comfortable, and drove in the direction of Sinaaq, towards the shadowing horizon.

SPARK

Tobias tried forgetting about the orca on the ice. The night he returned from the crime scene, he had stripped the bloody, frozen clothing off and stood in the shower for at least an hour. When he turned the shower off, he still imagined the gashes on the creature's side. When he made coffee the next morning, his hands didn't feel the pot's handle but instead the flesh and liquid oozing through the bandages.

It took less than twenty-four hours for Tobias to realize he was angry and wanted to do something about the poachers. He had heard of incidents around the Sea of Mortla but had never witnessed it before. The aftermath. It made him sick, as if he himself was slashed open from breast to navel and left to bleed out alone in the snow. For the first time in six years, Tobias Morgan called out of work.

"What?" said Stacey, the manager of the convenience store in Sinaaq. The store was also the post office. "How are we going to deliver mail?"

"Ask Bobby," Tobias said, putting a little sugar in the black coffee in his mug. "That's why we hired him."

"To help me with the store!" Stacey said, her high-pitched voice screeched through the phone.

"And if anything were to happen to me," Tobias said, trying not to let his frustration be heard. "I need a day."

He heard a heavy sigh on Stacey's end.

"Fine," she said. "I'm sorry, I'm just surprised that you need time. Is everything alright?"

"Yes," he said, hand shaking in anger as he grabbed a bag of oats from the cabinet. "I just need a day."

"Alright," Stacey said. "I'll take care of it. Better be back tomorrow, T."

"I will."

Once the phone was hung up, he prepared and ate a bowl of oatmeal along with his coffee. Then he bundled up and went outside. The weather was meant to be clear, with the sun beginning to shine over the ridge of trees by the hill. He hoped the ice would melt a little, but knew that would not likely happen.

When Tobias entered the sheriff's station, he saw a row of desks with matching chairs, but only a third of the officers at the desks. The sheriff, Abe Dolson, stood in the doorway to his windowed office positioned in the back right corner of the station.

"Tobias, what can I do for you?" Dolson called across the open space.

"Hi, Abe." Tobias hoped he could muster some semblance of social ability. "Can I speak with you in private?"

A couple of the other officers turned their heads to look at Tobias, and he felt warmth spread from his neck to his face.

"Sure." Dolson raised an eyebrow before gesturing for Tobias to follow him into the smaller room. "Want some coffee?"

"No, I already had some, thanks though." Tobias kept his eyes forward as he went into the sheriff's office.

Once the door clicked shut, Dolson pulled out a notepad and a pen. "What do you need to talk to me about?"

"It has to do with the whale poaching." Tobias said in a lowered voice, even though no one could hear them. "I was out on the ice, you know, like I am most days."

"Yep." Abe's face turned more serious, if possible, as he jotted notes down.

"I came upon a dying orca." Tobias kept his eyes open so he wouldn't see the sad dark eye of the beast.

"It was still alive?" Dolson said, surprised. "Still intact?"

"Mostly, I think." Tobias pushed his sleeves up his arms, feeling warm even though he took his coat off. "I don't know much about them, but the fins were gone. I thought poachers usually took the whole whale."

"They may have seen you coming," Dolson said, "And rushed off not to be spotted. They do usually take the whole creature as the bones are valuable on the black market, as well as the blubber and such. What time would you say this happened?"

"Oh, it was half-past three, roughly." Tobias said. "It was my direct route from Itcha Navak. I'm just surprised I haven't seen them before."

"There has been an increase in poaching activity, as you must have heard," Dolson said, looking tired. "I'm starting an investigation alongside the Fish and Wildlife manager, following all the information people have been bringing forward."

"We have to stop the poachers." Tobias felt anger erupt in his chest, not at Dolson but at the lack of knowledge and power he had in prevention. "Is there anything I can do?"

Tapping the desk edge with the pen, Dolson gave Tobias a

long, thoughtful expression. "Unfortunately, no. You need to keep doing your job, and if you come upon anything else, report it."

Nodding, Tobias took a deep breath, trying to calm his frustration.

"I appreciate you coming in, Tobias," Dolson said, putting the cap back on the pen. "How's life treating you here? It's been, what, eight years?"

"Six," Tobias answered, glancing out one of the windows to see the rest of the officers.

"Wow, right." Dolson laughed. "Sorry, it just seems you've lived here forever."

"Wish I had." Tobias patted the arm of his chair twice before sitting up straight. "Is there anything else you need?"

"Nope, unless you come up with any other information." Dolson stood and walked around the desk. "Let me walk you out."

Tobias left the office feeling unsatisfied and grumpy. The feelings festered as he made his way to his house, which was a little cabin in the back of the town. He could see the hill of stone burials in the distance, but then he turned down the lane toward his house and he could only see the trees. Before going inside, he checked on his snowmobile. It thundered on without a problem, but he still felt it would need to be checked tomorrow when he visited Itcha Navak. The town's mechanic, Citana Carver, could check on it during Tobias's lunch break. There must be something wrong with it for it to act up on the ice yesterday. It had forced him to stay with the orca.

All Tobias could do, besides be upset at the poachers, for the rest of the day was tidy up the house, listen to the radio that was always on when he was home, and read. The laundry that he washed and dried a week ago hadn't been finished folded, so he tended to that as Rob spoke on the radio. The only time

Tobias really listened to the radio was when Eirlys Wynn was on. Her comforting voice always helped him to sleep during her late afternoon and night show. He had only seen her in person a handful of times, all with her picking up mail and Tobias noticing her from the mailroom. One time as Tobias had been sorting mail into the name slots, he was putting a bundle of letters into a slot while Eirlys was opening her box at the same time. Their glances had met, startling each other. Eirlys had laughed, and Tobias immediately recognized her voice. He read the name of her mailbox, and it confirmed who she was. He muttered a sorry before she smiled and closed her side of the box.

He longed for her voice now, knowing it would quiet his racing thoughts about the poachers. He wondered what she thought about the whale killers, and remembered Eirlys was born and raised in Sinaaq. She must have been angrier than Tobias.

Once the laundry was folded and put away, Tobias made another pot of coffee. As the water steamed through the coffee grinds, he wiped down the kitchen and inventoried the contents in his fridge. He didn't have much and knew he should stock up in case another storm blew through. That happened two years ago, and he had to call Stacey for help. He had lost ten pounds from the lack of food, and he promised Stacey never to be underprepared again.

There was a knock on the front door, the noise pulling Tobias from his thoughts on the best type of breakfast to buy. Still holding a round canister of oatmeal, he closed the fridge and went over to the small front foyer. The translucent glass on the door suggested a feminine figure, and Tobias's eyebrows scrunched in confusion. The person knocked again, and Tobias reached forward and opened the door. His eyebrows now raised in surprise.

"Tobias Morgan?" The tall woman had high cheekbones that seemed to shimmer in the warm glow from the light above the front door. Tobias' noticed her dark pink lips, full and anticipating.

"Yes." He could not believe Eirlys Wynn was standing on his front porch.

"I'm Eirlys." She reached her gloved hand out, and Tobias felt shaky as he reached out in greeting. He realized he was holding the oatmeal box, so he switched it to his other hand, trying not to look any more lame. "I'd like to talk to you about the whale you saw yesterday. And the poachers."

Eirlys paused the pickup truck at the edge of the ice, hesitant about driving onto the frozen sea. Other trucks were parked around the edge of the beach, the citizens of Sinaaq ice fishing, enjoying an early morning with their friends and neighbors.

"Everything alright?" Tobias said. He was sitting in the passenger seat next to her, waiting.

"Yeah." She drove out onto the snow-packed ice. The only sound was of the tires crunching on the calm snow. "So, what happened to your snowmobile?"

She glanced in her rearview mirror to see his snowmobile in the bed of the truck. It looked old, or overused, but she didn't ask for a second time why he didn't simply drive a truck.

"It was acting up the other day," Tobias said, his voice gruff. "I would drive it today, but since it wouldn't have carried both of us, and the bag of packages."

She saw him glance at the bag, which sat in the narrow backseat behind her.

"I don't mind." She did, but she was forcing herself to face the thing that scared her. The ice. And to learn its message. "If it isn't fixed after lunch, I can give you a ride back."

"Then you'd have to drive me back tomorrow," he said, waving a hand. "I can stay at the mechanic's. We get along and he has an extra bunk."

The sun hadn't yet risen. The frozen sea looked like a starless sky, but Eirlys could see where the ice and horizon met as the actual sky was covered in tiny bright lights. She kept her eyes wide, looking out for cracks in the ice that may creep up in her headlights.

"You said you wanted to talk?" Tobias prompted.

"Oh, yes." She sat up straighter in her seat. "So, you pushed the whale back into the hole? Why?"

"Jumping right into it, okay." He gave a dry laugh that sounded like he was clearing his throat. "I don't know. I felt that was the right thing to do at the time."

"Are you spiritual?"

"No, not really."

Eirlys had been unsure if she should tell him about her premonition but now decided against it.

"Most of the people of Sinaaq are," she said. "Why don't you live across the sea?"

"It's quieter in Sinaaq," Tobias answered, and Eirlys could see him picking at his nails. "I know I'm an outsider, which is why I'm fortunate for everyone's acceptance."

"I don't really care about immigrants." Eirlys grinned, turning her head slightly so he could see her expression, "Some others do, but most townsfolk are happy when people move in since the population is so small."

"Yeah," Tobias said, "I lived in Itcha Navak for about a month when I first came out here and didn't like it. I don't mind visiting it, but I enjoy sleeping in a house without having to hear gunshots and drunk fighting."

"Does that actually happen?"

"Not every night." He met her gaze, and she forgot where she was. "I'll point out the hole. It should be coming up soon."

"Hole?" She looked back at the ice. "Oh, right... So what made you come out to the frozen middle of nowhere?"

"I lived in the city most of my life. Then I decided it wasn't for me," Tobias said.

"Wow," Eirlys said, "You don't act like other city folk I've met. You're much more relaxed."

"You think I'm relaxed?" His voice was mixed with surprise and a built-up chuckle.

"I hope that's okay," she said. "Is that it coming up?"

After a pause, Tobias said, "Yes."

Slowing down, Eirlys steered the truck a ways away from the hole. They climbed out and walked over to the jagged edge. The ice had a faint egg-shaped hue of red, but other than that, there was no sign that anything happened here.

"The orca was here." Tobias walked right up to the edge. "If you look at the rim, you can see some of the flesh frozen--"

"I'm good here." Eirlys stayed a good ten feet from the edge, focusing on Tobias's boots. He was dangerously close!

"Oh, okay, well," Tobias continued, pointing around, "I came from that direction, then stopped there. My snowmobile wouldn't start, and I decided to... check out the orca. Then when it died, my snowmobile started working again."

"Wait," Eirlys looked at his face, "Your snowmobile only stopped working when you were with the whale."

"Yeah." He shrugged. "There was nothing I could do for it, so I pushed it into the water. I didn't want the poachers coming back to retrieve it."

"They will just find another whale." Eirlys wasn't playing devil's advocate; she was interested in Tobias's reasons.

"Of course, they would." Tobias's glare snapped up at her,

his voice angry. "But what else was I supposed to do? Leave it? I tried, but my vehicle broke down."

"Would you have left it if you could?" Eirlys said, taking a step closer to see the water at a safe distance. "If you hadn't broken down?"

"I try not to think about that." Tobias shoved his hands in his coat pockets and walked back toward the truck. "I hope you have your answers."

"I guess." She walked back and climbed up to the driver's seat. Slamming the truck door, she felt agitated but couldn't really explain why. "From what Greg told me, and what Abe told him, you seemed pretty pumped up about the poachers."

"It's a shitty thing for them to do!" Tobias struggled to buckle his seat belt, and it finally clicked after the fifth attempt. "There won't be any whales left if those guys keep killing them."

Eirlys reached her hand over and placed it on Tobias's arm. "I know. I feel the same way."

He glanced at her hand in his arm. She brought her hand back to the steering wheel and started the truck. They rode in silence for a few minutes.

"Do you have a plan?" Tobias said.

"What do you mean?" Eirlys turned the heater on to the first setting and adjusted it to heat her knuckles.

"To find the poachers." He also adjusted his heater, except he pointed the vent at his legs. "You didn't want to see where the orca was killed. You wanted to go to the town."

"Tobias Morgan," she smiled and snuck a glance at his face, only to see him watching her, "You could have been a detective or something. What was your job in the big city, anyway?"

"Lawyer," he answered with a clenched jaw. "Now, answer the question, please."

She let out a loud sigh. "I'm going to ask around about the poachers. Discreetly, of course."

"No one is going to say anything," he said. "Not in that town. They don't like snitches."

"Then I'll ask where I can find some nice bone material," Eirlys shrugged, realizing she hadn't thought this trip through, "Or blubber for oil."

"No offense," Tobias raised a hand as if to shield her incoming wrath, "But most people will take one look at you and know where you're from."

She considered her blue jeans and boots, then looked at the ice in front of the truck.

"Isn't everyone out here wearing this?" she said.

"Yeah, but most people aren't native," he said. "They're outsiders, so they'll see your black hair and dark eyes and immediately know you're from Sinaaq. They'll tell you nothing. You need to be careful, too, as there are some folk who think poorly of your kind."

"My kind?" She clenched the steering wheel tighter. "You live with my kind."

"Eirlys, I have nothing against your kind," he raised his hands again, "I'm just trying to prepare you for what you might experience."

"I'm a grown woman." The only time she's ever had a conversation like this was when she was seventeen. She had been telling Greg about her newfound independence and how strong she was, just to get him to stop acting as her surrogate parent. This had been a few months after their parents died. "I take care of myself."

"I don't doubt it." Tobias said, lowering his voice as if to try to end the conversation. "I guess we should part ways then, once we arrive in town?"

She glanced at him and gave another sigh.

"I'll stop by the mechanic's before I leave." She told him. "Just to check up on you."

"I'm a grown man, Eirlys Wynn." Tobias's tone wasn't mocking but meant to make light of the argument. "I can take care of myself, but I wouldn't mind seeing you before you head home."

"I don't doubt it." Eirlys grinned, barely seeing the silhouette of the town against the white land beyond.

GONE; BY(E)

Eirlys Wynn had been to a bar before, but the one in Itcha Navak was very different from the one in Sinaaq. Where Sinaaq cultured respect and friendship, the town across the sea festered depravity. Eirlys thought of the kindest words, but all she could imagine were the cracked concrete walls and broken shingles falling off the roofs. Each street had at least two abandoned cars, hoods and tires taken off to expose the engine or wheel axles, where more parts were missing. The town had more people than her village, with people of different shapes and sizes as they were bundled against the weather. She didn't know what they looked like until she stepped into the bar.

As her vision adjusted to the dim indoors, Eirlys felt the almost-instant stare of everyone in the room. She could never meet their eyes, though. It was slightly jarring, knowing they were watching but not being fast enough to catch the stare. She hadn't believed Tobias when he said she would be treated differently. Now, for the first time in her life, she was conscious of her slightly-darker skin and non-European features.

The room was set up with round tables placed around the

room with wooden chairs. A long bar was set to the right with liquor bottles lined on the wall behind. Classic rock played through hidden speakers, loud enough to cover whispers of the other customers. What Eirlys didn't expect was the raised platform at the far back wall that projected into the sea of tables. The whole room was about the size of Sinaaq's town hall, which still seemed a bit smaller than this. The black walls caused it to look larger. An illusion. There was a metal pole fastened into the center of the floor of the stage and bolted to the ceiling. She knew what it was, but had never seen one before.

Fewer people were sitting at the bar, so Eirlys walked over and placed a hand on one of the stools. She felt this was the only place for her to go, even though there were other empty tables. She didn't know who to question first but approaching the men at the tables seemed dangerous. Stupid. Was she stupid for coming here? The plastic red covering that hid the padded seat flaked off onto her palm, but instead of brushing her hand off, she sat down and swiveled the seat toward the bartender.

"What can I get for you?" The white, middle-aged man set down a dirty rag on the bartop. He stared at Eirlys for a long time and it made her uncomfortable. It was rude but she didn't say point it out.

"Water, please." Eirlys said, returning the long stare.

"You looking for someone?" He said.

Eirlys glanced back at him and noticed his name tag: Andrew.

"Yes, but I don't know who." She leaned closer and lowered her voice enough that she could still be heard through the music. "I'm curious about the whale fishers."

Andrew raised an eyebrow and glanced around the room.

"Why?" he said, setting a glass of clear liquid down in front of her. "You don't look like a cop."

"I'm not." She took a long sip of water. "I'm just curious."

"Just curious," Andrew repeated, continuing his wiping of glasses. "Are you interested in whale parts?"

"What if I was?" Eirlys knew it wouldn't be this easy, but was unsure of what else to say. "Would you know who I could talk to?"

A grin spread over Andrew's face, and he shook his head.

"I wouldn't get into that stuff, hon'," he said, throwing his rag over one shoulder and leaning closer to Eirlys. "It's dangerous."

"So you *do* know?"

"No." Andrew's smile faded. "That stuff doesn't interest me."

"You must overhear things, though." She tapped her empty glass, and he re-filled it. "People talk to bartenders."

"Not here," he said. "People are quiet here when it comes to stuff like that. Look at them."

Eirlys glanced around again and made a mental note of the clusters of men. At each table, there were three or four men hunched over their beers. None of them looked in her direction but the way they sat, hushed.

"Not sure why you came all the way here," Andrew said, "Just for whales."

A buzzing erupted from the bartender's pocket, and he pulled a cellphone out.

"Oh, excuse me." He set down the glass he was polishing and walked over to the end of the bar. He picked up a microphone, sending a high-pitched squeak over the speakers positioned around the room. "Thank you kind men for coming here for the lunch-time show! I'd like to welcome to the stage, our favorite girl, Jessica!"

That was when Eirlys noticed a curtain behind the stage. With the curtain slightly pushed to the side, she could see it led to a back room. A slender pale arm pulled the curtain back completely, and in came Jessica.

The young woman, perhaps early twenties, wore purple high heels attached to her bare calves by ribbons that twisted and wrapped along her skin and were tied into a bow below her knees. She wore white shorts with purple lining, but Eirlys could have sworn it was a pair of panties. Thin fabric with glued-on sequins and rhinestones barely covered Jessica' breasts. If her breasts could get any larger, they would have popped out.

To Eirlys's surprise, the chest became exposed as the dance went on, and Eirlys slid out of her chair and turned toward the exit.

There seemed to be a lot more men in the room than before, and Eirlys wondered why they weren't at work. Did they come to see Jessica for every lunch break? What did their families think of them for lusting after this woman?

As Eirlys began stepping toward the front door, a hand wrapped around her wrist, pulling her to a stop.

"Hey, why aren't you up there?" said a deep, throaty voice.

Eirlys glared at who had grabbed her. It was a man with white hair and sun-burnt skin, and his icy blue eyes dug into her face.

"How dare you grab me!" Eirlys growled, attempting to release herself by twisting her arm away.

The man did not loosen his grip, grinning. "As much as we love Jess, we're always looking for new girls."

"Let me go." Eirlys lifted her hand to strike the man, but a familiar voice made her pause.

"Sawyer, let her go."

Eirlys's wrist was instantly free, and she stepped away,

toward the door. She turned at the direction of the voice and forced herself not to gasp.

"That's not how to treat a woman." Adam Locklear was standing in front of her, glaring down at Sawyer. "You need consent, or I'll cut your balls off."

Sawyer grumbled something under his breath and turned his attention to the stage. Another song had begun, and Jessica was still dancing.

Turning toward the exit, Eirlys stepped around Adam without a word. Once both of her feet were set in the snow outside, she turned around to face her old lover.

"What are you doing here, Eir?" Adam said, his lips turned up almost in a grin.

"Just visiting," she said, squinting at his square jaw. "I didn't know you stayed here."

"Yeah," he stuck his hands in his pockets, "I went to the city a few times but didn't find it enjoyable. Missed the great outdoors."

"You don't deserve the land." She wanted to spit on his feet, and she felt the saliva pool on her tongue. "The city suits you."

"You're still hung up on that damn fish, huh." He let a deep breath out, and he sounded like the wind in the trees. For Eirlys, the sound reminded her of her last year at the high school. The year she was with Adam. "You people are supposed to be more forgiving."

Eirlys took a moment before responding. "It is sad that you no longer see yourself as one of us."

"You all forced me out." Adam controlled his voice, but Eirlys could hear the anger in his words. "I had no choice."

"Yes, you did." Eirlys set her chin high, clutching the plastic compass that Old Lou had given her. She was used to grabbing her real one during times when she needed restraint. "You made the choice to break the law. You knew what would happen, no matter the reasons."

She watched the sadness pass through Adam's face, but then she stepped back and angled away from him.

"Thank you for helping me in there." She nodded to the bar's front door. "But I cannot see you again. You know this, Adam."

"I know." He lowered his gaze to the snow, and Eirlys observed the slouch in his posture.

He may have had more to say, but Eirlys didn't care. She walked up the road in the direction of the mechanic, wanting to get back home as fast as possible. She could no longer investigate in Itcha Navak, as she had vowed never to see Adam Locklear again.

BROWBEAT

Sitting at Citana Carter's dinner table, Tobias Morgan held a hot cup of coffee. He wanted to drink the liquid but also wanted to hold the warmth just a little bit longer. He was unsure which would keep him warm the longest as he waited for a diagnostic on his snowmobile.

Realizing the coffee pot was full on Citana's kitchen counter, Tobias sipped the black coffee, holding the cup in both shaky hands as he brought the rim to his lips. The space heater was turned to high, warming Tobias' legs. He stared at the small living room through the narrow doorway. There was a plaid blanket folded over the back of the couch, which faced the broken fireplace. For months, Citana had said it needed fixing but Tobias never really thought that would happen. Citana only had time for his trucks and his girl.

The door leading into the garage opened, breaking Tobias' concentration on the steam drifting up from his second cup.

"There is nothing wrong with your snowmobile." Citana drew out the last word.

Tobias laughed. "Still trying to sell me a piece of shit metal, after all these years?"

"Trying to keep you from freezing, that's all!" Citana poured himself a cup. "But yeah, everything checked out. You only got that ATV a few months ago, right?"

"Yeah," Tobias said. "It was acting up the other day."

"It happens," Citana said, then gave a lopsided grin. "Who was that pretty lady dropping you off?"

Tobias was surprised Citana hadn't mentioned Eirlys earlier.

"She's from Sinaaq," Tobias said, looking out the small front window as if Eirlys's red truck was about to pull up.

"I figured,"

"Why?" Tobias raised his voice a little. "Because of how she looks?"

"No, T, because where else are you going to meet a girl?" Citana gave an encouraging noise that sounded like a hum, but when Tobias didn't answer, continued his questions. "How long have you guys been going out?"

"W-We aren't seeing each other." Tobias recoiled but covered the movement with an empty laugh. "She just gave me a ride."

"T, come on." Citana sat down across the table. "I have offered to give you rides before, and you have never allowed me to help you. In all the years I've known you, you have never traveled the ice with someone else."

"I didn't want to risk driving the ATV." Tobias let out a sigh, then thought of the cold air escaping Eirlys' lips earlier that morning. "But now I know I never needed to come here."

Annoyed with his friend, Tobias stood up and grabbed his coat, which had been laid over the back of his chair.

"Hey, wait, wait." Citana held his hands up, not rising from his seat, "I know romance is a touchy subject for you. I'm sorry.

I just was getting all excited about you possibly seeing someone."

After a long pause of staring at the front door, Tobias sat back down, draping his coat over his legs.

"She's looking for the whale poachers," Tobias said, searching Citana's eyes for any spark of acknowledgement. "And... I want her to find them."

Citana gave a slow nod. "She has to be careful, T."

"Citana, do you – do you know anything about them?" Tobias said, holding his friend's gaze as long as he could. "Have you heard of anyone in the town, or out in the woods?"

"People rarely talk about breaking the law," Citana laughed but it was dark. "Even in a place of outlaws."

"You are the only mechanic in town." Tobias leaned closer, even though they were the only two on the property. "Everyone comes to you with their repairs."

Citana's perpetually friendly face tightened. "I'm the only mechanic listed in the phonebook."

There was a short pause before Citana stood up and set his half-empty mug into the sink.

"What does that mean?" Tobias said, annoyed that Citana wasn't saying more. "Citana, what do you know?"

"I don't want to get involved." Citana said, gripping the side of the sink with one hand. "If they hear that a mechanic snitched, they'll know it's me. Even if I wanted to help, I don't know much."

"Anything can help." Tobias stood up, as well, and noticed how tense Citana was. "Come on, Cit--"

A knock on the front door interrupted the conversation, and Citana straightened his posture before reaching for the doorknob.

"Hello, I'm just here to check on--" Eirlys glanced from Citana to Tobias, and smiled, "Oh, hi, Tobias."

"Hey, Eirlys." Tobias waved and stepped toward the door. "This is Citana, the mechanic."

"Pleased to meet you." Eirlys reached a hand toward Citana, who gladly took it.

"Very happy to meet you, Eirlys." Citana stepped back and gestured for her to come in. "Want some coffee?"

"Oh, sure!" Eirlys entered through the doorway and glanced at the kitchen counter.

As Citana grabbed an extra mug, Tobias stepped closer to Eirlys.

"I thought you'd take longer," he said, "Talking to the townsfolk."

"I did a little of that." Eirlys was unable to hide the uneasy look in her eyes, and Tobias wondered what had happened in the short time since arriving. "But I don't think I'll find my answers here."

"They have to be here, though." Tobias was surprised at how easily she was giving up. "Where else would they be?"

"I know, Tobias, I just..." She trailed off when Citana handed her the filled mug.

"Well," Tobias cleared his throat before turning toward Citana. "Citana said he might know something."

"Really?" Eirlys said as Citana spat his own mouthful of coffee back into the mug.

"He said he might know another mechanic," Tobias met Citana's intense glare with a small grin, "Who might know something."

"About the poachers?" Eirlys said, taking out a pen and small notebook from her coat pocket.

"I really don't want to say anything," Citana raised his hand. "At all. You know those poachers are dangerous. If they are willing to hunt and fish illegally, they probably won't mind killing those who get in the way."

Eirlys brought her hands down, clasping the writing instruments in both hands. "So, you're saying won't do anything?"

Tobias couldn't help but stare at the woman standing next to him. Her face showed controlled influence as if she could read Citana's thoughts. She was a few centimeters shorter than both men, but she seemed much powerful than either one.

"You know who my brother is?" Eirlys said, taking a small step toward Citana. "He is the head of the fish and wildlife team for the country. Do you know what that means?"

"Are you threatening me?" Citana said, stepping back and crossing his arms over his chest.

"No, no." Eirlys suddenly seemed ashamed of herself and turned her face toward the kitchen sink. "It's just that... every time a whale is poached, or some other beautiful creature out on the land, my brother has to go out to the scene. He sees the destruction done by the men, what they leave behind. Sometimes whole animals are left to die alone."

Tobias expected Eirlys to look at him, but she kept her gaze down at the sink, her eyes glazed over.

"I know some people," she continued, "Don't believe animals have thoughts and feelings. And I do believe in hunting, under regulation. But I'm sure if my people were few, I would be worried about extinction. Lastly, I would never want anyone or anything being alone, in pain, during their death."

"You can do what you want," she said. "But if you had the power to help and protect a species from dying out, what would you do?"

Optimistic excitement bloomed on Citana's face, and he laughed.

"I knew your voice sounded familiar," he said, stepping toward the door to the garage. "From the radio show? You really do know how to make people feel."

He left his two guests in the kitchen as he disappeared through the door to his garage.

"What does that mean?" Eirlys looked at Tobias.

Shrugging, Tobias picked his coat back up and pulled it on over his arms.

"What are you doing here, again?" Tobias said, rinsing his mug out and setting it on the drying rack.

"I told you I was going to check on you." She grinned. "Guess you're doing alright?"

"Yeah." He nodded, feeling his cheeks warming. "Will you be heading back, then?"

"I can't stay in this town for too long." A visible shudder passed from her shoulders to her arms. "But I wouldn't mind meeting you back across the ice later for dinner."

Tobias was speechless. His face got hotter, and he searched for words as she stared at him, waiting for an answer.

"Here." Citana burst in through the garage door, holding a piece of paper out to Eirlys. "I had a weird feeling about this guy."

Eirlys took the receipt, and Tobias read from over her shoulder.

"David Watson?" Tobias said. "That's it?"

"He used cash." Citana shrugged, rubbing the back of his neck. "No contact information."

"What makes you think he knows something?" Eirlys said, folding the piece of paper and placing it inside her notebook.

"Well," Citana faced both his guests, placing a hand on his hip. "The parts he wanted, I didn't think much of it at the time as they were scavenged from an old military truck. But after re-examining the receipt, I realized the parts can be jerry-rigged into a harpoon launcher."

SLIP

Many of the high school boys thought Eirlys Wynn was the most beautiful girl in town. She had the great bone structure that reinforced the long ancestral lineage of Sinaaq natives. Her hair always seemed unknotted, the straight black locks gleaming like moonlight on the dark sea during summer. Her hair remained smooth even after her trips ice fishing, hiking, and driving on her brother's ATV at top-speeds with the wind whipping through her hair. She was perfect, in every aspect, to the boys of Sinaaq. But she chose Adam Locklear, and he didn't know why.

    Adam had run with the same group of kids as Eirlys ever since they began schooling, so he already knew who she was. He even knew that her favorite treat was the chocolate chip muffins baked at the local bakery on Tuesdays and Thursdays. Once he found this out, he would wake up extra early those days, grab half a dozen of the muffins on the way to school, and hand them out to his friends. This way, Eirlys would get her favorite treat, and Adam wouldn't appear enthralled. As they grew closer to adulthood, Adam no longer needed to buy six muffins, and only bought one, as the circle of friends changed as people changed. Eirlys and Adam became best friends. Confidants. Some would say they were lovers.

Then her parents died. On the day they did, Eirlys did not leave the burial hill for hours. Four years older and now the adult of the family, Greg tried to convince her to come home. She finally did, but then stayed inside for days. Adam called her house phone many times and even knocked on the front door every day after school. Greg answered the door twice, and the phone three times, and he said the same thing: "She needs time, Adam. I appreciate your concern."

When Saturday morning came, Adam thought about the full day ahead of him and couldn't see him spending it without Eirlys. So, he went back to her house, but instead of knocking on the front door, he went around the side of the house and tapped on her bedroom window.

He would have never done this if Greg's truck was in the driveway. Though he began to doubt himself as Eirlys didn't answer the window.

"What are you doing?"

Adam turned quick to see her standing in the snow next to him. She was fully dressed, with her boots, and her almond-colored eyes squinting up at him.

"Trying to get you to talk to me." He approached her and placed his hands on her shoulders. "I've been so worried, Eir."

"I know." She stepped closer and placed her face against his coat. "I'm sorry."

"Are you okay?" His arms wrapped around her, trying not to focus on how close he was to her body.

Her head shifted against his chest, making a little scratchy noise from the coat fabric.

"I was sad." She pulled out of his embrace and looked up at

him. "I still am, but I need to move on. Old Lou said I've taken too long to mourn the dead."

"Old Lou doesn't know what he's talking about." Adam reached his hand up and cupped her cheek, wanting to take his glove off. "You should mourn as you want."

"If I mourn for too long," she blinked and her shoulders slumped forward, "Mom and Dad's spirits won't be at rest."

"That's bullshit." He saw the anger enter Eirlys' eyes, but he couldn't help himself. "You know it is."

"Adam, I know how you feel." She took another step back, but this time to distance herself from him. "But you need to respect our people's traditions. They are your traditions, too."

Taking a deep breath, Adam nodded. "Alright. I apologize. Can we go inside, now? It's freezing."

Eirlys took his hand, which made his heart skip a beat, and she led him into her house. She made him hot chocolate and herself a cup of green tea, and they sat in the living room by the fire, talking.

"Will you be back to school?" he said, holding his mug in one hand and her hand with his other.

"Monday, yeah." She stared at the fire, and he could see she was lost in thought.

"Everyone misses you."

She looked at Adam, then picked up her tea. The liquid appeared still very warm, but she took a large sip before responding.

"Do you remember the legend of the rainbow fish?" she said, staring into her cup.

Adam raised an eyebrow. "The one we learned when we were, what, like nine?"

"Yeah." Eirlys met his stare. "The ones we aren't allowed to catch."

"What about them?" Adam leaned against her, slipping his arm around her shoulders. Her body was warm.

"Do you remember the whole story?" she said. "How the fish was believed to hold magic that could bring back the dead?"

"You don't believe in that," Adam laughed, then paused. "Right?"

She shrugged.

"It'd be nice if it was real," she said. "I mean, myths and legends are rooted with truth."

"I guess." He placed his nose over his mug to smell the chocolate.

"Adam," she placed her cup on the side table and curled up against his side, "If I died, would you catch the fish to bring me back?"

Her eyes were squeezed shut, and Adam wondered what she was seeing.

"Yes," he said, and her eyelids shot open. "But we can't bring people back from the dead."

Their eyes stayed connected for a few moments before Eirlys reached her face up, and kissed Adam. With one hand already on her back, his other hand came around and caressed her neck. He still didn't know why she chose him, but she did.

* * *

Lying in Eirlys Wynn's bed, Adam woke up in a sweat. His dream was fresh in his mind, and so real. Eirlys had been running. He couldn't see anything except her body, eyes wide and filled with tears. Her mouth tight, teeth bared, as her fur-lined hood bounced around her forehead. Her arms were swinging fast as her legs propelled her forward, quickly away from the unknown pursuer.

Running too fast, Eirlys slipped off the edge of the sea,

which Adam could now see was thawed. There was snow on the ground, though, so Adam predicted it had to be late in the summer. Eirlys fell into the water. Adam expected her to surface, but she never did.

Now that he was awake, he could see her sleeping, peaceful, and content. It had only been a few weeks since their relationship went from best friends to lovers, but to Adam, it felt as if they were bound to each other for centuries. No one in town was surprised, even Greg, though he still gave Adam threatening glares when possible.

Being with Eirlys was all that Adam had hoped for in the last three years, but now that they were together, all he could think about was losing her. Every night, he dreamed of her death, and how he would have to help Greg cover her body in stones. He felt the same sadness that Eirlys had described to him when she lost her parents.

Adam climbed out of the bed and stood at her bedroom window. He could only see the brick building next door but could sense the Sea of Mortla. When he closed his eyes, he could visualize the beach at the edge of town. He imagined himself getting in a boat, alone, and staying out all day until he caught that special fish. He imagined himself having the ability to keep Eirlys safe, and never losing her.

"Adam, come back." Eirlys' hushed voice said from the bed. She reached out through the sheets for him.

He did as she said, holding her tight until she fell back to sleep. Slowly, he felt himself drifting off, thinking. What if the legend was right? What if the fish could protect her from harm?

The look on Eirlys' face when Adam showed her the fish almost broke his heart. No. His heart broke when, after the town of Sinaaq banned him from returning, Eirlys did not go with him.

"I did it to protect you," he said to her. They were standing on the outskirts of the town, with his truck packed and ready to leave.

"You knew what would happen, Adam." She had tears in her eyes, but she refused to touch him. "The fish is sacred. The elders are the ones protecting us."

"You spoke of the fish," he said, feeling angry, confused, sad, and in love all at once. "You thought about catching it, too. For your parents."

"Thinking about it is not wrong!" her voice raised, and her hands curled into fists. "I'm allowed to dream about it and wonder what it would be like to have that kind of power. But I would never--"

"That's why I didn't ask for your permission," he said, putting his hands in his pockets. "I knew you wouldn't approve."

"Then why?" She shook her head.

"I wanted you to have the fish," he said, "To keep, just in case you needed it. I knew you wouldn't have been able to catch it. I understand how you feel."

"Even if I hadn't given it alive to the elders," she said, "I wouldn't have used it. I would've tossed it back into the sea."

"Is that right?" Adam paused, feeling the words bubble up in his chest. "Let me ask you something. If I died, would you have caught the fish to bring me back?"

She stared at him, her mouth shut, and he felt panicked.

"If you one-hundred percent knew it could bring me back?" he said.

He saw a tear stream down her cheek before she turned away.

"Now I know." Adam opened the truck's door but then paused. "I will always love you, Eirlys."

"I never want to see you again." Her voice was heavy as if she had a hard time speaking.

"I know." Adam climbed up into the driver seat and gave a sad grin. "Let's hope the spirits don't follow me, huh?"

He closed the door with a hard thud. As he drove away from home, from town, from Sinaaq, he watched Eirlys' body grow smaller in his rearview mirror.

COLD CASE

The light brown of the corkboard was visible only through the twine. Red was used for connecting the murder cases. White was used to connect other leads. Black and white photos were pinned to the board with yellow tacks, with points dull from reuse. Some of the photos were accompanied by notes of paper, and some were scribbled on with a blue pen. If one were to follow one string, they would find a convoluted mess of knots that nevertheless were connected. And that's what kept Sheriff Abe Dolson going.

Staring at the board, which covered the top two-thirds of his office's far wall, Dolson pointed out the picture he took of a six-foot wide hole in the ice, with darker colors on the edge of the snow. A sticky note next to the picture pointed to the edge of the hole and said 'BLOOD'. He could still remember the chill that ran down his spine when he visited the crime scene earlier that morning.

"I wish he had left it." Greg sighed, pressing his index finger against the glossy photograph. "He said it was an orca, right?"

"Yep." Dolson watched the manager of Fish and Wildlife examine the presentation on the corkboard, waiting for him to say something. "Funny, since Tobias isn't from around here."

"What do you mean?" Greg asked, though he fully well knew what Dolson meant.

"Sure, Tobias has been a resident here for almost a decade," Dolson sat on the edge of his desk, "So perhaps he has adopted our culture and spiritual beliefs."

"Funny you should mention," Greg gave a dry laugh, "Since Eirlys has been talking to him, she thinks he is some kind of reformed Sinaaqan."

"Wait," Dolson held a hand up, "Eirlys has been talking to him?"

"Well, I guess they hang out, now." Greg tried to hide the protectiveness from his face, but Dolson could hear it in his voice. "Doesn't matter. She's a grown woman."

"Yeah," Dolson nodded, "I trust her judgment. It only makes sense that she'd fall for an immigrant."

"What does that mean?" This time, Greg didn't hide the malice in his voice.

"I didn't mean offense, Greg," Dolson waved his hand again, "I just meant all the boys drooled over her in school, and my sister was so jealous of her. Saying Eirlys could have any man in town that she wanted."

After a sigh, Greg turned and looked back at the board. "I know. I just hope her intuition is right about Tobias. Anyways, what type of tire tracks were near the hole?"

"All Tobias said was the 'typical kind,'" Dolson said, handing Greg the statement Tobias gave, "Goes to show you how little the man knows."

"Stay focused." Greg flipped through the statement, scanning the words. "And he didn't see anyone on his way from Itcha Navak?"

"No." Dolson grabbed his coffee mug, which now was his fourth cup. "But he said the tracks appeared to veer off north of the sea, so they must have gone to the woods and then went back home."

"And we are positive it's not here?" Greg asked, holding the statement even though he finished reading it.

"You know how many times we've checked." Dolson sipped the lukewarm liquid. "Even if the poachers *were* here, there are no buildings big enough to hide their tractors and equipment."

"They seem to change their routes." Greg wrote something on a sticky note, then placed it below the twine connecting the new photograph to another older one.

Dolson contemplated the older photograph of a harbor porpoise, examining the dead mammal before looking down at his mug. "Sometimes they travel north, sometimes south. Sometimes they seem to come straight at us before heading around the forest. I don't get it."

"They're smart." Feeling sudden exhaustion, Dolson pulled his chair out from his desk and sat down. "They know what they are doing. They know the land and our patrols."

"Patrols?" Greg laughed but wasn't smiling. "You mean Dan and Erik? Sorry, but between those two and us, we barely cover Sinaaq, the forest, and the sea. There's too much area."

"You know there's nothing I can do about that." Dolson took a deep breath in through his nose. "There's no one else to hire. It's not in the budget."

"Make another petition to the city." Greg sat in the chair on the other side of Abe's desk.

"No one cares about dead whales, Greg." Dolson kept his hands relaxed on his mug and took another sip. "We do, of course, but they aren't going to send recruits to fight poachers, even if it *is* against the law. Now, if it was drugs or prostitution, or murder, they'll send in an army."

"But they turn a blind eye to rising suicides and a dying village." Greg leaned his elbows on his knees and let his head fall into his hands. "I'm sorry, Abe, I don't mean to get upset with you."

"I know." Dolson did know, and had expected this outburst to rise from another whale finding.

"I was appointed to this position," Greg lifted his head and placed his chin on his knuckles, "To protect the natural resources. But I am failing."

"Greg." Dolson rose from his chair and walked around to stand next to his friend. He leaned against the desk and looked down at his hands. "You are not failing. You and your team have protected our land, and have protected many animals and plants from misuse. Every job has its challenges."

Abe reached down and placed his hand against Greg's knee. At first, Greg glanced behind him in a flurry of shock, but once he saw that the blinds to the office were shut from the rest of the precinct, Greg relaxed and placed his hand on top of Abe's.

"I don't like to think," Greg's fingers were cool against Abe's skin, "of this as a job. When I have a bad day, it's because another whale was found dead. Another spirit that needs to be guided to peace. I'm the one who attends the rituals with Old Lou."

Giving his friend's hand a squeeze, Dolson glanced at the corkboard. "I know. We will find them."

"We need help." Greg wrapped his fingers around Abe's wrist and ran his thumb over his palm. "We need more people and more support."

"I'll see what I can do," Dolson said. "I don't think it will be much, though."

"I know." Greg pulled his hand away and stood. "I have to

get back to the office and inform the team. We have to prepare for Survey Day, but afterward, we will work on this."

"Oh, yeah," Dolson grabbed a folder off his desk and handed it to Greg, "Surveying the invasive plants, right? Hopefully, the frost killed them."

"Haha," Greg grinned, taking the folder, "The snow probably killed everything *but* them."

When Greg left the sheriff's office, Dolson was sitting at his desk with a pen in his hand and a stack of papers under his other. From the way each man carried himself, no one would suspect the adoration strung between them.

REJECT

Since Adam Locklear was banished from Sinaaq, most cold nights were spent wondering what it would be like to return to his hometown. Every night was frigid living in Itcha Navak, even in the warm summer months of the northern arctic.

He never really thought about returning until he bumped into Eirlys in Itcha Navak. Her appearance was exactly the same as when they were seventeen, except the edges of her face were more rigid, and she looked more serious. Perhaps it was because she was being harassed by Sawyer.

Adam didn't think it was possible for her to walk away from him again, but she did. Barely looked him in the eye. He couldn't pull his focus away and wished she had paid more attention to him. He wanted to read her mind like he used to do back in school.

The way Eirlys pursed her lips together was the same when he left the village, an expression of such pity but disgust as if a fish deserved more respect than him. The whole village believed that, which was fine because Adam had only done what he did for her. But she rejected him, too, and he lost everything.

For the last rough decade and a half, Adam had been able to redirect his attention elsewhere. After seeing Eirlys, though, he couldn't stop thinking about her. So, he ignored his banishment from the village, drove his car across the sea, entered Sinaaq, and went to the radio station.

The village law was not always enforced by a government authority, and Adam could legally come and go as he desired. There were no cars in the front of the radio station, but there was a snowmobile parked on the side near the entrance of an alley. Glancing over his shoulders, Adam made sure no one was watching. The streets weren't busy as everyone was out helping with the regular weed surveys. The only reason Adam knew about the volunteer event was from growing up there. Adam guessed Eirlys would be helping, too, but hoped she stayed behind to watch the station.

The front door to the building was unlocked, and Adam walked in with his back straight and a sure footing. The first thing he noticed was classic rock music blasting in one of the back rooms down a tiny hallway. The front desk was empty.

"Hello?" he called, taking his gloves off before holding them in one hand.

He could hear the sound of a door opening, and the volume of the music grew before the door shut again. A scrawny boy stepped into the hallway and approached Adam.

"H-hi," the boy stuttered, wiped his hand on his pant leg, and extended it. "I'm Aguta. How can I help you?"

There was a line of sweat on the boy's forehead, and when Adam took his hand to shake, he noticed the sweat collected on the boy's palm.

"Adam." He grinned, giving the boy a firm handshake. "I'm looking for Eirlys Wynn. Is she available?"

"Oh, you just missed her by ten minutes," Aguta said. "She went to the invasive plant survey. I can take a message if you want."

"Sure." Adam watched the boy grab a notepad and pen. "Why aren't you out helping?"

"Huh?" Aguta shrugged. "I wanted to, 'cuz I love plants and all, but they needed someone to man the radio."

"Music's gotta play, right?" Adam laughed.

"Yeah." Aguta smiled a little, scribbling the pen on the paper to make sure it worked. "What's your message for Eirlys?"

"Just tell her that Adam Locklear wants to talk to her." As the name came out of Adam's mouth, he watched Aguta's face transform from blank and helpful to surprised and apprehensive. "If that's alright."

"You aren't allowed here." Aguta dropped the pen and stood tall, though he was a few inches shorter than Adam.

"I was hoping you were too young to know who I was." Adam smiled, keeping his voice calm and his body relaxed. "But I guess I've become folklore, huh?"

"My brother told me about you," Aguta said, stepping toward the office phone. "He said you killed the sacred fish."

"There's a lot of sacred fish, Aguta." Adam held a hand up. "You don't have to kick me out. I'm leaving in a minute. But let me ask first, who was your brother?"

There was a pause before Aguta's voice croaked an answer. "Kiiñak."

That's when Adam noticed the oversized boots on the boy's feet and recognized the bright blue laces.

"I give my condolences." Adam lowered his head for a moment. "He was much younger than me, but I remember him back in school. He was a tough kid."

"Y-you went to school with him?" Aguta said.

"You know how small the building is. We all knew each other back then. He had been a big theater geek before they defunded the program."

"Did Eirlys know him?" The muscles in Aguta's shoulders seemed to tense, but Adam definitely saw the boy shiver.

"Not very well, I don't think." Adam slid his hands into his pockets and felt the hard metal of his gun, and felt a pang of regret for packing it. "Kiiñak hung out with different people than her and I. At least, before I left."

This last sentence appeared to jolt Aguta, probably reminding him of the issue at hand..

"I'm sorry," he said, his voice no longer wavering, "But you need to go. I will tell Eirlys you stopped by, but you need to leave."

With one nod, Adam turned and faced the door. After two steps, he paused and turned back to see Aguta.

"It's good to see those laces." He gestured to Aguta's feet. "But you should find boots that fit you to prevent blisters."

Adam left the building and walked the short distance to his truck. Standing in the snow, he pulled his gloves on and felt the pinprick of someone watching. Scanning the street around him, Adam's found the onlookers.

Loading a truck with hot coffee boxes and cases of pastries, Ted and Mike had paused outside of the bakery to watch Adam. They had been squinting at first, but when Adam faced them head-on their faces furled with anger.

Adam's first instinct was to cuss and run away. Instead, he held his hand up and waved, smiling. As they continued to glare, Adam took his time climbing into the driver seat and buckling the seatbelt. He knew they couldn't do anything as he slowly backed out of the parking spot and drove by them. In his rearview mirror, he could see Mike's middle finger directed in his direction, and then they disappeared as Adam drove out onto the ice.

THEODOR & MICHAEL

Someone forgot to assign coffee duty. It was a day designated for volunteers to assist the wildlife workers in surveying the invasive plants east of Sinaaq. Starting from the bottom of the other side of the burial hill, citizens would do a vast line sweep of the fields and forests to observe and record any unusual or foreign weeds. And while some people brought their own thermoses of coffee, most people were not as prepared. So mid-morning, Greg Wynn asked his two closest friends to go back into town. Ted and Mike were happy to go get supplies.

"Grab some donuts, too." Eirlys told the men, holding a notepad open in her hand and a clump of weeds and dirt in her other.

"Chocolate chip muffins?" Ted knew they were her favorite.

"Of course." Eirlys grinned. "I just know the bakery got a new recipe for their specialty donuts, and I want to try them."

"Sure thing." Ted felt breathless as she bent down to tear out another green leaf through the thin layer of snow.

"I'll get him a cold shower." Mike told Greg in a hushed voice, and Ted felt his face turn red. "Come on, Ted."

The two men left the team and walked across the fields to the burial hill. Trucks were parked at the bottom, so they hopped into Mike's truck and made their way around the slope to get to Sinaaq.

Since everyone was mostly surveying, the town was empty. It made Ted feel uneasy, a prick in his subconscious telling him how odd it was to see the village so bare. Then again, he never had left Survey Day until everyone else was done, too.

Thankfully, the bakery was still open. It was an unspoken necessity for Niki to keep the blinking red OPEN sign lit from before dawn and after dusk, especially on the day of community gatherings.

Parked along the uneven curb, Mike hopped out and rearranged tools in the bed of his truck.

"How much does Greg want us to get?" Ted asked, helping Mike fold a tarp up before placing it in the corner of the bed.

"I got a list. Here, I'll finish this if you want to give it to Niki."

Ted took the piece of paper from Mike and walked to the bakery entrance. The doorbell jangled lightly, and Niki's warm smile and red cheeks met Ted's.

"I was wondering when one of you was coming," she said, one hand on her hip. Her other hand reached out toward Ted. "What'll it be, then?"

He gave her the list, chuckling. "Yeah, usually we're pretty organized but we slipped up this time."

"I get it," she said, filling up a large cardboard box with hot coffee. "It's been a weird year for events, I feel."

"Yeah." Ted studied the tiny storefront of three square plastic tables and unused coat rack, getting that eerie feeling again from the empty tables and parking spots in front of the large street windows. "Is there anything I can do to help prepare?"

"No, hun, I got it." Niki placed the first box on the counter and started a second one. "You just rest, now. Want a pastry while you're waiting?"

He didn't have to say anything as she used her free hand to grab a clean plate, place a cheese danish on it, and set it on the counter by the closest bar stool.

"Ha, thanks, Niki." He sat down and picked up the pastry. Flakey crumbs fell all over the front of his coat.

The doorbell sounded again.

"Is he harassing you?" Mike joked, sitting down and reaching for a muffin from the display case.

"You can wait, Michael." Niki shot him a glare, which made his hand recoil from the display case. "You don't just come in and grab things. You aren't a boy anymore."

Ted was trying not to laugh as Mike rolled his eyes.

"And no, Ted is not harassing me," Niki said, grinning. "Anyways, here's two boxes of joe. I'll fill up a third just in case, and then get the food."

"May I use your restroom, please?" Mike asked in a sarcastic tone, the words slowed down.

"Yep." Niki said, then glanced at Ted. "So, you find any cool plants out there?"

"Nothing really cool, I'd say." Ted watched Mike disappear into the back of the store. "But I know we're looking for something. These Survey Days are becoming more frequent."

"Yeah," Niki said, "I remember back in school we had them once a year. Now it's, what, every few months? And it's winter!"

"Apparently some plants thrive in the snow." Ted shrugged, dusting the flakes off his coat. "Just wish I understood it more."

"Yeah," Mike came back, wiping his wet hands on his

jacket, "You never paid attention to our wildlife classes in school. Could've paid off, now."

"Here's the third." Niki placed the box of coffee on the counter and grabbed a pastry box. "A dozen of these... half dozen these... dozen more of those..."

The baker talked to herself as she stacked the boxes on the counter.

"Looks like you'll have to close early." Mike took out a wad of cash from his wallet. "We're cleaning out your shelves!"

"Oh, I don't have anything else to do," Niki said. "So, I'll probably bake some more, test out some new recipes and such. Go through bills and invoices."

"You know, that's not true." Mike leaned onto the counter, and Ted felt annoyed at his friend. "You have things to do. Options."

Niki paused and gave Mike a flirtatious smile.

"You know," she said, setting the last box of donuts on the pile and leaning closer to him, "You're right. I have so many things that I could be doing. Ted?"

Ted felt his heart thumping a little harder.

"Once you've completed the surveys," Niki said, "Want to pick me up here and go to the shoreline together?"

Mike's mouth dropped open a little, and Ted felt a little nauseas.

"Only if you want." Niki continued smiling and held her hand out for the payment. "If you have nothing else to do."

It took a moment for Ted to regain his voice. "Sure."

"Great." She handed the change and receipt to Mike. "Enjoy, boys. Save us from those evil plants!"

Ted and Mike carried the coffee and food to the bed of the truck, and carefully arranged them so they wouldn't get squashed or shift around.

"And this is why you have me!" Mike told Ted, setting the coffee down. "I'm your wingman."

"I don't think that's what happened." Ted grinned anyway, a sense of excitement rising in his chest.

"That's totally what happened, man! Niki is so great, and..." Mike stopped talking mid-sentence, which he never did.

"What?" Ted followed Mike's gaze. "That's not..."

Ted also couldn't get words out of his mouth, and he steadied himself by leaning against the side of the truck. Across the street, standing outside of the radio station was Adam Locklear.

FAMILY GATHERING

Greg really did care about the whales. Just as much as he cared about the elk, the Arctic poppy, and the Quaking Aspen tree. He cared about the health of the soil, as well as bird waste. But even before he was paid to monitor the wildlife, Greg Wynn volunteered his time to monitor species and keep regulations among the people of Sinaaq.

Being the manager of Fish & Wildlife, he was in charge of the whole world, it seemed. Technically, the boundary for his position was supposed to be the county surrounding Sinaaq, as well as half of the Sea of Mortla and the forest encompassing that water, too. But because of the lack of an overseer across the sea in Itcha Navak, as well as most of the "local" territory called the arctic wasteland, Greg was asked to expand his perimeter extensively. His few employees and he were spread thin, but they made it work. Without assholes like poachers, days were spent counting animal and plant populations, writing reports, keeping up with regulations and scans of the territory, and providing educational programs to the younger generations of Sinaaq. However, whale killers made daily duties difficult.

Greg was pulled out of the manpower upholding the normal tasks as he worked harder on tracking down the poachers and cleaning up any whale carcasses. He was also the one to mourn the lost creature.

This meant that he would take a bit of the ground that the whale had died on, either snow or soil, and collect it in a bottle. The whale carcass was pushed back into the sea, rejoining the body back to its home. With the bottle, Greg went to Old Lou in the evening. The bottle acted as the body and was used in a burial ceremony for the creature. Then the bottle was set under a small pile of stones at the top of the burial hill. Greg was always the one to set the last rock on top.

This last time, though, the sheriff had gone out to where the orca had been killed. Greg had been so bogged down with organizing the Survey Day that he wasn't able to investigate the death. So, Sheriff Dolson was the one who collected the snow in a glass jar. When Dolson gave Greg the bottle back in town, it only held ice-cold water.

Now, the bottle was hidden by the stone piles. Greg nodded at Old Lou and walked down the dark path on the side of the hill. He was having a hard time focusing on his feelings of guilt and frustration as something else had happened today.

The drive from the bottom of the hill to his house was about three minutes, but as he turned the ignition off, he didn't remember any part of the short journey. He seemed to come to complete consciousness only when he stepped through the front door of his house and saw his sister talking to a man at the dining room table.

"Oh, hey, Greg." Eirlys grinned at him. She was leaning toward Tobias, the county postman.

"Hey." Greg nodded at his sister, and then paused as he examined the dark skin of Tobias's body. "Hi, Tobias. Didn't see you at the survey earlier."

"I was working." Tobias had a tense face as if he had conflicting thoughts and couldn't decide what to say. He always had this expression, but it made Greg annoyed, nonetheless, deeming it indecisive and weak. "I wish I had gone, though."

"We could always use extra hands." Greg slipped his coat off and hung it on the oak hook by the door. "But people need their mail."

"I was just telling Tobias," Eirlys said, "about how you were helping free the orca's spirit."

Greg paused as he put his scarf on the same hook. "Yeah, just came from Lou's."

"Do you do that for all the poached whales?" Tobias asked.

Turning around, Greg stepped toward the dining room table. He noticed how close Eirlys' hand was to Tobias', almost touching.

"Yeah." Greg went to the kitchen sink, grabbed an empty glass, and filled it with water from the tap. "You know, I didn't see your car out front. Did you walk here?"

"His snowmobile is on the side street," Eirlys said, smiling. That was when Greg noticed the notepad in front of her. The top page was three-fourths filled with notes.

"Right." Greg nodded, then took a big sip of water. "Tobias Morgan and his snowmobile."

"There's nothing wrong with that," Eirlys turned to glare at her brother, and her hand rested on Tobias' arm, "And you know that. Snowmobiles are just as good as trucks."

"Sorry," Greg set the empty glass in the sink, "I don't mean to be rude. It's been a long day, and I need to speak with my sister."

"Yeah," Tobias' voice was soft but low, almost a whisper. "I should get going."

"You don't have to," Eirlys said loudly, and Greg turned to see her stand up, "You shouldn't feel unwelcome here."

"I have to wake up early for the long ride tomorrow." Tobias stood and set his hand on Eirlys' shoulder, before turning to Greg. "It's nice seeing you, Greg."

The only response Greg gave was a nod and polite side-grin as Tobias picked up his coat and walked out of the house.

"What the hell was that?" Eirlys' voice was three times louder than before.

"Can you not yell, please?" Greg pinched the bridge of his nose.

"I don't know why you don't like him." Eirlys said. "You both have the same views. He could help you hunt down the poachers if you let him."

"Eirlys." Greg refilled the filled glass. "Have you been seeing Adam Locklear?"

Perhaps the air shattered, but there was no lighting nor thunder. The house seemed to disappear above them, but Eirlys still felt crushed by its walls. Eirlys' face screwed up in a sense of anger and surprise.

"No."

"Then why did he come looking for you down at the station?" Greg felt the chill of the cold water seep through the glass and into the skin of his palm. He wanted to believe his sister wasn't making the same mistake she made back in high school. She had grown to be smart, level-headed, and careful. Not weak-kneed for some traitor

"He what?" Eirlys hadn't been to the station all day as she had been mostly by Greg's side helping identify invasive weeds. The shock in her voice alerted Greg that she was more surprised than he was.

"He spoke to your intern." Greg set the glass down and leaned his hip against the counter. "Ted and Mike saw him driving away from the building, so they went in to check on the place."

"Adam spoke to Aguta?" Eirlys sat down at the dining table again and set her forehead in her hand.

"The boy didn't seem to say much," Greg said, "Only that Adam asked for you."

"Fuck." Eirlys slammed her palm against the tabletop.

"I know you went across the sea," Greg said, then quickly as Eirlys opened her mouth, "And I know I have no say over your life, and you're independent and all, but I need to know if you've been associating with that traitor."

"I would never." Eirlys spat, banging her small hand against the tabletop. "I went to investigate, about the whales, and I bumped into him. I didn't even know he was still in the county."

"Apparently he moved back a few years ago." Greg grabbed the glass of water and sat across from Eirlys at the table.

"How do you know that?" Eirlys's eyebrows furrowed. "You haven't been in the office since the morning, right? Unless..."

Greg said nothing to guide her conclusions as he took small sips of the water.

"You've been watching him," Eirlys said with confidence. "You think he's the poacher."

"Yes." Greg gave a cough as a drop of water caught in his throat. "Watching has been difficult, though, with the lack of employees."

"Hasn't Abe searched his place?"

"Government won't let him." Greg sighed. "There isn't means enough. It isn't like a sex offender or ex-con. He broke Sinaaq law before it was an official law, and he was technically a minor. He doesn't have one misdemeanor or arrest on his record."

"Really?" Eirlys focused on a dark spot in the spruce table. "I'm surprised."

"I know, right." Greg looked down at the half-filled glass. "It's almost like he's a good guy or something."

The Wynn siblings gazes at each other.

"I can't forgive him for what he did," Greg whispered. "Even if you do."

Eirlys looked away and blinked. "I never could, but I've tried."

RUMBLE

They were just trying to help. Perhaps they did in the long run, though things could have gone differently.

Ted was furious by the trespassing of Adam Locklear. He should have never traversed the frozen Sea of Mortla and stepped foot in town. When Ted found out he was there to see Eirlys, every molecule of carbon, oxygen, nitrogen, and phosphorus twisted into tiny flames.

Ted and Mike already carried their switchblades, but Mike brought a hammer. The two men didn't ask Eirlys or her brother for permission, because they believed Adam only deserved to be asked questions later, action now, for he should have known better.

However, the two young bachelors of Sinaaq didn't know much about Itcha Navak, nor the rugged acquaintances of Adam.

As Mike drove into Itcha Navak, he didn't pause at the edge of the sea and snowy sand. The tires dug into the icy ground with no hesitation.

"There's his road." Ted pointed at a worn street sign, his

other hand clutching a map. Niki let him use her updated map, and she was eager to help him. Ted wanted to dwell on their special moments last night, how innocent they were, but he focused on the mission at hand. He would see Niki again tonight, and things would be okay.

"This building?" Mike paused in front of a small house. The structure was no different than the other houses, except there was no truck out front.

"Yeah." Ted re-read the address on the paper and back at the house number. "This is it."

"His truck isn't here." Mike pulled over into a side street and parked. "We'll wait."

"Wish we knew where he worked." Ted sighed, staring at the windows to see if anything was moving. "I'm itching to get back home."

"Not until we make him learn," Mike growled. He grabbed a pack of cigarettes from the middle console and lit one up. "Want one?"

"You know I don't like that." Ted waved a hand at the smoke.

"I know, I know." Mike rolled his window down a bit.

"So, what's the plan?" Ted asked, patting his jacket. "We can't kill him."

"Who says?" Mike raised an eyebrow.

"Come on, Mikey," Ted said. "We're just going to scare him a bit."

"Yeah." The smoker took in a large puff of smoke, held it, and then let it out. "We should cut his hair off. Can't believe he's still letting his hair grow out like us."

Ted had been fiddling with his own long hair, and let it go. He reached for a bottle of water and took a sip.

Catching their attention, a black truck pulled up in front of

Adam's house. A thin man hopped out and went behind the house.

"That isn't him," Ted said.

"Not his truck, either." Mike tossed the cigarette out of the window and rolled the window back up. "But I bet he'll lead us to him."

They waited for the man to return to his black truck, and they followed him down the road, keeping a distance. After about five minutes, the black truck pulled off the road and parked in front of a large warehouse.

"This looks sketchy, Mike." Ted checked the barren street on the edge of the town. There were no residential buildings, and the other warehouses were abandoned.

"There's Adam's truck." Mike pointed, and sure enough, Adam's pickup truck was parked on the side of the warehouse.

Mike stopped his truck in the lot and turned off the ignition.

"We're doing this?" Ted asked, grabbing his switchblade, and holding it hidden against his wrist. He was angry but was beginning to think this wasn't the right way to deal with Adam. Ted acted tough but the last time he beat someone up was junior year in high school; Mike threw most of the punches that time.

"Yep." Mike did the same with his switchblade and the hammer, and as they walked up to the entrance of the warehouse, Ted couldn't notice the weapons up Mike's thick sleeves.

The glass warehouse door was covered in a black cloth, so Ted and Mike couldn't see inside. Ted knocked.

"So polite," Mike grumbled.

"There's other people here," Ted whispered.

The door creaked open toward the inside, and the man from before stepped out. He looked as if he just graduated high school, but something about his emotionless face and blank eyes sent tremors along Ted's skin.

"What?" The man asked, sounding annoyed.

"We're looking for Adam Locklear," Mike said, his voice booming and confident.

"He isn't here." the man said.

"His truck is." Mike took a step forward but the man didn't flinch.

"Yeah, it is," the man said. "But he isn't. He won't be back until later."

The man went back inside and closed the door.

"What do we do now?" Ted whispered.

"He's in there." Mike's glare didn't move from the door. "We're going in."

"What?" Ted didn't know what to think as he watched his friend raise the hammer in his fist and slam it against the front door.

Glass shattered inward and outward, covering and mixing with the snow around the doorway. The hammer ran against the black cloth, making it flap from the force and sudden airflow. Mike jumped through the doorway, so Ted followed.

The warehouse was large and tall inside, filled with metal cranes, pickup trucks, and tractors. From what Ted could see after pushing past the black cloth, Mike had run across the floor in search of Adam.

"Mike!" Ted called, panic setting into his blood.

He heard a scuffling behind a tractor and rushed around it. The young man who they had followed was on top of Mike, holding a wide blade to Mike's chest. Ted ran up behind the man and used both hands to shove him off Mike. Then he felt a thud behind him, and pain erupted from his head.

"Ted, no!" Ted heard Mike's voice, saw his lips moving, but couldn't help falling to the concrete ground.

Feeling limp, Ted relaxed, feeling his fingers becoming numb. His vision was fuzzy around the edges, but he kept his gaze toward Mike.

The young man had retrieved his blade, rushed over to Mike, and sank it into Mike's chest multiple times. Not once, but more. And Ted didn't say anything as he felt like sleeping, even on the hard, cold floor.

* * *

Ted woke up cold. Wet. Pins and needles. His face was laying on the white snow outside. Outside where?

Moving his head around, he felt pain spread through his neck and scalp. He saw tall evergreen trees surrounding him for as far as he could see. Tire tracks were imprinted into the snow next to him, but no vehicle or person was around.

The worse part: Ted had no clothes on.

Like a sick joke, his wrists were tied behind his back, so he couldn't even keep his dick warm with his hands.

Sitting up made Ted's vision fuzzier, and the world spun around him. He realized he couldn't feel the skin of his right thigh, the one that had been laying against the snow. His fingers had no feeling, either from the tight bindings around his wrists or from the cold. The only thing keeping Ted warm was his long black hair, which fell free down his back and shoulders. He tried to grab the ends of his hair with his fingers but didn't know if they were moving.

He knew he had to get up and move. Any movement would create heat, and no one would find him out here. In time, at least.

It took him a few minutes to roll to his feet and saw the strange coloration on his toes. The sight made him nauseous, but he squeezed his eyes tight to calm himself down.

"Focus." He breathed, noticing how sore his throat felt.

He set his gaze forward and took a step. Then another. He had to walk carefully as he couldn't feel the ground well with his numb feet, so he kept a lookout for sharp sticks and rocks hidden under the snow. His whole body ached, especially his wrists. He didn't know what bound them, but it didn't feel like a rope. Perhaps it was a metal chain. Maybe that's all they had. The young man clearly had a partner, the one who hit Ted in the head. But why didn't they kill him?

Suddenly, Ted remembered Mike. He remembered the switchblade in his friend's chest, but it was too cold and the air too dry to let out a sob.

His ankles were cold, but Ted pressed on. After some time, he could no longer feel his feet at all. He refused to regard the colors blossomed on his extremities. Through the trees, he could see a clearing and hope coiled around his ribcage like a warm campfire smoke.

Stumbling past the last tree, Ted let out a dry gasp. The vast, empty surface of the frozen sea extended out in front of him, with no town building or road in sight. No fishing holes. No pickup trucks.

As time grew, Ted did not know if he was walking. He felt as if he was swimming. He thought to himself that maybe he had slipped through the ice and become a fish, and started flapping his blue skin against the current of saltwater. What would he see? Where would he go? The coldness never left, but it no longer bothered him as his body felt comfortable in the abyss of the liquid. No longer falling. No longer rising. Just unmoving. Hush.

STILL LIFE

His hands never shook so bad.

Adam Locklear was able to handle most situations, or at least bullshit his way through. Not with this. There had been so much blood on the floor of the warehouse, Leo was still wiping it up when Adam arrived after sunset. There was a lump covered in a tarp, but black snow boots verified that it was a person.

"What the fuck?" Was all Adam could say as he stood over Leo.

"Is that blood?" David Watson, who had been with Adam all day, came up behind.

"What's the difference," Leo spoke calmly, not slowing in his activity, "Between whale blood and human blood?"

"What happened?" Adam asked, searching for Sawyer.

"Bastards attacked us." The old man came out of the backroom with trash bags, and he tossed one toward Leo. "Came looking for you. They were armed."

"This is just one." Adam didn't want to look, but stepped over to the body and lifted the tarp. "Goddamnit, no!"

"If we didn't get rid of them," Leo still spoke with an eerie calmness, as if he was just cleaning up after a whale kill, "They would have exposed us. They saw what we had here."

"Where's Ted?" With a tightness in his chest, Adam tried appearing composed.

"Old friends of yours?" Sawyer laughed, lighting a cigarette while leaning against the truck. "We let the other one go into the woods. He won't make it."

"Like hell, he won't!" Adam shouted. "He could walk all the way back home and tell everyone."

"Not without his clothes and boots, haha." Sawyer took a long drag, his shoulders relaxing. "Not even your kind can withstand frostbite."

There was a crack of discomfort, a raw and epiphanic sensation that started from the crown of Adam's head. It trickled along his spine, encircled his heart, and made its way to the soles of his feet. The feelings of doubt, for the choices he made in the last fifteen years, he no longer ignored the guilt as he realized one full truth: He fucked up.

"That whole town will be looking for him," Adam jabbed his finger toward the body, "in less than twenty-four hours. They will look here first, most likely, since these two probably talked about us with all their friends."

"No, no," David said through heavy breathing and began puking into a bucket.

"You two," Sawyer pointed at Adam and David with the butt of his cigarette, "Seem to think this line of work isn't dangerous. That we won't have to keep people quiet to protect ourselves. I'm surprised, Adam, to see you so worked up."

"You guys aren't being smart." Adam said, thinking. "Alright, this is what we'll do. Ted and Mike won't be reported missing until morning, hopefully. We have all night."

"I mean, the blood is almost gone," Leo shrugged, holding

up a bloody sponge before tossing it into the black trash bag. "We just have to dump the body and the bags."

"Where were you planning on bringing them?" Adam put a hand on his hip, ignoring the loud second round of vomiting from David.

"Since David was going to the city tomorrow," Leo said, grabbing a clean sponge, "He could bring everything and dump it somewhere."

"What?" David exclaimed, standing up. "I'm not doing your dirty work! Fuck that."

"No." Adam nodded, turning to David. "You already have enough to worry about, with the buyers and all. We will take the bags tomorrow when we go out on the ice."

"And what about the whole body?" David gestured to the tarp without glancing at it. "People are going to notice you dumping a body-shaped trash bag."

"It isn't whole," Leo said, matter-of-fact.

For the first time, David pulled the tarp back to see, and had a much harder time than Adam in composing himself.

"What the fuck is wrong with you?" David stepped back and clutched his stomach.

"I'm proactive," Leo had finished sponging up the blood and stood up. He brought the trash bag over to the tarp and started rifling underneath. Adam could hear light thuds, trying not to imagine the body parts piling up against the stretchy plastic.

"You gonna help us or not?" Sawyer stepped up to David, a new cigarette in his grasp. "Or you gonna pussy-out?"

"He will help, Sawyer." Adam held a hand up between the two men, and touched David's shoulder to comfort him, "Help me carry some of these bags to the pickup truck?"

Adam handed a tied-up trash bag to David and grabbed one

for himself to carry. They said nothing until they were on the side of the warehouse.

"I need you to be strong, David," Adam said as he placed the bag in the back of the truck. "Don't lose your cool."

"How can I keep calm?" David's voice was raised, but Adam wasn't worried about being overheard as there was no one else around. "This is scary shit. I didn't sign up for this."

"No one did." Adam grabbed David's shoulder to make him focus. "No one will see us driving out tomorrow. No one follows us, anyways. Once we drill the hole, we'll dump the body."

"I need to throw up again," David said, his hand on his stomach again, "But there's nothing left."

He wiped sweat off his forehead even though the four-thirty evening chill hadn't set yet. With the van loaded with human remains, Adam handed David the keys to the pickup truck out front.

"If you leave now," Adam said, "You should get there before dawn."

David said nothing as he took the keys.

"What will you do until I get back?" David asked, shifting from one foot to the other.

"Stick around here for a bit." Adam nodded toward the warehouse. "I don't want other people following me to my house; can't have that right now."

Nodding, David walked toward the front of the warehouse.

"I'll be back in a few days," David said over his shoulder.

"Get us that money." Adam grinned, walking to the corner of the warehouse and watching David get in the truck..

He watched the pickup disappear down the street. When the taillights were no longer visible, he turned and went back into the warehouse.

"Leo!" Adam called out, examining a medium-sized metal machine hooked to one of the large trucks. "Is this ready to go?"

The scrawny young man slunk over and smiled. "Oh, yeah. We can use it tomorrow."

"We're still going out?" Sawyer asked, standing next to a pile of harpoons.

"Why not?" Adam glanced at him. "Unless you have a problem with blood now."

Sawyer wobbled over with an aggressive expression. But then he grinned, showing missing teeth, and let out a deep, gross laugh.

"That David boy makes you act weird," Sawyer told Adam, slapping his hand on the side of the truck, "Makes you all sensitive and shit."

"To be fair," Adam said, forcing his own laugh, "You separated a man's head from his body. I've seen a lot but not that."

"Are you two done?" Leo asked, impatient with male bonding, "I want to show you how this works."

WATERCOLOR

When Tobias heard the news, he was at the post office. He had arrived at Sinaaq from his mail run early and was hoping to clean his house before Eirlys came over for dinner. It would be their third dinner date, but because there weren't any restaurants in town besides the bakery cafe, they had been having their dates in her dining room. Now it was Tobias' turn to host, and he was nervous.

As he unpacked the letters in the back room, his nerves disappeared, transformed into confusion, sadness, terror, as Stacey told him about the death of Ted.

"All I heard was that he was stripped naked and left to freeze.," she whispered to him. They were standing in the backroom and he sorted mail into the residents' labeled boxes. "And Mike is missing."

Tobias' hand clenched around a random letter. He thought of the two goofy men that always hung around Eirlys and her brother. Tobias knew Eirlys saw them as family.

"Stacey, I have to go." He set the envelope down in the mailbag.

"What?" The short plump woman asked, no longer whispering. "The mail isn't done being sorted."

"I'm sorry, Stace." He grabbed his coat and gloves and pulled them on. "Can you take over? Please."

He didn't wait for an answer as he headed out the door to the front of the building. He heard a sigh before the words, "Fine, T," followed behind him.

Tobias didn't see Eirlys's truck parked across the street by the radio station. Nor did he see Dolson's in front of the sheriff's station. Glancing down the road, Tobias could see a small gathering of people on the top of the burial hill.

As much as Tobias desired to join them, he knew he didn't belong. He wasn't of these people, no matter how long he lived here. The only reason he wanted to climb the hill was to find Eirlys and comfort her, and the last thing she probably wanted was him. She needed to be with her friends and family while mourning.

Going by the bakery, Tobias walked in and smiled at Niki.

"Hey, I'm sorry." She gave a sad smile, "But we're closing early."

"Oh, can I grab a muffin real quick?" He asked, pulling out cash from his wallet.

"Alright," she gave a shrug, grabbed a white paper bag, and a pair of tongs.

"Just a chocolate muffin, please." He laid the bill on the countertop.

Niki handed the bagged muffin to him and took the cash.

"Keep your doors locked, Tobias," she said, placing the cash in the register.

"Always do." He opened the front door. "You do, too."

Climbing onto his snowmobile, Tobias noticed the funeral crowd had dispersed from the hill. The sun was setting, making the figures look like the stones, but moving. He rode over to

Eirlys's house but slowed down as he saw the driveway was packed with trucks. All the lights were on in the house, and loud male voices clamored from inside.

Instead, Tobias directed his ATV back toward the road and toward his street. He put the muffin in his bag; it would have to wait.

Arriving at his house, he saw someone sitting on his front steps. It was hard to see who it was in the dim twilight, but he recognized Eirlys as he parked in his dirt driveway.

"Hey." he spoke quietly, approaching her.

"Hey." She didn't move from her seat, her arms wrapped around her knees.

Sitting down next to her on the step, Tobias set the bakery bag down.

"What's that?" Eirlys said, her voice thick like molasses.

"It's nothing," Tobias said, waving a hand, but Eirlys picked it up and looked inside. "I got you a muffin when I heard about what happened... and, I know it's stupid to think chocolate will help, but..."

"Thank you." Eirlys closed the bag up and took his hand in hers. Her eyes rested on the ground in front of them.

"What are you doing here?" Tobias asked. "I went by your place."

"Then you saw how insane it is." She gave a dry laugh. "I can't be around all those men right now."

"But you can be around me?" He smiled, nudging his shoulder against hers. "I'm a man, too."

Eirlys met his gaze. "You're the only person I want to be around right now."

The intensity of her gaze caused Tobias to suck in a deep breath before speaking. "Do you want to come in? You must be cold."

Taking her gaze away from his, she nodded. Tobias stood and unlocked his front door.

"You always keep your doors locked?" Eirlys asked as they walked in.

"Yeah," he shrugged his coat off, "It's a habit from when I lived in the city."

"There's a lot of murders there, right?" Eirlys asked, stripping off two heavy sweaters and putting them on the back of the couch.

Tobias saw her sad expression. "I'm sorry, Eirlys. I'm sorry for what happened."

"So am I." She walked into the tiny kitchen and leaned against the counter. "So, what's for dinner?"

"Did you still want to do that?" He opened his refrigerator and took out a dish of gumbo.

"Yes, I need something to distract me," she said, "Did you prepare that?"

"Last night, yeah." He put it on the counter and set the oven to preheat. "That's why I left you early."

"Oh," she laughed, taking a step toward Tobias, "I thought you ran away because of my brother."

"No." He remained still as Eirlys placed her hand on his arm, the distance between their bodies diminishing, "Though he provided a great excuse for me to do so. I wouldn't have had time this morning."

Eirlys' face was close to his, and he wanted to lean in toward her. But the depressing events of the last hour prevented him from closing the gap.

"I know you want a distraction," he said, placing his hand against her cheek, "But that's not what I want to be."

The dreamy expression on Eirlys' face vanished, replaced with sorrow.

"Here," Tobias held his hand out toward her, "Let me hold you."

Eirlys took his hand and allowed him to pull her into his arms. With arms wrapped tight around her body, Tobias laid his cheek against the side of her head. His heat mingled with hers, and even standing, clothed, in the middle of his kitchen, he felt as if they had melted together.

"Ted's wrists were bound together," Eirlys whispered, "With the chain of his compass."

She began to cry, and Tobias let her. He listened to her incoherent sobs and understandable phrases of agony. He didn't let go of her except to put the prepared dish into the oven.

"I'll give this about twenty-five minutes," he said, closing the oven door.

"That's alright." Eirlys wiped her sleeve over her eyes. "What should we drink?"

"I have water, beer, or coffee," Tobias said.

"Beer," she said, sitting at the kitchen table.

He popped off the tops of two bottles and gave one to Eirlys. Sitting across from her, he took a long gulp.

"There's going to be a search party for Mike," Eirlys said after taking her own long sip. "I know you have to work, but maybe you can join us afterward."

"Where will you be looking?" he asked.

"I don't know yet," she said. "Abe will let us know. He's working on it right now."

Tobias sighed, impatient.

"I know you have a lot of questions," Eirlys said, reaching across the table and taking his hand in hers. "I do, too, but I need to stop thinking about it."

Nodding, Tobias gave her hand a squeeze. They sat in silence until the oven alarm dinged.

"That smells so good," Eirlys said as Tobias took out two plates.

"Hope so," he grinned, pulling the platter out of the oven and setting it on the stovetop. He scooped a serving onto each plate and set them down on the tabletop. "Voila."

"It's so spicy," she said after two bites, "It's different. I like it."

"My mom used to cook with all sorts of spices," Tobias said, "She taught me a few recipes before she passed."

"She must have been a lovely cook," Eirlys said, glancing up at him, "How long has it been?"

"She died about ten years ago," he said, pausing to think about the time.

"I'm sorry." Eirlys looked back at her plate.

"It doesn't upset me anymore." Tobias shrugged. "It still makes me sad sometimes, but using her recipes makes me happy."

"It's a legacy of sorts." She grinned.

The plates were empty in a matter of minutes. Tobias took another serving as she finished her beer.

"I'll meet you in the living room," Tobias said, standing at the kitchen sink, "Once I'm done cleaning up."

Once Eirlys left the room, Tobias imagined her scanning his shelves. They were packed with books, CDs, and trinkets. He wondered if Eirlys would focus on the books or the music.

With the dishes clean, Tobias went to the living room and found Eirlys examining the worn wooden rosary dangling on the wall.

"I thought you weren't religious," she said as he came up alongside her.

"I'm not," he said, reaching out and touching the wooden cross. "This was also my mother's. I like to hold onto it during tough times, helps direct my thinking."

"It's like our compasses," Eirlys turned so her body was facing Tobias.

"Yeah, something like that." He dropped his hand to his side. "Except compasses have a practical purpose."

"So do rosaries." She wrapped her arms around his torso. "They help people believe. Press on during times of need."

Before Tobias could say anything else, Eirlys stood up on tiptoes and placed her lips against his. He didn't wait to respond. The room dissolved around them as only they existed, only mattered. Tobias no longer worried about his humble furniture. He didn't care about their cultural differences. He no longer cared about being her distraction, and let her use him if that was what she was truly aiming for. He gave her comfort, safety, pleasure. All that mattered was their feelings, now, pressing together, reacting to each other in each domino chemical reaction of passion.

CRISIS

There was less mail needed to be sorted upon arrival at Itcha Navak. With the extra time, Tobias was able to attend to personal tasks. It really wasn't personal as David Watson hadn't done anything against Tobias, but he was a lead for the postman-now-citizen-detective. He wanted to identify the poachers, and he wanted to do it soon.

"Call me if you find him," Eirlys had told him last night, the sheets pulled around her body.

"What should I say?"

"Just tell him you're asking all the neighbors," Eirlys ran her hand over his shoulder, sending goosebumps up his neck. "For a survey for the sheriff."

"He won't tell me anything," he laughed, pulling her closer by the waist. He pressed his nose against her temple and breathed in.

"It's a start." Eirlys pulled back. "It's something."

David Watson's house wasn't remarkable to look at. The small house sat one block over from Main Street. The dull green exterior paint peeled like the rest of the houses in the neighborhood, and the pickup truck that sat in the driveway didn't stand out like any of the others.

Tobias parked his snowmobile in the driveway and went up the steps to the porch. He knocked on the wooden door a few times and waited.

The house was quiet, and the sound of his knock echoed inside. He knocked again but after waiting, he peered inside through the tiny window by the door. The living room was dark and motionless. There was only the couch and a side table. There weren't any pictures on the walls, and the shelves were empty.

Walking to the other end of the porch, Tobias glanced into another window. The kitchen was neat, with the cabinet doors open showing no contents. The house was vacant.

After a few moments of thinking, Tobias walked back to the driveway and peered into the truck's front windows. The keys were in the driver's seat, with a note. It didn't feel like anyone was around, so Tobias opened the door and read the note. It was an address further north of town.

Tobias closed the door. Stepping next to the bed of the truck, he felt an odd sensation ripple inside his chest. He shivered and rubbed his palms together.

Pulling the cover back from the truck's bed, he could see cardboard boxes filling the space. There were no labels on them. He reached over and pulled the flaps up of the closest box, exposing gold statues.

Eyebrows furrowed, Tobias pulled a few of the statues out. He could see a white object below them, and realized this visit was not in vain.

Hard, cold bones rested on the bottom of the box. Polished, with a tag tied to one end. The tag only had a series of numbers and letters. Next to the bone was a black velvet pouch. Inside were white triangles, each about the size of Tobias's index finger. Some larger and some smaller. Seeing them reminded him of the dying orca's gaping mouth. The tragic event seemed so long ago now.

Tobias felt a sudden flush of adrenaline and put all the illegal objects back. Putting the cover down on the bed, he went over to his snowmobile and pulled out of the driveway. As safe as possible, he rushed to Citana Carver's place, the only one who would let him use a telephone.

Every time Tobias had visited Citana, the mechanic had his radio blasting throughout the garage and the doors open, even in the winter. As Tobias entered the office door, he heard nothing swirl through the doorway leading to the garage.

"Citana!" he called out. "Are you here?"

He had to be here as he never went anywhere else. Tobias saw the telephone on the desk, but hesitated to pick it up. Leaning in through the doorway, he peered around the garage for any sign of a human.

Sitting in his prized 1977 Ford Bronco, Citana waved a lazy hand out the open window. His other hand brought a bottle of rum to his lips, and took a long sip.

"You never drink," Tobias said. He didn't really know this for sure as he never hung out with the man, but the only beverage he'd had during these limited visits was coffee.

"Jess left me," Citana said, laying his forehead on the steering wheel. "She just quit her job at the bar last night and left town."

Now at the driver's door, Tobias could see a pool of vomit on the concrete ground. He focused on his friend's face, noticing the bloodshot eyes.

"I'm sorry, Citana."

"Everyone told me we wouldn't work," Citana threw his hands up in the air, which made some of the rum spill out of the bottle. "But you know how hard it is to find someone here?"

"I know," Tobias reached up and patted Citana's arm. "I'm here for you, but I need to borrow your phone."

Citana turned his head to squint down at Tobias, then gave a shrug. "You all just take. I just give. I won't argue."

Pausing, Tobias felt an urge to open the car door and drag Citana to his bedroom upstairs in the loft. He wanted to take care of his friend, make sure he didn't drown in his own regurgitated rum. But that urge was small in the wake of Tobias's more urgent mission.

"I'll be back, Citana."

Tobias made two phone calls. One was to Abe Dolson. The sheriff was very adamant about Tobias coming back to Sinaaq.

"I appreciate your help, Tobias," Dolson said, his tone tense, "We have a lead now, but I need you to stay out of this. It's dangerous."

"I have more work to do," Tobias said, pressing his thumb and finger against his forehead, "But thank you for your concern."

He hung up before Dolson said anything else. The second call was to Eirlys, who picked up after the first ring.

"Did you find David?"

"No," Tobias felt a little of the weight rise from his chest when he heard her voice. "But I think I have the address to the poachers."

"What is it?"

As Tobias told her, he could hear the scratching of a pen on paper from her side of the line. "I told Abe, so he'll let Greg know. I bet I'll meet them there."

"Wait," Eirlys paused, "You aren't going there."

"I'm just going to drive by," Tobias said, "Don't worry."

"I can't believe I'm saying this," Eirlys said, "But let the cops deal with this. It's dangerous, especially if they were the ones who hurt Ted."

"I'm just going to check, Eir. I'll see you soon."

After hanging up, Tobias glanced through the doorway at Citana. He was out cold, snoring against the steering wheel.

Back on his snowmobile, Tobias headed north. He knew the roads that led to the street that address was on. It took around fifteen minutes, and he was aware of how distant and remote the building was. Not that crime wouldn't happen in the middle of the town, but having less people around still made Tobias nervous. This was a first in six years, since he moved away from the city, where having more people made him uneasy. The quiet wilderness was comforting. Except at this moment.

Out of the all the abandoned warehouses, one had a car out front. Tobias stopped his vehicle but didn't turn it off, and knocked on the front door. There was no answer, and he couldn't see inside. He walked to the corner of the warehouse and glanced around. On the side were two wide garage doors, both closed. It had snowed early that morning, and two tractor tracks were imprinted in the fresh snow. They led away from the building and out toward the northwest part of the forest.

Eirlys's recent words churned through Tobias's brain, but he climbed onto his snowmobile. He paid attention on the large tracks. They led him toward the forest, but soon they veered east onto the Sea of Mortla.

HOW THESE THINGS GO

Accelerating, Tobias directed his ATV over the fluffy snow covering the frozen sea. The speeds he was going weren't safe, and the icy wind scraped against his layers. He had no weapons on him except two fists waiting to break a nose or jaw. He knew that wouldn't be enough. He had heard stories of poachers carrying harpoons and saws, but as most humans set hard on a path, he wasn't thinking straight.

The open plain was empty as usual, with occasional gusts of wind that shifted shallow snow dunes. The horizon ahead was clear for many miles, but soon there was a blip on the line between white and sky.

Tobias wondered if he should use the snowmobile as a weapon. It could take out one, possibly two people. But as much as he wanted to bring civilian justice, he didn't want to solve a crime by committing one. He would have to leave the scene before Dolson arrived, and Tobias wanted to stay in Sinaaq with Eirlys Wynn.

Slowing down, Tobias felt the distance between the tractors and his snowmobile was safe enough. There was nowhere to hide and he stuck out like a black splotch on a white page, but he didn't know what else to do.

No longer moving, Tobias turned his snowmobile off and listened. There was a low rumble under the snowmobile, a shallow vibration that reached up through his toes and into his ankles and calves. They were drilling.

To the right, Tobias saw movement out of the corner of his eye. Glancing in that direction, he saw tiny dots on the horizon heading toward Itcha Navak. Gasping, Tobias reached behind him for his emergency bag. Untying it, he pulled out an orange gun. It resembled a toy. He grabbed a flare from a small box and inserted it into the short barrel. Pointing it at the sky, he pulled the trigger. Expecting a loud bang, Tobias flinched at the tiny click created as the flare exited the barrel and flew above him. It made a small arc to the left, a bright orange and red flame barely visible in the blinding-white environment.

The air stilled. The ice didn't move but felt no longer inanimate. The casual wind shifted to a consistent breeze, pulling at Tobias's knit cap and fur-lined hood. The pressure in the air goaded all moving dots forward toward the trucks, and Tobias obeyed.

Starting his snowmobile, Tobias moved toward the trucks. The dots to his right closed in, becoming two more pickup trucks. The tractors in front also grew in size, and the small distant figures were now larger men bundled against the weather.

One of the tractors had a drill twisting down into the ice. One of the figures was forcing the drill up, trying to ready the tractor for departure. Another figure was dragging a black trash bag away from the hole. The third figure disappeared into the cab of a pickup truck.

Tobias arrived a few moments before the sheriff and Greg, but was unsure of what to do. So, he observed, ignoring the feeling of helplessness as he stayed in the seat of his snowmobile. Abe's truck stopped behind him, and Greg's truck next to it. Tobias listened to the doors opening and the readying clicks of guns, but he didn't want to shift his attention. He had a feeling that the minute he looked away, they would disappear and he would never catch them again.

"I told you to stay away!" Dolson came up along Tobias's ATV, and the postman could see the barrel of a shotgun in his peripheral. "Are you even armed?"

"No," he pointed at the black trash bags, "But look."

Dolson followed Tobias's finger and stepped closer to the scene. "Take Eirlys home."

"She's here?" Tobias finally turned around to see her standing next to her brother's truck, her brother coming up next to Dolson with his own rifle.

"Greg." Dolson gestured to the trash bags, "Call backup and tell them where we are."

"Aw, hell!" A loud voice came from the younger man, and everyone witnessed one of the trash bags ripping open from the hard ice. A ball-shaped object tumbled out of the bag, with a mess of long black hair. The longer the object lay on the snow, the more red liquid spread out from underneath it. It was a head.

"Put your hands up!" Dolson advanced on the man, pointing his rifle at him. "All of you!"

The man dropped the bag and put his hands in the air. There was another rumbling from the ice, but the drill had already been lifted out of the hole.

The other figure put his hands up and stepped forward.

"Adam."

Eirlys had walked up to Tobias and now stood next to his snowmobile, but she was staring at the man holding the drill. Looking back at Adam, Tobias saw him lock his gaze with

Eirlys. Fists clenching, Tobias climbed off his snowmobile and stepped in front of Eirlys, his back to her.

"We need to go," he said.

Abe and Greg had stepped a few feet closer to the men before a loud bang rang out from one of the tractors. It echoed across the ice before the world quieted once more. The old man who had gone back to the cab of his truck returned with his own gun, and fired with shaking hands.

Adam's hands were no longer up but clutching his chest. His jaw dropped as well as his knees.

"Leo, come on!" said the old man with the gun, and the last guy rushed over to the pickup truck.

Abe and Greg ran around the hole, firing at the pickup truck as it began driving away. The spinning wheels kicked up snow and ice and the truck lurched forward.

Eirlys pushed around Tobias and ran to Adam, who was now lying on his side in the snow. Blood leaked through his hands and onto the ice. Following, Tobias watched as Eirlys pushed the man to his back and placed her hands on the wound. There were tears in her eyes, but they didn't fall.

The rumbling from the ice transformed into an earthquake. The earth seemed to break, and there was nowhere to hide or hold for support. Tobias placed his hands on top of Eirlys', and he felt the warm blood seep through his fingers. It reminded him of the orca he tried saving, and the sensation of the liquid on his skin grounded him as his teeth chattered.

There was a shout, and Tobias and Eirlys turned toward the escaping truck. Greg and Dolson had stopped running toward the truck and were now running in the opposite direction, toward Eirlys and Tobias. Tobias imagined their faces pulled back in fear, their teeth bared. The ice cracked and creaked, but the fractures couldn't be seen from where Tobias knelt. In the distance, the pickup truck's rear tires disappeared.

Standing up, Tobias could see a hole had split open and swallowed the truck. He could hear the front tires spinning at full speed against the edge of the ice, but the weight of the truck pulled it backwards and into the hole. Then there was no noise as the truck disappeared.

The rumbling tapered off, and a high-pitched wind blew toward the hole. The edges stretched out toward each other, and little by little, the ice healed and connected. The fissure closed. The scar painted over by a light dusting of snow.

The group's amazement was interrupted by the gurgled speech of the injured man.

"Don't speak," Eirlys said, her hand still on the wound.

"Eir-" Adam tried, but coughed up a pink foam.

"If we get him on a stretcher," Greg turned toward his pickup, "We can meet a helicopter and..."

He trailed off, and Tobias saw Dolson shaking his head, a mournful expression on his face.

"I... wrong..." Adam forced out two words, staring at Eirlys' face.

"It's okay," she brushed the hair off his forehead, "We all were."

RECLAMATION OF STONE

His ancestors wouldn't have allowed an outcast to be buried by stone. Old Lou was trying something new, though, with the boys of Sinaaq. He didn't think that what his father, grandfather, and greaters did was wrong, just different. Two ways of handling a situation. Following tradition wasn't saving the lives of his people.

Adam Locklear wasn't of his people, but his misunderstanding of the Sinaaqan tradition wasn't his fault, but Old Lou's. It was the Elders' duty to guide the future generations in the ways of the land and the cautionary tales, and Old Lou had failed. To start anew, he would let Adam's spirit rest with the ancestors, near the bones of the whales murdered by his hands.

There were two adults standing next to Adam's burial site, Eirlys Wynn and Tobias Morgan. It was odd, Old Lou thought, for Tobias to have joined as he never knew Adam. But Old Lou appreciated the support and presence the postman provided for Eirlys. She had always been a spirit who attracted misery, but what she did with her gifts was what surprised Old Lou.

Eirlys Wynn didn't stop living, always moving, in a direction very different to any compass he'd witnessed. Eirlys was guided by multiple elements, more than one future, and she followed all of them instead of just the one. Her versatile destiny would be the savior of Sinaaq, but she would never know. Old Lou had believed himself to be the link between the old ways and the new age, but he was just guidance. Eirlys was the connection.

Eirlys stared down at Adam's face for many moments before settling the last stone. Tobias stood beside her and did not waiver, did not leave, but remained by her side in case she needed him. She wouldn't. He would. It didn't matter.

As the couple descended the hill, Old Lou stepped up to the stone pile. The sun had set a quarter of an hour previously, and the top of the hill was dimming. The elder pulled a small bag out of his pocket and opened it. He took a pinch of grain, a mixture of spices and ground flowers, and sprinkled it over the grave. He performed the ritual in an ordinary fashion, as if Adam had never been banished and had never learned of heartbreak, greed, nor loss. He had followed his compass, which had been in his coat pocket when the body was brought to Old Lou's house. The compass had been used, with scratches, the metal torqued at the hinges so it didn't close properly. Through all the terrible deeds Adam did, the compass guided him. In finality, it brought him home, even if only by stone.

ABOUT THE AUTHOR

Gabrielle Rupert is from Framingham, MA, and has a B.S. in Biology and an M.S. in Marine Biology. She is currently working as a fisheries observer in the Northeast Atlantic Ocean, fulfilling her dreams of making the world more sustainable. While she's not working on fishing boats, she writes short stories and novels. Her work has been published in Pif Magazine, Ripples in Space, Transfer Magazine, In Parentheses, the Coffin Bell Journal, and Forge & Flint.

UNDERWATER EYES
BY BRIAN PHILIP KATZ

Marta

was in three places.

She stood in the back of the room defying the nakedness forced upon her by keeping her hands at her sides. She had space around her, a solid foot of space between her and the throng of other women screaming and pressing towards the closed iron door. The woman to Marta's right was trying to calm her daughter, a slight thing almost her mother's height, and pressed into her mother's flesh as if they were trying to become one, "They're only going to wash us. They're going to clean us, you see."

Marta thought of her two-year-old son, Allen, who was given to her younger sister, Pauline, months ago as passage to Switzerland was secured for two and only two by their grandfather, *Andere Vater*, or "other father," in a prescient act of desperation.

Marta was now with her son wherever he was, preferably playing in a park, and he was fine, he was alive. She knew this.

"*Wasser!*" someone ordered.

"*Wasser!*" they all screamed.

Marta, herself in the large, filthy sterility of this "shower" alone in the mass of various fleshes, became what was left of herself, a lone pile of clothes, mostly woolen, next to a heap of tatters.

Allen

Ivan Schwartz and his son, Will Schwartz, were quite alike on the surface – they looked like father and son and despite a lifetime as peripheral characters in each other's story, they shared the same mannerisms. As far as the depth of their relationship was concerned, there was no bond; they existed light years from each other even when in the same room – no vitriol, no panic, no anguish, no remorse, just two bodies too remote to size up the possibilities, both peaceful and pertinent and too inherently stubborn to embrace their similarities.

Allen remained cloistered in a physicality that called for action, for experience. The recipient of two manilla envelopes tendering two separate divorces, he still cared about his looks. A solid ten years younger in appearance with most of his wavy hair intact to his pride, Allen was as strong as a man half his age. Tempered and hard-working, he lived alone in a large Park Slope apartment while contemplating an early retirement from his Wall Street law firm.

He never questioned what went wrong or what he could've done to repair the damage. He just accepted the separations from wives and children. No guilt, no concern, just alone; and that was okay because he still had most of his hair.

Will

sought the world as he knew it, the great expanse of America, but found nothing much – a strip mall surrounded by a strip mall surrounded by an even larger strip mall. At twenty-nine, trailing memories across the characterless stretch of Route 70 in an earnest attempt to find a question worth asking, he was drawn to this nothingness of uniformity. The landscape was attractive because it didn't take much thought *and isn't that just what they want? Not much thinking?*

He was heading back home.

The product of a black-Irish girl and a self-hating Jewish boy, Will withstood the loneliness of a world full of family historians, each with their own story as to how he got here:

Dana

said, "I'm going out," just as Will walked through the door of their one bedroom apartment on West 122nd St.

"I'll join you," he said and she looked at him and he looked at her in a way, that way, "or not."

"No, no, it's okay. Come. But I'm heading over to Balthazar," which meant that he was too dirty – covered in drywall plaster, sawdust, and paint – and she wanted him to opt out.

"I clean up good, don't worry."

"I'm already late."

"I'll meet you there," and he never did.

That was what their relationship was all about, being together but never meeting-up.

Allen

lived on the fringes of the Styrofoam landscape maintained by a few disembodied divorcees who shuffled in and out of the downtown pillaging of the meek of which they were once – a type of anthropophagy, prosecuting others just like themselves and saving a few chops for later consumption. It was there, in a real Brooklyn brownstone, that Allen lifted a mug of freeze-dried coffee while sitting in the light shining through his bay windows overlooking Prospect Park. He felt something, perhaps a loneliness evidenced by the near six-mile run he completed on that Sunday morning – a morning so distant from Boomer expectations that nary a page from the Sunday Times existed in his apartment.

The pewter mug with a peculiar dedication engraved on its moldering surface: "First Lieutenant Schwartz, US 4th Infantry, an Ivy League Man Despite his Flower Power Ambitions, 2/12/72." The phrase lent itself to metaphor. The "Ivy" referenced the IV roman numerals of the Fourth Infantry and the "Flower Power (Fourth)" was the moniker that the Infantry wore during Vietnam. Why this mug existed and who, exactly, gave it to Allen remained a mystery even to himself. His first ex-wife, Will's pregnant mother, found it when she, in *Good Housekeeping* mode, dumped the contents of his dusty duffle bag in the center of their garage. The mug safely landed on top of a pile of woolen greens.

Will

ends every evening in the same fashion: From junkyard to natural landscape to mound of transforming clay: The soft haze of a divide, an undiscovered valley, that separated the two realities, one less defined than the other, often displayed an inspired pastoral beauty. The first hill, piled with the remains of the past, filth and litter of an earnest existence, sloped sharply, almost cliff-like, toward the wash. The other side changed its form, its structure, in the wind that blew in bursts unpredictable yet expected. A window slammed, a neighbor groaned in an apneatic fit, someone searched for their keys in a midnight stupor, Dvorak crescendoed a marching standard, a bus whined and wailed its way down Broadway, a deep fryer gurgled overused, and the sickly numbers of the digital clock marked the episode as having just begun.

My feet are wet.

While traversing the continent on back roads he became all too familiar with the similarities of the many towns with their remnants of industry – abandoned or rediscovered factory buildings that seemed as natural to their environments as the maple trees to Vermont. These buildings sometimes serviced the communities offering public space or transformed into art spaces and museums, condos, shopping districts, malls even, or rediscovered industrial parks. But most remained unresolved and it was in one of these dilapidated locations where the ruin of a former society stuck out in the pasture of the human commune; and he returned, every night, naked and wet without reason, to that complex.

When I am here, in the empty rooms with unknown machinery, I allow the logic and recognition of place, yet neither what is known or inherently understood – instinctually – fails to absorb the purpose of this moment, this half-moment. This is reality, this is real, neither dream nor dreamy. Believe me: this is real, an abduction unto myself.

Ever since he was a little boy, William was terrifyingly drawn to brick buildings.

Allen

being Jewish and not wanting to be Jewish defined the majority of his experience. To him, "Jew" meant, "Self-Hating." But even that didn't capture the whole truth of his identity. It was not hatred; it was the assumed limitations of self and spirit in reference to the world's history of Jewry.

Allen was fatherless and referred to his aunt Pauline as "Mutter" – a word he used under his breath in both embarrassment and fear. Although raised Jewish by this "Mutter" and her husband, a podiatrist in Philadelphia, Allen was, despite his ambitions, an outsider. In this post-war mock-up of a family, he became the eldest of five faux-siblings, all of whom were really his cousins; but they were raised to believe he was their real brother and neither he, nor the podiatrist, nor his aunt ever told them otherwise.

The Jewishness of his family was not his. They were Jewish and he was of Jews; they came from once-orthodox families and now, under conservative guise they simply kept kosher and observed high holidays. There was a difference between Allen and his family: he was beyond reformed – he was Other. So when he left home for college on a partial scholarship to run track for Boston University, Allen, when asked if he was Jewish, always said he was adopted (which wasn't really a lie) and that he was Swiss – the implication of such was the he must've been Christian; but when pressed, he had no affiliation.

Deep within the recesses of his use of English lay a subtle accent that at times made it sound as if his tongue were thick with drink.

But Allen never drank.

Anya

met Will for drinks at a bar they often frequented in the East Village. She on her third martini and he on his fifth IPA, Anya finally, with some remote concern, asked how he was doing.

"No remorse," he smiled.

Anya bounced and lifted her legs and sat, Indian-style, on the cracked vinyl seat.

In her dyed auburn quirkiness and expressive brown eyes, Anya played against the expectations of her studies. She was a philosophy MA candidate, ardently looking forward to a PhD. Hers was a world of written and practiced morality; a road from Aristotle to Aquinas to Butler to Hume to Kant to Mill (or Mill to Kant) to Bentham to Moore to Gauthier to Larmore – an enormous "old boys network," she once said. Despite the stodgy bulk of her academic pursuit, she had this idea that philosophy should, nay "ought" to be for the people. At the neophytic age of twenty-four and newly minted, "scholar," she was writing a column for a free New York weekly newspaper, answering various questions as they related to her moral understandings and studies and, more importantly, to her intuition.

Anya was a practical ethicist and, despite his growing attraction for her, a lesbian.

She, tangled in her own hair, body and mind, offered solace. Sitting with her, just sitting there in a bar with a decent jukebox, Will forgot himself long enough to lose track of his heartbeat. Anya's dark eyes continued to fuss over him.

"I love Dana, but she was reckless with you," Anya said.

Knowing the lack of complexity to their relationship, Anya commented on his slacking disposition, his abstract insecurities, and his lack of a backbone – he slouched through his relationship with Dana like an acquiescent, self-centered Neanderthal in a B-movie teen flick – as she cheated on him "recklessly."

"And that's just it. You could love, I could love, someone who cheats, someone who wants to live a life pretending, but your idleness allowed for her fantasy to become a reality," she could've said; but instead, she smiled at the boy sitting across from her.

Marta

reclined in the center of a room piled high with bodies, a lone woman stirring. When the soldiers dragged them through the iron door and tossed them onto the flatbed -- leaden sacks of organs, lengths of flesh -- her skin was riddled with goosebumps. Marta's.

A soldier noticed. She was shot in the head.

Her flesh remained aroused.

Will

was halfway through his second year of graduate school

when in the midst of a collective, indefinable panic, a strange conspiracy took hold of him as he tried to identify *or not* as an artist. He went to Health Services complaining of various ailments, some legitimate and others of a more hypochondriac disorder, and was prescribed an antidepressant. But he was given a choice: Paxil, Prozac, Zoloft, Wellbutrin – for each character, a character correction or displacement. Paxil, just recently introduced, and, in a more pronounced, handy assessment, Prozac both seemed to match his profile and after being told what the various side-effects may be – somnolence, insomnia, agitation, tremors, increased anxiety, dizziness, gastrointestinal constipation, nausea, diarrhea, dry mouth, vomiting, flatulence, asthenia, abnormal ejaculation, sweating, impotence, libido decreased – he settled on the one that would also "mellow you out" and "help you to sleep," as the doctor distractedly droned: Paxil. The doctor, a dry, old Jewish borscht-belter, gave him a free month's supply, followed with his prepared shtick: "May take some time to take effect, perhaps a month; but it will help to lessen these bouts of anxiety your symptoms seem to predicate. Sooner than later, you'll be able to move beyond your fears – they'll be put to the peripheral – and you'll be able to function in a more assertive manner."

When Will returned to his apartment and read the diagnostic insert and directions that came with his first week's dose – a rhetoric more diffuse than a lawyer's legal jargon – he mulled over the possibility of a personality transformation and how it would influence the style of his work, his drawing and constructions, and after an extensive three seconds of weighing the repercussions of taking something to reduce his anxiety, he committedly decided to forgo the trial. He could live with the somnolence – *Fuck, I wasn't sleeping and I was plagued with twilight visions as I stumbled through my days in a perpetual state of* R.E.M. – and the ability to sleep, no matter the catalyst, would be a blessing; but of the relative familiarity he had with all the side effects, he had no idea what "asthenia" was, and he had no desire to increase his anxiety nor willing to lose control of his nether-region; and the percentages didn't support his fears.

A week later he traded the pills for a case of Guinness and a newish copy of *Ulysses, The Corrected Text*. Wondering why anyone would use them without a prescription (or why anyone would use them at all), he was told that the friend of a friend with whom he was trading was a recently graduated MFA in poetry with no health insurance. "But why these?" he asked. The answer: "He grinds the pills into a dust and snorts them after a long night of drinking and smoking." Will walked away with the better deal. *Let someone else suffer from the "anal leakage."*

After the transaction, in the midst of an unprovoked anxiety attack about the anxiety of not taking the anti-depressants and experiencing the rush that goes with the paranoia of his first and only foray as a new age drug dealer and trying to beat back the spirit of his fears with the very same stout he earlier bartered, Will read in a nutritional guide that Dana left behind that "when you check your wrist for a pulse, you ought not use your thumb. The faint throbbing of a pulse in your thumb may confuse your ability to gauge your heart rate."

Maybe this categorically defined my problem: I counted two heartbeats for every one contraction. Then having mastered the correct techniques to check his pulse he noticed that his heart skipped a beat every ten or so seconds – a little internal gasp. These skips became dropped moments and the compulsive manner in which he monitored heartbeats to assure himself that the maddening fluttering represented nothing but a harmless arrhythmia of sorts, to assure himself in the most desperate, consoling fashion that he, at age twenty-five, was not having a heart attack, started to control his routine. Descending the stairs of his fifth-floor apartment he would pause to place his forefinger and middle finger, in a gesture reminiscent of a secret greeting among Masons or Star Trek fans, at his carotid artery on his neck to count the beats and the growing pauses between them. Even on a crowded subway or in the middle of a seminar, he approached the pulse of his wrist without drawing attention to his actions – as if anyone were watching. He continued to seek the answer for his panic by visiting a series of university-associated physicians, several off-campus, who all diagnosed him in the same fashion, "Anxiety." Their proposed methods of treatment were vastly divergent; and despite the offering of various prescriptions, all in the convenience of trial packages that he declined, he did, in fact, enjoy the only drug, besides antibiotics and painkillers, that he would ever take – Ativan, an antianxiety panacea that rarely stopped him from checking his pulse but did help him to rest... with his hand still in the aforementioned greeting to his neck. *What if it has something to do with the bricks? I read somewhere that the lime in the mortar is corrosive and can burn. Am I having trouble breathing? I was drinking... No...*

He was drinking rather heavily at the time, not alarmingly so but probably enough to associate his beering with his state of being and enough to heed the warnings on the labels. He didn't feel depressed – "gloomy, down, holed-up, paralyzed" – although he remained sleepless if not also, surprisingly, artistically productive.

* * *

In that almost half-alive, hazy, dizzy, dreamlike state with distant sirens as his lullaby – a momentary respite from heart obsession – he saw the building. It just loomed in the shadowy distance of twilight, a small New England factory, brick and mortar, with the first few lights of evening revealing some interior. Nothing spectacular, nothing foreboding; just a medium-sized building in a darkening landscape. But he knew this place.

And then he took to running, and ran for his life; ran in flailing desperation through the deciduous woods, through the empty town on Sunday morning, past the park along the river; ran past all that was recognizable and then forgotten. He ran west.

When he roused, if not awoke, the following morning, he made his way to an appointment at the health clinic. He was introduced to a new doctor who, after reviewing his "fine" bloodwork and growing chart of complaints, suggested he try meditation.

The following day he met a therapist who was also a hypno-therapist, not a psychologist, not a psychiatrist, in a sterile, campus office. There was nothing remarkable to her office space: slot rack shelves lined with paperback books, a few family portraits, a squeezy doll with popping eyes. The chest crushing agita was upon him and he counted the blossoming rapidity of heartbursts as he sat across from her and her enormous length of brown, curly hair. She reviewed the plan with him – what it was they were about to do and what "we" needed to accomplish. She said something about "self-hypnosis" and he balked; but as she began to count and constructed the scene – the cliché-ridden pastoral or bucolic scene – he was brought back to the factory and with a little less dawn on the horizon he saw the word "Hardware" stenciled in fading yellow on the brick façade. And then walking forward and settling into the scene as the therapist's voice hummed in the distance, a sharp, bright light burst a fraction of a second in his mind's eye with a grating, metallic crunching in the back of his memory, and as he was jolted back to awareness, a large, red brick fell from the ceiling with a thud.

Brick.

Anya

's brooding little frame was devoted to the contact of women and her mind more often than not allowed, and often expressed, a true or righteous condescension of the male. Employing this recognition of his inferiority, she took pity on Will from first introduction and let him into her heart – a place much healthier and more expansive than his own.

. "I keep having this recurring image, as if in a dream," he said for no apparent reason feeling left out of the cuddling of herself occurring across from him. "This enormous, immortal brick – you know, industrial-sized, not a Morse brick, but a fifty-pound red brick heavy..."

"I have this recurring dream," Anya interrupted. "I'm driving a scooter – a motor bike – and it's attached to this cart and in the cart is the Pope in a glass cube, a bulletproof cube and I'm driving him in a parade. But I have this tremendous fear that I don't have a bulletproof jacket on."

He backed off in embarrassment and readdressed Anya, "Something to do with Catholic guilt."

"Sure," Anya replied, "and it has a little more interpretive scope than a brick. Is it really red?"

She pitied him; and out of pity, she kept him around, took him to gay bars, allowed him to dine with her at her apartment and even once took his hand as they left a party early in the morning.

Will

was reared as the divorced child of divergent personalities. Born and raised in Long Island, his father left him in his all-too-young mother's, Bria's, care as Allen pursued a career and a family to match his idea of what a man's life should be. As a boy, Will suffered terrible earaches – a malady he now blamed on his mother's inability to breastfeed. He had little recollection of having these infections, although he knew he'd had them.

Bria told a story of them visiting her aunt in Baltimore and Will, six-years-old and in mid-drive antsiness, started to complain of a building pressure in his inner ear. Sensing the outcome, Bria informed her nurse-aunt and Will was placed on antibiotics. Bedridden on the second day of their visit, Will, in an unparalleled state, took his mother's hand and pulled her into a closet repeating, "It's okay, mom, they're not going to get us in here."

Dana

hosted at a SOHO haunt and during the day shuffled from audition to audition for a soap opera or off-off Broadway play or commercial selling shampoo or a photo ad depicting the young woman in aisle eight searching the cereal prices – no matter the gig, the same vapid expression was required but for some reason her vapid expression – eyes wide, quirky smile, forehead slightly creased – left her in the cold dark room in the back wishing she could enter the next room and lie on the couch. Rejection became life and left her bitter... very bitter; and when she accepted a role in an update of an Oscar Wilde play off-off-off Broadway (really just a bunch of 20-something players fresh from a downtown university), she ended up having an affair with the lead actor. Will's various neuroses at first kept him blind to the infidelity and then numb to realization; *but looking back on it now, I'm glad she got away from me.* He was busy being himself and she was busy being herself, smoking cigarettes only when in the company of other actors, fawning over the guy or gal with an agent, kissing the assistant director's ass, kissing the gaffer in the backyard of an apartment in Sunnyside, touching someone somewhere all the time; and Will knew, sort of, who she was and it really didn't matter. He was so busy dying that he actually did what was right for his relationship – he lived in the moment, albeit a very blind moment. They were barely compatible by even the loosest standards. She needed attention and Will was too self-absorbed to shine the light on her.

Anya

said, "These retro Japanese toy robots pale in comparison to the originals."

"You think so?"

They were having lunch at a bar that only served pastrami sandwiches on hard rolls and he was holding a tin toy robot in his hand – a kitschy wind-up he bought for $23.99 in a comic book store on 32nd street. He was both trying to justify the purchase and trying to distract Anya from launching into what was fast becoming a daily rant of hers – one that he would never disagree for fear of her rage – a too-coherent rage: "And there's something to the manner in which those who regularly eat fast food, stream TV, pay for the newest Marvel movie, and manage their lives in order to get more processed food, fast food fix..." – when she digressed in the most unnatural manner: "A few weeks ago you mentioned a dream you keep having, something to do with a brick."

"Yeah, I think it has something to do with the earaches I

routinely developed as a child. No idea why I mentioned that – I was being flighty, neurotic."

"Well, I felt bad for trivializing your story. I noticed that I hurt your feelings."

Pause.

"You didn't hurt my feelings. I was... a little drunk. You put me in my place."

"I want you to know," she began in mea culpa mode, a new side to her personality, "I want you to know, I had terrible earaches as well."

There's this beast of a brick – industrial, huge – and a grating noise as if the weight of a wrecking ball were being unleashed, chainless, upon relics – a force that didn't match the space, torqued, sharp, grating, crunching, crumbling – without a boom, swinging repeatedly through the air with more intention, more free will than a man.

"In my case it has something to do with not being breastfed; had terrible allergies, still do – my mother gave me none of those antibodies," he said.

Anya laughed, knowingly, and he caught himself in the embrace of his own beginning revelation. They ate in silence.

"I always find a way to tell a balding person that he is going bald," Anya said. "But not right away. I will be making small talk, comparing my small height to the person idly chatting me up, and when the change in the weather fails to garner an appropriate response from me, I sense the balk in conversation and begin, in the most haphazard fashion, a one-sided conversation on the virtue of hair. In other words, I have a knack for offending or finding the most politically-correct person in a room and saying something downright loathsome or putting on a buck-toothed, goofy grin as a man or woman with a misplaced shelf of a lower jaw turns to pass a pint to a friend."

"You're as abstract as me," he said.

"I wasn't breastfed either but I sure as heck found a way to make up for it." This marked the first time she used her sexuality as fodder for humor in his company. Sure, she sometimes had an amiable way and the depth of her observational humor rivaled George Carlin's and she laughed at Will's attempt at humor and his inane stories, but up to that point in the time of their friendship, nary a self-effacing barb about her lesbianism. And now levity, abstract and tangential lightness, was mutually explored, they rejoiced in their shared misery – formula babies of the Catholic Modesty Brigade.

"Must be why I'm a lesbian too," he said and effectively killed the mood.

Before they left the bar she blurted out in a seemingly uncharacteristically extemporaneous fashion, "Just for the record, you know, most women don't compare vagina sizes... size really doesn't matter."

Again, in her way, she was apologizing both to Will and for Will.

Dana

said he smelled like raspberry bunny farts. "I never liked the way he stank; and he moaned when we fucked, the only boy who ever moaned in bed with me. A crying moan."

Will

ventured into the caverns of his subconscious – all ending on the outside of the iron door to an imposing, dilapidated factory and the motif of the brick somehow, someway entering the landscape of his imagination – and he started to refocus the obsessive sense of his falsely failing health and became more interested in the redundant patterns of his dreams and visions.

He took on the half-life of a sleepwalker and started to draw pictures of walls, brick walls; and no matter how one may want to associate these drawings to the artist's sense of self-isolation, no matter how a critic may choose to analyze the pictures as representative of his condition, all of this, every last little bit excluding that which is already commonly known, is built for the sake of the metaphor, the construction, the brick, the mortar, the brick, the hard, full, little boxes zipping through the air, Ignatz's most precise aim, and plunking off of poor Krazy Kat's noggin, Pow!

He just needed to get out of his own way.

His therapist said that he should be more upfront and try to keep the less-repressed memories in a separate category for the sake of all those hidden truths.

Come to think of it, I do feel much better.

But the more digging he did, the more depressed he became.

Allen

met his second wife shortly after his separation from his first. Trudy was a fine woman, maybe a little jealous that her husband had a previous wife, but she tried to keep Allen and Will together and, as often as Allen would bring his first son home, which was rarely, she would try to feed Will the various lasagnas and pies she baked for his all-too-slight body. She thought he wasn't treated fairly, by father nor mother – but she needed to feel that way even if she was partly incorrect. But Will held firm to the hunger strikes of his discontent; and, in full, mature awareness, he knew, at the unripe age of 6, that he did not belong in their company and that his father, probably subconsciously, didn't want him there either.

So, as stated above, he held firm to his rare weekend hunger strikes... for several years... and poured himself into the small pile of comic books he brought with him as a security blanket. *Ben Grimm, aka the Thing, dressed in his disguise outfit of a large-brimmed hat and massive overcoat to cover his hodgepodge, rocky bulk, found himself in a remote alley after hearing screams from a seemingly defenseless woman about to be raped. Stepping into the alley, he takes off his coat and reveals his form in the light of a lone streetlamp. But to his dismay and relief, there is only a small brown and red cat behind a dumpster.*

Will

inevitably roused to the urgency of his heart in his ears and a pain, spreading like a fire-soaked towel, across his chest. The sugars of his diet pulled him from the two missing hours of his evening routine and he often landed in front of his sketchbook, one of many hardcover, black books he purchased for $5.95, both scribbling inane passages and tracing the images in his head, all that stuff that he so abhorred. He was onto himself.

Another of the three items Dana left behind was a small, pink television that received, rather clearly, all the local NY channels: 2, 4, 5, 7, 9, 11, and 13. The box was in the bedroom on a stack of magazines he subscribed to but never read and maybe once scanned for insightful photographs of wildlife or horror or illustrated lewdity – a pile he carted from destination to destination out of guilt and pretentious expectancy. Pushing the channel button like a morphine-addled, terminally ill patient, he searched the seven channels for something worth watching – part of an early, early morning-after romp through the scheduled detritus – but never once found a show worth the hour wasted.

She also left behind a fancy-looking brush with an enameled handle and a web of her tan hair in its bristles and a t-shirt with some manga or anime girls in a Charlie's Angels pose – an arc of primary colors haloing the smiling, gun toting pantomime. He tried on the shirt, but, as expected, it barely made its way over his chest and he ripped the sleeve as he forced his biceps through the sleeve. But he wore the shirt for a day, his burgeoning beer belly hanging out.

He sat in his apartment and drew some abstract ideas, shapes to be made with brick and mortar, processing the inspiring little sparks that dropped from him like heavy loads into a toilet, and nursing a Guinness while wearing her t-shirt and questioning whether or not he ever really loved Dana.

Shiffren

was a regular at The Lion's Head and he was onto Will's schtick.

"Your last name is 'Schwartz,' you must be a Jew," he whispered when Will introduced himself.

"Well, sort of," Will said. "I have Jewish blood, but I was raised by a Catholic mother. I'm a McJew. I love to drink but hate to pay for it."

Not amused, Shiffren called out in a shockingly deep voice, "Next!"

Will

met Anya at Donegal's for cheap yet tasteless burgers and modestly priced pitchers of beer. The bar was alive and in no need of assigned personality – it had personalities, any number of customers, and moved to the aggressive nature of burgeoning alcoholics, the pining of flirters, the dilettante's unbearable offerings, the stoic's listless reproach, caromed around the room and jumped from person to person in an unfailing attempt to be of the many. The bar was an unintentional, careless succubus and its denizens were all perfectly fine with that.

They met on Wednesday evening earnestly looking to blow off steam. Anya arrived with her new girlfriend, Sam.

Watching Anya watching her girlfriend, them holding hands and kissing made him want to bolt like a shamed seventh grader from the school dance, a boy embarrassed by the girl he likes liking another boy, or girl, and humiliating him publicly by kissing him, or her, on the lips. *On the lips!*

It was on this evening when the loneliness of his imagination, the depths of his artless despair, got the best of him and he promised himself and Anya that he would be leaving.

"Where would you go?" she asked, while stroking her lover's arm.

"West. California. I have an opportunity."

Anya

and Will had their last dinner together at a pub on Smith Street in Brooklyn.

"When you get there, I have someone for you to meet. She's an old friend from high school," she said. "But there is a caveat: I know this sounds a little over-the-top, but she gets what she wants. Be careful."

"You would introduce her to me after Dana."

"She's no Dana. She's not mortal."

"You're serious? You make her sound like Circe."

"In every way," and she winked at him. His lesbian friend, Anya, winked at him.

It was at that moment that he wished he had had the courage to ask her, "Why not me?" but he already knew the answer. Everyone knew the answer. The bartender knew the answer. The couple at the next table knew the answer. The lady staring at the menu posted on the door knew the answer. And the waiter in his natty uniform knew the answer.

He was not made for this woman.

"When I first moved to the city," Will began as an attempt to share some of his feelings, "I used to pass this street artist on St. Marks. You know, the guy that created those fantastic images out of chalk on the cement. He would take over a huge portion of busy sidewalk and people had to skirt his canvas. Well, I always hated the product but admired the endeavor – the impermanence of it all. I often dropped what change I had in his hat. But one day, a hot July afternoon when the streets were abandoned, I saw him as he finished his daily piece and saw him empty his fedora of the money he had acquired. And then I watched him count the bills. His tongue seemed to hang from his mouth and he licked his index finger like an old-fashioned bank teller as he sorted the bills. I waited until he left and proceeded to trample his pastoral scene, scraping the soles of my shoes over the pavement. I hated him."

Anya paused. She seemed impressed with him. "Good," was all she said.

Will

packed up his Volvo 240 station wagon, a hand-me-down from his mother, and, after committing to leave for the West Coast, a place he had never been, tried his best to make activity a reality of sorts. He tried to justify the escape from Art Central but instead donned sunglasses for the gloss of a less understood radiation. He needed to go somewhere and began by driving his boxes of books, comic books, toys, and tools across the country to take an adjunct position in LA – a job offering pittance, no insurance, and little respect; but he had the sense that he needed to leave New York and left for the Hockney horizon.

BY BRIAN PHILIP KATZ

Chanie

's transformation from schoolgirl to young woman was more remarkable than could've been expected. Her hair was down – a marked improvement from the pulled severity of her yeshiva hairdo. As he tried to avoid looking directly at her, a scattering of his wayward vision to everything else in the room, his eyes quickly crossed her chest and he noticed the shape of her body for the first time revealed in a form-fitting t-shirt.

Words like bricks...

Will

was alienated from his many familial cultures, from his stereotyped masculine identity, and from the puritanical culture rising up around him. Will, a thinly-veiled protagonist, was a half-Irish Catholic and half-German Jewish artist, searching for his father twenty-odd years after being abandoned by him on a cold, mysterious island off the east coast of America.

Chanie

struggled with her orthodoxy and tried to embrace the secular world.

Anya

smiled.

Will

sighed.

Art

is either "A Cursory Review of Where It All Went Wrong" or "Hanging on the Wall of the Contemporary Museum of Art":

A Rawlings outfielder's glove, style number "6592," "U.S. Pat. No. 3.602.915" with an Andre Dawson signature, a "holDster" for my pointer finger, and "Edge-U-Cated Heel," "Basket-Web," and "Deep Well" Pocket." Underneath Andre Dawson's name I wrote "Sucks" out of the mocking peer-pressure I received for having the glove of a non-New York player – it was given to me as a gift from my father after his first son with his new wife was born.

I was eight.

Allen

held a faded wallet-sized picture in a gilded frame of a teenage Marta, with her long, brown hair tightly pulled back, an ardently attempted smile on a sweet yet sad face, and a summer dress with a panicked pattern of flowers.

Will asked, "Dad, did you ever wonder who your father was?"

"My mother was raped by..." he started in full anticipation of his son's query. "You see, I'm not even really Jewish."

Will said, "But your mother was a Jew."

"To Jews I'm a Jew... and then again, a son of Hitler. Believe me Will, the latter forsakes the former. I am my own worst enemy."

Allen opened a shutter to the bay windows of his apartment and surveyed the autumnal park with mayoral intent – this was his block and this was his life now: a life in the shadows of his own personality and the betrayer of a people by mere circumstances of birth. He rounded himself out – shoulders lost their sense of purpose and Will knew it wouldn't be worth the follow-up. This was everything the son ever needed to know.

He was the grandson of Hitler?

Will

found a converted garage apartment one block from Venice beach. The owner, who happened to live in the main house, was an old yet spry woman, who stated, before introducing herself, that she was a vegan and asked him if he ate meat.

"Uh, no," he lied as he looked upon the yellow structure with a skylight, a prolific spray of white roses wending their way up a trellis leaning on the clapboard siding, and a half barn door for an entrance.

After telling her what he was doing in Los Angeles and making his teaching job sound more interesting, more secure, and more important than it was.

She said, "Hah, my ex-husband taught there for 33 years."

"Who?"

"That shit-spewing stoner, Moses."

"Ed Moses?"

"Yeah, that fucker."

Rent was only $800 a month, about a third of his monthly salary, and there was no need to check references or sign a lease. She looked into his eyes and said, "I trust you even though you lied to me about not eating meat."

"I don't care about the messes," she said. "I just want to feel like someone is living here."

"Then I'm your someone," he said.

I

remember asking my father to read Curious George *every night at bedtime. I remember him reading to me about the monkey that finds himself in the most ridiculous and precarious situations. I think I remember the monkey being reprimanded, punished and spanked. I remember my father's beard, soft as he kisses my cheek before shutting off the light. I remember watching him watch television on Saturday afternoons,* The Wide World of Sports, *and watching him nap, stretched out on the couch, arms behind his head. I remember his duffle bag and the heavy lock that hung from the clasp. I remember his running sneakers and the rubber sole separating from the heel and every time he took a step it was like a cartoon character opening and closing its mouth. I remember his record collection organized in milk crates. Simon and Garfunkel, Bob Marley,* Revolver *and the mess of people growing out of heads of hair, Cat Stevens, The Mommas and the Poppas, The Doors, Goat's Head Soup. I remember his sunglasses perched halfway down his crooked nose and the imprint the nose rests made on the side of his nose. I remember his perfectly polished car, a convertible orange Triumph, and his leather driving gloves and their patterned air-holes, his fingertips poking through. I remember that there was no place for me to ride in his car. I remember him calling me Bebop and I never questioned what the nickname meant. I remember so much about him but I can't remember the truth.*

Will

received a one-year appointment as an adjunct instructor. The art department chairperson happened to be the partner or lover or ex-lover of Will's graduate advisor. He warned Will that his classes might feel like remedial tutorials – mostly students who had to take a creative arts requirement – but he welcomed Will's presence and said he enjoyed the packet of slides he had sent with his application and the chair was impressed by a small review Will received in an art publication for a group show he participated in in the East Village and his mention on the list of "Young Artists to Pay Attention to" that appeared in another publication where Will was number seventeen with an exasperated exclamation and heading, "Again, When Ugly is Beautiful, Again!"

He never intended on being a teacher, but this was, at this time, the only profession that he was qualified to pursue. Making art didn't make ends meet and his art wasn't marketable – grotesque, enormous brick structures that required space to build – space he could not afford in the post-graduate world of New York rents – and although he went to graduate school to secure a future, he came out making less money than he ever would have as a carpenter or mason or plasterer, but he had an official-sounding moniker, even if not exactly true to the definition of his position as "adjunct lecturer."

Chanie

tugged the band from her hair – *too curly, not attractive at all – no lipstick, no blush – an unbleachable stain on the pocket of my blouse. If I could only brush my teeth right now – look how yellow they are – and my shoes, these dowdy, clunky shoes. What I would do for something pretty to wear, to burn this uniform, these rags of conformity, to slip into something form-*

fitting because if there is anything attractive about me it is my body and I wish...

She, a combination of teen Ava and adult Gardner, entered his office. Her kinky hair was pulled back into a soft knot. A brown canvas bag strapped over her shoulder defined the space between her breasts, her white bra clearly outlined through her white oxford shirt. Will's stomach dropped and despite being only four years older than she, he beat back the chauvinistic impulses – those wandering eyes that can frame a woman's presence in a mere glimpse – and refocused the design of his attraction on her face... and then the outline of her body, the flower print skirt above her knees, her bespectacled grey eyes, and she caught his wandering and tossed it back at him with a coy, all-knowing smile – *a brick weighing two tons.*

All the old anxieties started to beat at the door. He scratched the back of his head and looked away with a paralyzed half smile. Again, he was caught off-guard by her form – the mystery of an orthodox, Jewish woman. She entered, bare stretch of calf, sandals revealing painted toes, quirky, casual, and wholly disarming. He looked away again, nodding, feigning disinterest.

"I think you're the first person to come to my office hours."

"Not much going on here," she said as she surveyed the room.

He had few scattered portfolios and tabletop art books and a few pretentious posters on the wall. She noted it all and shook her heading knowingly – knowing what, he didn't know.

"I don't have the time to decorate," he said.

She chuckled, "Seems to me like you have nothing but time."

What did she mean?

She opened her bag and procured two sandwiches

wrapped in wax paper. "I hope I'm not being so bold as to suspect that you haven't eaten any lunch."

"Here, take a seat," and he brought his chair around the desk so as to sit near her.

He usually tried to remain distant from the students, especially the attractive ones, but from the first day of meeting Chanie, wearing her religiosity in the prescribed dark tones but counterbalancing the weight of her clothing with a perky smile and perfect teeth, he let his guard down. She was safe, pious, and soon, he found out, quite intelligent – smarter than he, and a damn fine welder. She was the only student in the class that had some training with an arc welder having learned during her two years of conscription in Israel.

"Tuna on rye. Your favorite," she said as she crossed her legs and leaned forward and placed the gift on his desk.

"How did you know?"

"You told us the other day in class when you said you were hungry after looking at Donald's painted cardboard still-life of a 'Midwestern Supper,'" but he didn't remember saying that and he thought Donald's piece, slathered in red, was unreasonably critical for a boy who had never been out of the Valley until he went to college on the other side of the Hills.

"Well, it's delicious," he said.

At 23, Chanie was older than she looked despite spending over three years in Zion's sun before returning to Los Angeles and college.

"New York 'delicious'?" she asked.

Even at his relatively young age, he had developed that academic paranoia that all college professors wear on their sleeves: It was always best to say something positive, light, nonsexual, impossible to misinterpret: "What brings you here?"

"I wanted to talk about my project – the 'Reading Man'."

"I think you're using more scrap metal than the entire class combined."

"Yeah, that's the problem." She tucked a loose strand of hair behind her ear. This little action charmed him and although he was wearing a professional face and talking in adult tones – an opaque facade – he was drawn to watching her, staring at her. Her presence, distant... no, sheltered, had reawakened something in him. He was becoming that creature driven and derided by sexuality, that creature that he brought to the city of vanity in order to repress, to hide, to lock away in a little yellow garage apartment by the beach. They sat in silence for a minute or two – *felt like a long time, even longer now*. Finally, she just smirked and looked away.

"It's taking a long time," she continued.

"I can help," Will said. "I can help you tonight. Just tell me what you need."

The smell of tuna and mayo and a whole dill pickle reminded him of 2nd Ave *before you were born*.

"That would be great," and she smiled at him. "You can help with the base – I need to arch his feet into the metal platform."

"My pleasure."

"I'm not comfortable with the Acetylene yet and I need to cut a three foot disc."

"I'll do it."

"Thanks."

They chewed on the moment of silence.

"You're Jewish, " she said. "Do you know anything about Judaism?"

Thinking of his father sitting in his office, poring over numbers, he said, "A bit."

"I mean, do you know anything about orthodox Judaism."

Thinking of his young grandmother and the bulldozed pile, "Not much. They're the real Jews, right?" *Not like me.*

He began to lose his appetite.

"They'd like to think so," she said under her breath. "It's against Jewish law to create a complete representation of another human. My 'Reading Man' isn't proper. On top of it, I'm trying to reproduce the image of a Rabbi."

"I know," he said. "Worshipping false idols."

"It's my father."

"I never would've considered that."

Chanie seemed flustered but she carefully re-wrapped her sandwich and placed it back in her canvas bag. "I just wanted you to know."

She turned back to face him from the door – the door had been open the whole time – her eyes wide, suggesting that he should ask her something else before she left.

"Thanks for lunch. No one has ever brought me lunch before."

"Then tonight?"

"Okay, sure, I'll be here."

"And just so that you know, I'm not orthodox. My family is," she said.

Will

knew how he was made – neither natural nor divine, but constructed on an assembly line by two workers who fell in love with vanity reflected in each other's eyes.

He had this image of himself looking at himself in a mirror, the hideousness of his masculinity, wretched under the plump of increasing beer fat.

He watched himself looking at himself and ignored the bloat, the beard, the wires from his nostrils, the useless muscles, and then the cause of all his anxiety – the true cause: He was not his father.

What an ugly thing, a Will.

He became the handful of his crotch, a bent rod stripped of its destiny, pocked-marked and pimpled – the corpus of its history – and terminally intrusive.

Tara

had every sexual identity and followed the impulses of her desires. For her, making love to someone was really a simple act.

Bria

was a storyteller. Shortly after Will's father left, she created this little tale for her confused son:

Once upon a time in a land on the other side of the mountains, a woman lived in a small house with her only child, a son. Her son was almost in his sixteenth year and devoted to their small piece of property where he gardened and, through the grace of the spirits of the land, was capable of growing just about anything from seed. Their plot of land produced more than enough food to last them through the winter and on Fridays during the summer months the young man sold their large surplus at a farmer's market in town.

One day in late summer, the son set out for the market to sell his tomatoes and peppers. Neither fruit was like anything else ever grown in the region. The tomatoes were striped with yellow veins and when sliced would smell like cherries but tasted like savory, cooked meat; and the peppers were thin and long and orangey red and upon tasting them, one bite would be as sweet as rock candy and the next as hot as fire. No one had ever tasted anything like the son's produce and he was usually emptied of his basket with a pocket full of coins within an hour of his arrival. But on this one Friday in late summer, after selling his basketful, a huge and unexpected rainstorm took over the land. His journey home was to be stalled, for the roads became impassable rivers.

To avoid being saturated to the bone, the young man sought shelter and food at a local inn. He was greeted by the owner of the inn for he too was a customer of the young man's and often advertised the gardener's delicious and exotic produce in his recipes. The owner brought the young man a pint of ale. The young man almost declined the offering placed in front of him for he had never tasted alcohol and was often warned by his mother of its effects. But the foamy, bubbly amber smelled like the earth and tasted like the earth – a sensory experience that the young man immediately recognized and loved. As the hours passed and the inn gained more patrons, the young man sat in the corner and drank ale after ale. After his first pint he felt no pain – the calluses on his hands seemed to disappear. After his second he became a little giddy and smiled at everyone who passed in front of his little table. Upon completion of his third he became chatty and talked to anyone who would listen. And after swallowing the last drop of his fourth, he became dizzy and sensed that he was not totally in control of his body; but he couldn't stop. He drank a fifth and then a sixth and stumbled to the counter to order his seventh when the innkeeper said to the young man, "It might be best if you go home."

The young man said, "Nonsense, I would love another," in the uncharacteristic growl of an insulted man's challenge.

"Just one more," the innkeeper said as he slid a half-empty pint onto the table.

Infuriated by the paltry amount, the young man threw the pint across the room and left the inn.

The next day the young man tended his garden in a stupor. At around noon, a small brigade of armed soldiers came looking for the gardener. Apparently, when he threw his mug in utter disdain he struck a man at the bar; and despite the fact that he had no recollection of the event, he apologized profusely and asked the soldiers to whom it was he gave offense.

Their answer, "Not just an offense! You concussed his royal highness!"

The young man, having carelessly confessed to the act, was immediately arrested and shackled behind the largest horse. His mother came running out of the house, pleading with the soldiers to tell her why they were taking her son, her only child.

Their answer, "This villain is responsible for the attempted assassination of the king; and at this moment, the king lies in his bed bleeding profusely above his temple. If his condition doesn't improve, your son's crime may be raised to 'regicide.'"

"Regicide?" the mother and son almost queried in panicked harmony, for neither knew what the term meant.

The young man was dragged to the castle and presented to the queen who sat upon her throne weeping. When the shackled, dust-covered young man was thrust in front of her royal highness, who, in midstream, saw the innocence in front of her, she struggled for words.

The innkeeper was then brought into the royal hall.

"Is this the man... the boy who attacked my husband?" the queen, between sobs, asked the innkeeper.

"Yes, your highness." There was a pause and the innkeeper continued, "He is the gardener who grows the tiger tomatoes and spicy/sweet long peppers, your highness. I know him well. He had many pints of ale..."

"He is *the* gardener. How many pints did this boy, for he is really a boy, drink?"

"Almost seven, your majesty," the innkeeper responded.

The young man now deemed "boy" remained silent – his head hammering, his mind swirling, and his eyes welling with tears of fear and remorse. The queen noticed his sadness and it almost matched her own. She looked to the innkeeper who had a nervous smile on his face.

"And you allowed this boy to drink that much?"

The innkeeper tried to protest, but the queen waved her hand in a dismissive fashion and, gaining composure, had the innkeeper removed from the royal hall.

The king, to the great joy of the queen, did, in fact, recover but he lost the hearing in his left ear; and after returning to the throne, he promised his wife that he would never again foray secretly into their kingdom to partake in the excitements of the common people.

The innkeeper, in the most surprising turn of events, remains, to this day, in the prison tower while the boy, who was a young man before being arrested, was sent back to his mother's arms and his garden where he now grows vegetables exclusively for the royal chef who cooks exclusively for the king and queen.

Will

was one of those kids who never understood the moral of a story.

Was his father the innkeeper and was he the boy? Certainly, his mother was the mother; but maybe she was the queen? No, wait, his father was the king? If so, was Will still the boy? Or was he now the innkeeper? No, wait, Will was the king.

Anya

said, "We don't think in a linear fashion so why should we live in a linear fashion?"

Tara

looked too much like his own mother ... *and my father left her not because she wanted more but because she wanted much more for herself and needed to expedite matters by finding herself posing nude for a man who would become her lover after Allen left...*, too, too much like his mother – flirty, flouncy auburn hair skirting, if it could, her moon face; and her skin was very cared for, illuminated to the depths by organic creams and facials and herbal infused steams. Then he blinked and she still looked like his mother looked when he was a boy, but her eyes were grey, not hazel, and she had a toned heft to her flirty body whereas Will's mother was thin, sometimes very thin.

The assertion that something belonged to me and it was silver...

She greeted him with the all too overused, "I've heard so much about you," and he thought, *How? Why?*

"Same here," he said.

"But not all good," she responded and before he could follow with another piece of small-talk cum greeting-cliché he realized in the aggressive winking of her response that the "not all good" was, in fact, about him.

Tara was sharply dressed in big, flared, flowing cream-colored pants and a snug silk shirt mostly unbuttoned; her hair tucked behind her ears and flowingly held at bay by the wide-rimmed sunglasses on top of her head. She drank a martini and seemed to know the man sitting to her right, who in turn seemed to know the woman sitting to his right at the bar.

No one else feigned interest in the dusty newcomer, but Tara more than made up for the slight of not being introduced properly. She ordered a drink for Will without asking what he wanted and then offered a toast, "To Anya."

To Anya.

Afflictions

Various Types of Tumors	Expected Survival
Glioblastoma multiforme	One year
Anaplastic astrocytoma	Two Years
Astrocytoma	Over seven years
Oligodendroglioma	Over six years
Mixed glioma	Over five years
Medulloblastoma	Nine years
Brain stem tumors	Nine months
Pineal region tumors	Five years

Tara

broke hard on yellow to red – there were cameras everywhere – and looked over the top of her leaden, Jackie O. sunglasses and smirked a smirk that said she knew that he was full of shit.

He *was* full of shit.

The bulk of her enormous Cadillac rocked to the rhythm of maximized cylinders.

She pulled into a gated industrial complex in Burbank.

Will's first time at a movie screening.

In a matter of minutes, the forty-seat theater filled to a chatty capacity with people who all knew each other and all dressed fashionably; but his paint-stained self didn't seem too out of place. Soon, he became the answer to the "Who is he?" question. When someone asked if the seat to his left was taken, he volleyed a few yeses and nos before Tara, leaning across his lap, nodded No.

Numbers filled the screen.

The countdown to extinction.

Hesse.

Wild head of windswept hair topped by a fur-lined hat and the camera pulled its focus to reveal Eva walking the streets of Washington Heights in New York City. Grainy, seedy and the scene – like an early seventies PBS Masterpiece Theatre external shot – in the middle of a winter day – no leaves on the trees and Eva wrapped in a tattered overcoat, stumbling, drunk and desperate and damaged. The image was impressive, if only for the fact that the film crew was capable of clearing blocks of New York City of people. The camera matched Eva's walking pace, joggled and jarring and dodgy, and the only sound was that of shoes on pavement seemingly dubbed into the soundtrack – crunchy, distant, and unmatching. As Eva progressed, someone, a vagrant, stepped out of a liquor store and yelled a syphilitic pun on her name, "Evil," and then a window opened and a painted mouth yelled her name, and then another person stepped out of a door, and then another, and another, all calling her name – or some play on her name – until the street, full of people, screamed her name. She continued, unfazed in her disorientation, specter-like.

The opening credits.

The film progressed with an irregular staccato of imbalances – beautiful images juxtaposed with the mundane, the art of making art versus the story of a woman beating back the conventions and the establishment, the story of desperation and depression modified by a husband's shadow, and a lot of images of the title character roaming the Bowery like a 60s version of Camille Claudelle. He remained absorbed by Eva making her art – the phallic, floppy, stranded symbolism of it all –; at least, he thought her desperation seemed real but he couldn't care less about her real life: her husband, separation, lover, family, breaking of tradition... the story suffered from plot – and just like Will's life, or any life, the dream in oddities, eccentricities, absurdities was preferable to reality.

The woman who portrayed Hesse performed well – stoic the neurotic (*I know her well; used to dance around a bonfire chanting her name*) – and her death by brain tumor was one of the better deaths by brain tumor scenes of recent memory (*I try not to laugh*) – a solemn, defeated face covering wild, agonizing eyes.

The end.

Overall, the weird silence of the film made it more poignant without the addition of a score.

After the movie, a woman, mid-thirties in clunky brown boots, tough-guy demeanor, breasts as pectorals through a blue oxford shirt, khaki pants, nerdy eyeglasses on a round face that mirrored the look of a young man, came over to Tara. Their conversation escaped Will – a conversation pariah – in its hushed tones but Tara then, for the first time that evening, introduced Will to someone, the screenwriter. Carly gripped his hand like a man and he found it disarming, emasculating... *and fucking sexy.*

"This is Will Schwartz. He's in a show over at Bergmont," Tara said. He wanted to correct her with "group show" – a show with faculty peers in the art department – but "Nice to meet you, Mr. Schwartz," Carly said. The "Mr. Schwartz" made him feel old. He said, "Will, same here. Your movie is really engaging."

"Will like in *Good Will Hunting*," she paused to assess him. "Engaging, huh? Thank you."

"The movie has taken some of my... eloquence," he said.

Tara smiled at him.

Will was both oblivious and obvious.

Eva

Hesse once wrote, "If I'm O.K., I will abandon restrictions and curbs imposed on myself. Not physical ones, but those restrictive tabs on my inner being, on solely myself. I will strip me of superficial dishonesties."

Tara

drove them to a French restaurant where she knew the host.

"So, now tell me. Honestly."

"Ah, the rub."

"I need a critical response. You're an artist and an educator. Tell me. Tell me what you think."

"I'm not much of a critic."

"Bullshit." She sipped her wine, "You're a fucking college professor."

BY BRIAN PHILIP KATZ

Over 637 kids have epileptic seizures after watching an episode of Pokemon.

"I teach art, Introduction to Studio Art. I'm only 27. I know nothing. Minimalism, Postminimalism, I know nothing. I honestly didn't understand the critiques I received for my graduate show. Just words."

"Okay then, as a member of the audience, what do you think?"

"I like it."

Will swirled his wine.

"No, you don't. I can tell."

"That's not true. I do like it."

"Can we stop with the simple, monosyllabic responses and move to a complex analysis. I've been nursing this idea since college and developed the script with Carly..."

"The screenwriter?"

"And I really wanted to capture the mind of the artist. Not just how she behaved but how she made art, how she was art. You know..."

"You chose a good example to reflect your ideas."

"She was driven and derided by her past, by Germany, and the form – her sculptures are all informed by her history and psyche and Jewishness. That is why I'm asking you."

"Again, I..."

"And your real opinion is...?"

"I thought that your dream images, your search for the soul of Eva and her art-making was innovative. It has that European cinema pastiche quality. It's the rest that I can't quite relate to. You review, too briefly, both her upbringing and the turning, the escape from the past, but you are relying on conventions of storytelling to tell a story about a person that isn't, wasn't, well, quite conventional."

"Less story, more soul."

"Depends on what you mean by 'soul.' But I really don't know. I mean, the visual things – I know the story, I think. That's what I'm talking about; and even so,... I suppose 'soul' like the Russian use of 'soul.'"

"'Russian soul?'"

"I suppose."

"'Less artifice and more art' I keep saying to myself," she said.

"And what does Carly think?"

"Too wrapped up in making Eva a feminist icon. I couldn't give a shit about making a feminist statement or turning her into an icon. I just want to tell a good story, make a good movie, try to do something original." She paused and looked into him and past him at the same time. "I hate all of this." Part of him suspected that she was drunk, but another part of him thought that her contacting him, her interest in his opinion based on Anya's review of his interests, his personality was that she, like her dinner guest, was struggling to find her voice; and no matter how trite the depiction of this search was, the same search that she tried to depict in her film, and no matter the language, the words used to describe the reason to wake in the morning, or lack of, they may have been kindred in their torture of exposition and desire to find a task to complete.

"Truffaut died of a brain tumor," she said.

"Who?"

"Fancois Truffaut. You know, *400 Blows*?"

Later that night Will would suffer a seizure and be diagnosed with a brain tumor. In the meantime, he will drink and begin to care less about his unavoidable diagnosis.

"Oh, and Bob Marley," she added.

Tara

's Cadillac made her appear smaller, but the heft of the car rumbling down Venice Blvd. also created the illusion of toughness, self-reliance. There was a masculine air to her performance as chauffeur and Will was drawn to her sense of control, this power of a little woman over a heavy machine. *Was this what Anya felt like when they met in college?*

He didn't even remember what he had for dinner, if he even ate, and her thin lips and Cheshire smile, painted wine with wine-stained teeth all moving to justify herself and her endeavor, instilled in him the want to kiss her, but kiss her quickly, as if he could steal something from her, and run like a child-thief from a deli.

When she drove down the alley and pulled up to his bungalow, she commented on the overgrowth of flora and maybe some vagrant fauna – his owner's cat – and the bags of mortar mix and the neat piles of bricks.

As he turned around to wish her a good night, her face, like a sun in front of his, kissed him, not passionately, not desperately, but lovingly as if he had known her for years.

Lifting her face, eclipsing the light of the neighbor's house across the alley, she kissed his eyes, his forehead.

"You're sweet," she said.

He closed the heavy door of her car, feeling the latch grab the bulk, and he smiled; he smiled for the first time in his life.

But he felt used.

Will

's first solo show in Los Angeles took place at a reasonably respectable little gallery not far from his house – a gallery not often used to showing sculpture, especially an extemporaneous hodgepodge of wood, brick, cement, plaster, glass, and anything else found and unfound.

"Gog, Magog, Golem, and Baal: Four Figures":

Will built the substructures from weathered 2 x 4s he stole from a construction site on Lincoln Blvd. and slabs of peeling plywood he bought from a surfboard shaper on Grayson Ave. He framed the forms in an impulsive fashion, allowing for the figures to develop naturally according to the pieces being placed and hammered and screwed together with his Makita drill – the first tool he ever bought with his own money. Skeletons bending, reaching, praying, prostrate, supine – he reinforced them with steel plates that he fashioned in the welding studio on campus and then ran a web of wire from one support to another. When the skeleton could stand on its own without any tested and visible weaknesses, he began to wrap diamond mesh lath around the bulk of the body and wove pieces of wire, bending and securing, within the cavities. The forms began to look like horrendous trees, abstracted beyond organic recognition. He coated the structures, inside and out, with a layer of cement and plaster and then pressed chips of brick and broken glass onto the wet surface, a bric-a-brac of abandoned pieces; and the four figures took shape. He complemented the "demons" with a dozen charcoal drawings based on the sculptures – large, disenfranchised shapes that moved in panicked smears off the long lengths of newsprint.

The review said, "While feeling somewhat dated in their masculinity, Schwartz's sculptures occupy the storefront gallery leaving little room to appreciate his illustrations. Despite the imposing, dangerous forms, there's something comforting about the fact that they're inanimate and unlikely to kill the viewer... unless they fall on you."

BY BRIAN PHILIP KATZ

Allen

overcame the burden of his responsibilities to ex-wife and ex-child and came for an afternoon visit – what was once supposed to be a weekend retreat for father and son – and reclined on what was once his couch and watched *The Wide World of Sports* on what was once his color television.

... Spanning the globe to bring you the constant variety of sports, the thrill of victory and the agony of defeat, the human drama of athletic competition, this is...

Playing in the den just to be near him, Will stacked his many Lego blocks until he created a little wall to hide behind.

Will

and Tara stood at the gates, three o'clock in the morning, and the dream reasserted itself:

She said, "I know you want to kiss me," and the truth was he really knew nothing else. She turned on the heels of her heavy London shoes and walked away; and over her shoulder she called out, "I'll see you soon," *the violent scraping of metal claws within the rusting pipes and the cursing of an electric drill hammering, yes, "hammering," the screw into the wood – the peeling whine of something not meant to fit...*

...there are men working – always men working – but they remain in the shadows as complexities unto my imagination, full-bodied ghosts wrecking the space and rebuilding brick by stupid brick until the box rises higher than the complex down the block

...and then the pain in my groin, behind my testicles, and the feeling that someone is putting all of their weight into violating a place on me, in me, of me that has no means to be violated...

...and then in the balmy return to base, the collision of sleep-

lessness and consciousness, I stumble from the building, alone, liberated, and in the field between the river and the brick façade, the robins guard the blades of grass in isolated perimeters mere feet apart from their neighbors, my sweat evaporates in the late March gusts of unaccepted early spring.

Bria

was a storyteller, but her son didn't always understand the point. When he asked what it all meant, she said, "Well, it takes two to tango."

Will

once tried to tape his penis into his pelvic ridge, pushing its circumcised, moon face into its turtleneck and securing the whole, little beast with clear strips of tape. The mad face pressed against the sticky barrier, a trick still up its sleeve, and a burning erection defied the cover and burst from its jacket.

He was six years old.
What's his excuse now?

Tara

said, "I met someone the other night that you know."
She had invited herself over and arrived with a magnum of champagne, Vuvee Clicquot, and a pungent, potted azalea.
"You did?"
"Someone you know intimately."
Initially doubting that it was someone he knew intimately – there was no one he could recall who knew him "intimately." Tara relished the idea that he had a history that she knew about

and that she knew someone he must've known well beyond the surface.

"Guess," she said.

"I have no clue."

"Want a hint?"

"No, just tell me who it is."

"Her first name ends in the letter 'a.'"

"You're kidding me, right?"

"'A.'"

"Okay, ah, Anya."

"Ah, so you know Anya intimately?"

"No, I mean, my god, no. She..."

"She's a lesbian and you're a boy."

"Yeah, and..."

"And I said, it's someone you know intimately, not me."

"Really, I don't have a clue."

"Begins with a 'D.'"

"Fuck, you're kidding me."

"Who is it?"

"Dana. Dana's in Los Angeles. I suppose that makes sense."

"I met her at a small soiree in West Hollywood. She came with this tall, spindly guy with a goatee."

"Fuckin' a."

"Actually, I was talking to him – he was just cast in a friend's movie, the friend who was throwing the party – when this cute brunette came over to reclaim her man. Well, one thing led to another and we both found out that we knew Anya – although it sounded like she hadn't spoken to Anya in forever – and then I asked if she knew you. I think she also said, 'Fuck, you're kidding me.'"

"Small world, no?"

"Can't escape it," he said.

Will

understood that there were many uses; every part of the beast had its purpose. The skin as leather; the hair as stuffing or woven into fabric; the bones ground into fertilizer; and the innards stewed for other lesser beasts' dinners.

There were moments when nothing was spared, nothing to waste; but then there were so many dead beasts, so many shaven carcasses that the storehouse behind the brick factory building could no longer contain the pieces.

Marta

knew how to knit before she learned how to read. Every evening for the entirety of her fourth year she sat with her *bubbeh* knitting lengths of scarves, drab stretches of tight rows of garter stitches, and the woven moss-stitched tubes that became hats when stitched into a knot on the top or sewed into a seam to create lengthy, bulky, heel-less socks that her *zeyda* would wear; and by the time she could read, Marta could fashion multicolored sweaters made of creams and browns and grays and reds and greens – circles piled on top of each other that changed course down the sleeves in a reverse pattern emulating the bulk of the body. Then, by the time she completed Louisa May Alcott's classic on her own, Marta was cabling complex cardigans and seamless gloves.

Here, in the den of her grandparent's apartment in Oranienburger Strasse, the apartment where both she and her younger sister were raised, Marta knit from childhood through youth to teens through *Kristallnacht* through an inability to attend university through the endless night of repeated thievery to recovery through pregnancy to the birth of her son and then the forced removal from her den as she tried to hold firm to the cliché of knitting outfits for her son who just days before was sent away with her sister and as she nearly pierced the soldier's cheek with her wooden needle and as the young man, no, boy, lifted the grip of his pistol to strike down the madwoman and her bulk of no consequence, and as the boy feigning soldier, swimming in parallel and horizontal lines, destroyed her in seconds of anger controlled by a burst of destiny – a destiny compounded by destinies of people – one fate at a million parts to that whole.

Anya

said, "All storms and stars are lost and nothing more or less at dawn."

Will

's hands had been burning since he was 19, the year he discovered cement and mortar and the calcium hydroxide, the lime, that helped to create the cohesion of the elements. It was the lime that burned and burned some more, but he was young and hardening and then accusing his obsession as the cause of his panic which was beginning to take shape in mid-night, mid-sleep anxiety attacks that sent him across the room, soaked in his sweat and gauging his temperature. There were times when more than something deep within said, "Build," build... and he did, not knowing what. He wrote, too; but he was always more comfortable building even if it wasn't art. But it was art to others and he was praised. He wanted to be a writer – stories were buildings too. Writing, however, was just a matter of that

– write or don't write. When he finished college and took a job as a set builder he stopped writing and didn't really build for the sake of building.

Like most male art students at the time, Will was drawn to the Macho Brigade of Judd, Serra, Caro and lesser-known sculptors like Irsherwood and Long. He wanted to build big, burly, industrial pieces that moved his bowels; and so he tried, to varying effect, to create his manhood.

At 19, he was given an early assignment by his sculpture teacher, a brother of one of the Macho Brigade. Instructions: Simple: make a leaning sculpture. Easy enough. He built a huge frame, aping the structures built to set sidewalk cement, laid a latticework of rebar as a substructure, and poured concrete, ten 100 lb bags of the stuff. Three days later, fully set, he took his 10' x 5' x 5" slab and leaned it against a wall in the student gallery. It took four friends to carefully place the cement piece in its leaning position.

When he returned the following morning, cup of coffee in hand, the weight of his cement wall had crashed through the gallery drywall crushing an exhibit of pottery on the other side. Cement chunks and jagged slices of plaster littered the floor and the metal rebar, almost fully exposed from about halfway up the facade, poked out like newly discovered dinosaur bones in sandstone. The dilapidation was far more beautiful and relevant than the polished piece – a ruin. Looking at the mess offered the same thrill he had as a child when he would build a wall, using all his beloved blocks, and then knock it down. Every childhood structure was built for the purpose of knocking it down.

Will lobbied the art department to let the piece remain and promised to build a new gallery wall after the art show. Fortunately, the potter whose work was also ruined, was too high to really care and laughed off the destruction.

BY BRIAN PHILIP KATZ

After college, Will became sick, had palpitations, thought he was having a heart attack, but he was only 22. Then graduate school made him an artist again... and gave him an artist's pain again. And he began to build more and learned more about building, more about technique.

* * *

In graduate school, Will discovered bricks and would raid abandoned lots and dumpsters for bricks that he would pile into the trunk of a friend's Subaru. No brick was too shoddy, too chipped to not be used; and many retained the brickmaker's name on one side. Will chose only the red, clay bricks that could fit in his hand, the basic, nominal modular size of 4 1/2" (width) x 3 1/2" (height) x 8" (length) – the standard soldier in the field of masonry, the common brick – and assigned those that retained their stamps to key positions in my structures. The stamps were as varied as the manufacturers: family names (Evans, Kane), names and initials of companies (Acme, Empire, Puritan, Star, H.C., R.U.S.C.S), places (Buffalo, Buffalo Clay, London), combinations of symbols and logos, and dates, the oldest of which he found in an abandoned lot in Yonkers, 1863.

* * *

Will had been building ruins his whole life and now he got to call it "Art."

* * *

Having not lobbied for renewal of his adjunct contract, Will was surprised to receive a phone call from the Art Department chair saying that they had a full time, temporary position as a replacement for someone who was either on sabbatical or retiring – it was vague as to whom Will was "temporarily replacing" and why he was being called upon above all the other viable, experienced, and, simply put, better adjunct instructors in the program.

"It's a one year contract."

"Benefits?"

"Health included," pause, "and your own advisees."

Knowing that just about everyone in the Art department was an adjunct instructor (only 11 of 47 instructors, including the chair, were tenured or tenure-tracked, four of whom were Emeritus – among the ivory-towered, an ancient Hollywood photographer, a well-known painter of photo-perfect realism, a conceptual artist who made soap, and a potter), Will couldn't believe his good fortune. Along with the yearlong position came his own bigger "office and studio space" and, he assumed, a computer. He was impressed with himself.

Chanie

wasn't looking for a lecture.

"I suppose that's what separates us," he said. "You believe that someone created life. I believe in the Big Bang and evolution – from lifeless energy came life force. All this stuff is alive with energy and moving, constantly moving." He grabbed two bricks, one in each hand as if he were lifting weights and presented a tan, porous block to Chanie.

"This is a universe, created like the universe of atoms, of matter, of fire, of stone – deep within this universe are infinite universes. For all we know, the future of cosmic beings relies on this brick."

Chanie, unfazed, said, "You looked like a savage standing there with your two stone tools. Now you sound like one too."

BY BRIAN PHILIP KATZ

Will

became Paul "Fred" Varjak, just more bloated; yesterday disconsolate, but today champion in white with a mink prowling the perimeter.

Tara screamed, "Let's celebrate!" into the phone with panic and anticipation and relief and commitment to drinking, drinking something good and getting loose and maybe even stoned, and aside from several teachers he had befriended – people to whom he could not brag to considering his upgrade and their more earnest plights – and Chanie, his orthodox "I'm not orthodox" Israeli student – *Why leave Israel? Why leave the Promise Land?* – who was probably preparing Shabbos this late Friday afternoon *This is really a put on, right; you're not really an orthodox Jew? No, I'm not. My family is. My father is a rabbi and a principal of religious studies at a yeshiva high school. He is a representative of Israel, a representation of why the young men should return to Israel for two years after they graduate. I'm not even a Zionist.* Tara was the only person, even after twelve months in the terrible polish that is Los Angeles, with whom he could revel. She said, "I was just thinking of you," when he called and followed with, "Hell yeah, I'll join you. Do you want me to make a res?" "How about just meeting at my house. I'll cook something." "You will, will you, Will?" And she agreed, and said she would be leaving her office in Santa Monica early and forsaking the traditional Friday night scene of industry parties and various happenings, all of which he had remained firmly oblivious to except for the screening of *Hesse* which, she informed Will the week before, had been accepted to Sundance. She said, "See you in a couple," and he realized that he had never been invited to her house in Beachwood Canyon.

Chanie

lived in mid-Wilshire; but aside from her father being a rabbi, that's all he knew of her home life. Circumstances would dictate that she was one of many siblings – many as in more than five – and probably a middle child, a forgotten child, considering that she was seeking a separation of self and attending university and lunching with her teacher four years her senior, and just about to kiss him, to lean over and kiss him with her lightly painted lips.

Will

stopped at Trader Joe's for some finger food and booze and facing the Friday blitz of blue people, he reached for a six-pack of some eclectic stout, the last six-pack of its kind, at the same time as a balding anti-cavalier hulk of a man. The beast looked at him with that "You got a problem" glare and snatched the beer from his reach.

Everything was rent asunder. You coward. You vermin. No appreciation of life. No sense of the future.

Will said, "Damn man, what's your fucking deal?" Crowds always bring out the worst in everyone – Will played into the hunger to confront.

"Fuck you," Hulk said under his breath as he turned his cart around in mid-aisle.

With the spark of flint that was about to make the best red-orange-blue flame black, Will pushed the man in the back as he walked away; the man stumbled a few steps forward while still holding onto his cart – his heft was superior to Will's thrust. Will was calling him out, but they never made it out. The man turned, a heap of useful flesh, and reached for Will's throat, but he dodged and Hulk grabbed Will's jacket collar and flung him into the pet food – a peculiar landing on kibble and cans and rawhide dog bones and rope toys. Will recovered as quickly as his shock would allow and two Hawaiian shirt-wearing employees, both men larger than Will but smaller than Hulk, grabbed the bull before he could charge. Fuming, every epithet in the *Oxford Dictionary of Inappropriate Words* that began in f, s, and c, burst forth from the man as he tried to muscle his way toward the now-frightened boy. *I once sat in dog shit, he said to Chanie. It was among the most embarrassing moments in my life. All the neighborhood boys and girls just pointed at me as I ran home covering my ass. "He sat in shit. Will sat in shit." They all screamed the obvious.* Another employee came and he was all but pinned to his position and Will, heeding the words of someone behind him, skirted his way around the rage, reached into the man's cart, extricated the six-pack as another surge mounted.

Placing a ten dollar bill on the Customer Service counter by the exit, Will walked out of the market with only his trophies – six dark tan bottles of a microbrew stout he had never drunk with labels depicting a smiling man with severe eyes and a halo above parted hair, dressed in a pin-striped suit holding a blood red pitchfork – and an exaggerated sense of victory.

Dark victory.

* * *

In a way, violent confrontations balance the fancy of extremes of self-isolation in Los Angeles, a city of enormous expanse and unreasonable layout. Will was a new breed of the antisocial, socializing dude: hermetic, yet in touch; sexually active, yet mostly with myself; unfashionable and unconscious; uncharismatic and removed; unintelligent and irresponsible – he knew that he was a mean-spirited ...

Spectre of his own visions, a nightmare within a nightmare;

but at least the ghost of his conscious self spoke to him in his sleep. *Will, behind that rusting door is the answer to your unasked question: Who made these brick buildings.* And he answered: "The, the, the very same people who, who diedin here. I mean, in here, here, here, here, and here. Will pointed everywhere...

Marta

was gassed with the same shit they used to kill lice. You see, the story is told over and over but nobody really talks about what's what. Dad died. She died. They all died. So, nobody knows. Not even the witnesses of extermination – they're always on the other side of the door with earnest fascination. Some were fascinated cowards, of course. Oh, but she was pretty, still pretty as a corpse, her breasts still firm despite having given birth. And her blue eyes... She had blue eyes? Her blue eyes exhibited no fear or darkness, looking beyond the pile... They were in a rush to kill at this point. Marta was still strong and lovely and would've lived if not for the panic of killing. Something to do with more Hungarian Jews, a large number, a city large. Coming to Vernichtungslagerville or Todeslageropolis. *He heard it called, "das Lager der Vernichtung." These are memories, not his own... Apart from being a part of the gassing operation, they marched in with them to alleviate the panic. Everyone panicked. Everyone feared the water. The water became the fog. The fog became death.*

Will doesn't have much more to say.

Tara

gently pulled Will's hand up her leg to the meeting of her thighs and whispered in his ear, "First base is not a kiss."

BY BRIAN PHILIP KATZ

Will

    's sense of victory retreated. There was too much to do. The phone rang and his mind flitted. There was always the expectation of news being bad, but the calming second wave of "What bad news could there be?" was beaten back by the idea that he was defeated waiting, waiting, waiting every other weekend for the phone to ring, for his father to be on the other side, to even hear an excuse that could validate the waiting; and he had been waiting for thirty-four years, every moment of thirty-four years, but back then he was in his late twenties, bent on overcoming his telephonaphobia, or phonophobia, and he turned the ringer on the handset to too loud. He didn't have reason, an anticipation of a call from someone important, to do this or that, but a premonition, or something akin to sensing something on the horizon, nudged him – things were about to change. When he flicked the little switch, he resigned to whichever fate – Klotho, Lekhesis, or Atropos – may have been in charge – the taut umbilical measuring more than the few feet from the wall to the cradle of phone, phone machine,.... *The phone will ring and he will want to answer it. And of his condition? Faith – a matter of constipation.* He said, "The phone will ring."

* * *

Someone placed a list of phobias and their definitions in Will's school mailbox. At first he thought the gesture was specific to his condition – a statement of sorts or perhaps a criticism; everything was about criticism and perhaps someone was taking a cheap shot. But he noticed that the pink flyer was placed in everyone's box and he sat at his desk, drank his weakly-brewed coffee from one of the campus cafes and read the small type covering both sides of the sheet. According to

said list and compounded by his already too prevalent hypochondria – can someone know that they're a hypochondriac and still be a hypochondriac? –, and in conclusion, this was his condition:
AndrophobiabogyphobiacancerophobiacardiophobiaclaustrophobiaclinophobiadementophobiaAnyaquoted,*MuchMadnessisDivinestSenseToadiscerningEyeMuchSensethestarkestMadness'TistheMajorityInthisasAllprevailAssentandyouaresaneDemuryou'restraightawaydangerousAndhandledwithaChain*hadephobiahelminthophobianovercaphobiaophthalmophobiaouranophobiapolyphobicjerkofftelephonophobiabecausesomeoneisgoingtocallandsaythatsomeonediedandhe'snotgoingtogiveashit

Tara

passed Will the remaining ember of her cigarette. "I haven't smoked a cigarette in years," he said as she poured another glass of champagne from the magnum that seemed to come with the package of her personality.

"I'm a bad influence," she said, "but you look like you need one," and before she could even light it with the fancy box of matches from one of her haunts she had him pinned to the only soft cushion in his place. He worked on the buttons of her blouse, but she, sitting on him, yanked her shirt and her bra off all in one motion – a seasoned pro. Her breasts were small, soft and pointed, and she hovered over him and they, in their natural response to the gravity of her position, reflected his returning pubescent disbelief. He moved his hands up the ridge of her back in filmic fashion, aping the romance of movie stars in chick flicks or 9 and 1/2 weeks – which he watched several times in succession in his teens –, but she plowed into him indifferent to the tenderness and grabbed his wrists and forced his hands above his head and her head and in a sadist fashion, she smiled, an evil smile, and he lost ego and sensation and pulled himself up enough to have his lips on her breast, but she pushed her chest into his mouth and dropped her full weight onto him, onto what was left of him.

Will

would like to say that his was a heroic endeavor: Odysseus returning from years at war, overcoming the wiles of enchanted, wicked women, and travels to get home to take Penelope firmly for the duration of the hero's prescribed roll in the hay; but he was more like a man who was released from state penitentiary. Everything worked, but worked like an eager, first day employee faced with months of probation.

Andere Vater

said, "Will, the only burning necessity is to burn necessities."

Will

wiped the sweat from his overworked brow and worked the perspiration through his hair. Chanie knew he was anxious, worried but she kept talking and his eyes kept searching the campus café for people to fear, shrieking ghosts, and the kid at the next table produced a nasal diatribe on Tolstoy: "Now about Ivan Illych and the cancer in his side, colon cancer, and the cancer is personified as a god and it talks to him, or so he thinks, but he is really talking to himself, finding the god of 'I.'" The cancer is his god *and, and my god? My god, look who is sitting across from me and all that I crave hovers twenty-five feet away, hidden specters haunting the brick buildings, over my shoulder, pitch-forked nemesis whispers dirty, nasty things to me like, "I think I'm falling in love with you." Save me... but don't you think this is a good time to make a split? There is only one truth and it is here, right here in front of you chewing on a piece of arugula. Can you see me? You think I've chosen you, but you've chosen me. Me? I chose me? Would you like another? Nod yes. These fingers are on my hand and this hand to this arm and this arm to this torso, but this is not my head, this is not my life. These are not my words. Marta is that you in there? You weren't good enough for the first wave of executions, always second string, and even though I am here and you suck, I love you son... son... I love you grandson sa – un, man, ssssssss. Are you listening?* and then she asked him a question and before he could answer, before he could imagine her perplexed response to his answer, before he could take in the absurdity of this recycled Hollywood experience, professor with student, before he could discern the sarcasm in her voice *he was on the little fucker like a bloody halo, my fist to his face, but he moves his head slightly and his mouth meets my swing and I can feel the crunch of my knuckles against his teeth. He stumbles backward, stirred and shaken, bruising the gin, reaches for his mouth to check that all his teeth are there, then looks at the bit of blood on his fingertips and passes out. It was a sucker punch, and not much of one at that and my knuckles are bleeding more than his face. Tara ignores him entirely and determinately walks up to me and slaps me with brute force, my ear rings a terminal feedback. With my bleeding hand I reach for my face, but Tara grabs my hand, pulls me toward her, and in full view of* Chanie smiled at him.

"You're miles away."

"It's just that I'm the teacher here."

"I suppose."

"And you're twenty-three years old."

"Twenty-four next month."

"Twenty-four."

"Twenty-four."

"What's the difference in age? A few years? My father is ten years older than my mother?"

Father? Mother?

"I'm your teacher," and then Ingrid, a painting instructor, slipped into view holding a cup of coffee. She nodded at Will approvingly and he prepared to excuse himself. *She turned and grunted at Chanie and made a gesture as if to slap her but Chanie defiantly stepped forward to meet her face as Ingrid held back another swing.* Ingrid attended to the line of students leaving the café and he finally excused himself, recused himself, helping himself to his feet and the woman, the girl, the young woman, the students looked up at him, a confused angel, those dark eyes like flaming hosts *and she screamed, "I can't believe you fucking punched me."* He left.

"Are you angry at me?"

"You're a religious woman; I'm an atheist."

"You assume... but we would both be on the same train," she responded.

Kathy

, a Freshman in his Introduction to Sculpture class, welded two enormous loops out of scrap metal and called the sculpture "Earrings." She had no interest in explaining the title after being queried by one of her classmates. Despite the warm, too warm, temperature in the studio, Kathy kept her denim jacket on proudly displaying patches and bumper stickers of punk and hardcore bands – bands he was listening to over a decade ago when he was her age: Murphy's Law, D.O.A., Agent Orange,

Cro Mags, Agnostic Front, Minor Threat, Minutemen, and the Black Flagg bars. *The adolescent fever lights no moon, sends no meteor, snuffs no star; but mention the book, the book, the book and the laws become obsolete and no boy, no girl bends whose modesty modifies his/her appearance under Hashem.* But her jacket with its various, outdated yet newly hip labels didn't fool him. Her black Converse high tops didn't fool anyone. Her arms remained covered, and her skirt, her prickly, black skirt, covered most of her legs and safety pins created a lattice along the hem. She seemed to be saying in her pouty, Hellenistic manner, "Criticism is bullshit," and he didn't all too much disagree with her. He tried to shift the rhetoric of art to a more organic level of review – a language suited to the makers of art, not the writers on art, the critics; and he believed, and still does, that artists ought not be leveled by soundbytes *sound bites* but by genuine constructs – emotions, the medium's output, the tools, design, and perceived intent. Criticism is for non-makers, wannabes, rhetoricians, not for artists, not for neophytic creators of stuff, of scenes, of life, of man in nature. So, he told the class, in a state of self-imposed humour of self and situation, that the earrings actually hang in space from the head of god and one kid, a Larry if he'd ever known one, said, "god doesn't wear earrings."

"Are you sure? Is this a Judeo-Christian God?"

"It would have to be if she intended such," said another Larry.

"Why's that?" he asked.

"I mean, look at her, she's obviously Jewish," he answered and Kathy cringed and then scowled and then Will feared for Larry.

"You don't know that," Kathy almost growled.

"Well then, my fucking mistake," Larry said, and Will asked, "Why the hell can't god wear earrings?"

Kathy turned and said, "If these are earrings of a Jewish god, he can't wear them because he's Jewish; but they're not earrings of god they're just big, fucking earrings."

Will brought a picture of Buddha with his enormous, pierced lobes to the next class but Kathy was absent. Kathy, with her angry mousy moon face, never returned.

I

am the adopted child of St. Stephen of Hungary, patron saint of bricklayers; a bastardized version of a bricklayer, I am still making sculptures of brick, but now I make my own bricks. At first, when I moved to Los Angeles, I learned from a Mexican contractor, a man more versed in the history of native bricklaying than I in just about everything I've ever done combined, how to make Adobe bricks.

"It would be my pleasure, man," he said in perfectly Spanish-tinged English when Will called. A photographer in the Art Department recommended him and gave Will his number. He'd worked on her house.

They met at a storefront office on the otherside, the farside, of Sunset near Dodgers Stadium. Bags of mortar mix, cement, and clay and sand spilled their contents all over the cement floor and his bodega windows looked like they had been washed with plaster. Several short, muscular Mexicans in baseball hats milled about, and Mondo, a man of his name, met Will at the door.

"You want to learn how to make bricks?" he asked.

"I want to learn how to make bricks," he said.

"Well, let's see," he said as he looked him over. He reached out for Will's forearm. "Need to work on your streng't," he said. "Practice your mixin'."

He went behind his counter, the cleanest surface in the

shop, and procured a large, sandy stone. "You start with this simple brick. Like Adobe."

"Hector," he called to one of his foot soldiers, "Hector, set 'im in back, show him sand."

Behind the shop were more stacks of bags, and in a courtyard that severely outsized the size of his shop, columns of standard red bricks piled on pallets, platforms of bricks lay drying in the sun, and mounds of sand of varying browns and grays and carbon, men shoveled various mixes into large, black plastic tubs and barely mechanized mixers; and two large kilns with half-sized iron doors open to their cooling contents, looked, just seemed, as illegal as the men milling about.

Hector never said a word and pointed Will to a cask of fermenting sand and liquid. He held his fists out and pantomimed a churning like a milkmaid.

Will churned for an hour until Mondo returned, "You come back and micks for me everyday for one week and then we make bricks. Okay?"

Nothing about this felt authentic, and despite all the stoic faces on all the workers, Will got the sense that the joke was on him. But every day, for one week, he came and turned sand and water into thicker sand and water.

On the eighth day, after an afternoon faculty meeting, Mondo handed Will $10. "Go and buy as much beer as you can" and he pointed to a bodega across the street. Will bought two six packs of Tecato and chipped in another $20 and bought a six of Heineken and a six of Bud Tall Boys. When he returned, the store was empty and he went straight to the back where some redundant jingling and drumming muffled through the piles. Hector was the first to meet Will and he took the beer, patted him on the back, and all of a sudden all the men seemed taller, much taller. The Heinekens went around followed by the Buds and Will was left with a brown bottle of Tecate.

Ingredients

1. Measuring cup (a tin can will do)
2. Mud, preferably fine grain
3. Sand *He surreptitiously filled sacks of Malibu Beach on midweek nights.*
4. Water

Directions

Make a mixture of approximately 4 cans of fine mud and 1 can of sand. Mix together. Add water to make a mud ball. Play with the mixture until you can make a ball that will stick together and not crack. Tightly pack the mud mixture into a shoe box. Move the box to a sunny place and turn over. Remove the shoe box and let the mixture dry in the sun for 3 or more days.

* * *

Winning, preparation, moulding, drying, burning... when I was a boy my mother took me to Brooklyn to go clothes shopping at a store in Brownsville run by German Jews; and I remember this because the men and women working the store had those numbers tattooed on their arms – numbers like bricks on their arms – and thick, Yiddishy accents and referred to me as boychik *and* bubelah. *The clothes were cheap and the little that Allen gave my mother for child-support went further in this store as my mother combed through boxes of denims and corduroys and underwear and tee-shirts usually with the help of a gruff little pince-nezed man with one of those enormous Karl Malden* schnozzes, *donning a cap on, not a yarmulke, and nudging me with his cloth measuring tape while a woman of almost equal stature and appearance as the man probed the other end of the box.*

My mother, the goy with her halfling son, left with more items for me than money spent, "Mensches *all,*" *my mother said,* "Mensches *all.*"

Brick

brick brick
brick brick brick brick brick brick brick brick brick brick
brick brick brick brick brick brick brick brick brick brick
brick brick brick brick brick brick brick brick brick brick
brick brick brick brick brick brick brick brick brick brick
brick brick brick brick brick brick brick brick brick brick
brick brick brick brick brick brick brick brick brick brick
brick brick brick brick brick brick brick brick brick brick
brick brick brick brick brick brick brick brick brick brick
brick brick brick brick brick brick brick brick brick brick
brick brick brick brick brick brick brick brick brick brick
brick brick brick brick brick brick brick Anya brick brick brick
brick brick brick brick brick brick brick brick brick brick
brick brick brick brick brick brick brick brick brick brick
brick brick brick brick brick brick brick brick brick brick
brick brick brick brick brick brick brick brick brick brick
brick brick brick brick brick brick brick brick brick brick
brick brick brick brick brick brick brick brick brick brick
brick brick brick brick brick brick brick brick brick brick

BY BRIAN PHILIP KATZ

brick brick brick brick brick brick brick brick brick brick brick
brick brick brick brick brick brick brick brick brick brick brick
brick brick brick brick brick brick brick brick brick brick brick
brick brick brick brick brick brick brick brick brick brick brick
brick brick brick brick brick brick brick brick brick brick brick
brick brick brick brick brick brick brick brick brick brick brick
brick brick brick brick brick brick brick brick brick brick brick
brick brick brick brick brick brick brick brick brick brick brick
brick brick brick brick brick brick brick brick brick brick brick
brick brick brick brick brick brick brick brick brick brick brick
brick brick Marta brick brick brick brick brick brick brick brick
brick brick brick brick brick brick brick brick brick brick brick
brick brick brick brick brick brick brick brick brick brick brick
brick brick brick brick brick brick brick brick brick brick brick
brick brick brick brick brick brick brick brick brick brick brick
brick brick brick brick brick brick brick brick brick brick brick
brick brick brick brick brick brick brick brick brick brick brick
brick brick brick brick brick brick brick brick brick brick brick
brick brick brick brick brick brick brick brick brick brick brick
brick brick brick brick brick brick brick brick brick brick brick
brick brick brick brick brick brick brick brick brick brick brick
brick brick brick brick brick brick brick brick brick brick brick
brick brick brick brick brick brick brick brick brick brick brick
brick brick brick brick brick brick brick brick brick brick brick
brick brick brick brick brick brick brick brick brick brick brick
brick brick brick brick brick brick brick brick brick brick brick
brick brick brick brick brick brick brick brick brick brick brick
brick brick brick brick brick brick brick brick brick brick brick
brick brick brick brick brick brick brick brick brick brick brick
brick brick brick brick brick brick brick brick brick brick brick
brick brick brick brick brick brick brick brick brick brick brick
brick brick brick brick brick brick brick brick brick brick brick

UNDERWATER EYES

brick brick brick brick brick brick brick brick brick brick brick
brick brick brick brick brick brick brick brick brick brick
brick brick brick brick brick brick brick brick brick brick
brick brick brick brick brick brick brick brick brick Tara
brick brick brick brick brick brick brick brick brick brick
brick brick brick brick brick brick brick brick brick brick
brick brick brick brick brick brick brick brick brick brick
brick brick brick brick brick brick brick brick brick brick
brick brick brick brick brick brick brick brick brick brick
brick brick brick brick brick brick brick brick brick brick
brick brick brick brick brick brick brick brick brick brick
brick brick brick brick brick brick brick brick brick brick
brick brick brick brick brick brick brick brick brick brick
brick brick brick brick brick brick brick brick brick brick
brick brick brick brick brick brick brick brick brick brick
brick brick brick brick brick brick brick brick brick brick
brick brick brick brick brick brick brick brick brick brick
brick brick brick brick brick brick brick brick brick brick
brick brick brick brick brick brick brick brick brick brick
brick brick brick brick brick brick brick brick brick brick
brick brick brick brick brick brick brick brick brick brick
brick brick brick brick brick brick brick brick brick brick
brick brick brick brick brick brick brick brick brick brick
brick brick brick brick brick brick brick brick brick brick
brick brick brick brick brick brick brick brick brick brick
brick brick brick brick brick brick brick brick brick brick
brick brick brick brick brick brick brick brick brick brick
brick brick brick brick brick brick brick brick brick brick
brick brick brick brick brick brick brick brick brick brick
brick brick brick brick brick brick brick brick brick brick
brick brick brick brick brick brick brick brick brick brick

BY BRIAN PHILIP KATZ

brick brick brick brick Allen brick brick brick brick brick brick
brick brick brick brick brick brick brick brick brick brick brick
brick brick brick brick brick brick brick brick brick brick brick
brick brick brick brick brick brick brick brick brick brick brick
brick brick brick brick brick brick brick brick brick brick brick
brick brick brick brick brick brick brick brick brick brick brick
brick brick brick brick brick brick brick brick brick brick brick
brick brick brick brick brick brick brick brick brick brick brick
brick brick brick brick brick brick brick brick brick brick brick
brick brick brick brick brick brick brick brick brick brick brick
brick brick brick brick brick brick brick brick brick brick brick
brick brick brick brick brick brick brick brick brick brick brick
brick brick brick brick brick brick brick brick brick brick brick
brick brick brick brick brick brick brick brick brick brick brick
brick brick brick brick brick brick brick brick brick brick brick
brick brick brick brick brick brick brick brick brick brick brick
brick brick brick brick brick brick brick brick brick brick brick
brick brick brick brick brick brick brick brick brick brick brick
brick brick brick brick brick brick brick brick brick brick brick
brick brick brick brick brick brick brick brick brick brick brick
brick brick brick brick brick brick brick brick brick brick brick
brick brick brick brick brick brick brick brick brick brick brick
brick brick brick brick brick brick brick brick brick brick brick
brick brick brick brick brick brick brick brick brick brick brick
brick brick brick brick brick brick brick brick brick brick brick
brick brick brick brick brick brick brick brick brick brick brick
brick brick brick brick brick brick brick brick brick brick brick
brick brick brick brick brick brick brick brick brick brick brick
brick brick brick brick brick brick brick brick brick brick brick
brick brick brick brick brick brick brick brick brick brick brick
brick brick brick brick brick brick brick brick brick brick brick

brick brick brick brick brick brick brick brick brick
Chanie

Will

's red wine, face-slapped hangover was exacerbated by the continued ringing in his ears – "Tinnitus," one of his university doctors said – and the bounding of his heart, a coronary thud he thought he lost months ago, surging in his ears. He couldn't even take comfort in watching Tara sleeping next to him, the sheet, the lone white sheet, drawn down her back and he thought, *She is lost to me until, at the soonest, Sunday while she performs her daughterly duties and attends to her father.*

And what of her father? Did he suspect that his daughter had feelings for her Introduction to Studio Art teacher, a half-Jew with a self-hating Jew for a father, and an S.S. soldier for a grandfather.

The weight of his head had the effect of a buoy – an out-of-place mass perched atop the water in a manner both hideous and earnestly effective in the most ineffective manner. The rest of his body, the anchor beneath the waves dropping through the still waters running too deep, tingled with the anticipation that he was about to have a heart attack even though he was too young, in reasonably good shape, and not a smoker.

Tara slept, or at least she seemed to sleep but he wouldn't have doubted that she was faking. *My hand, while nursing the throbbing of my right arm, fills in the grade bubble – after some consideration I've decided to give Chanie an A...* And then he finally fell asleep, arm numbed beyond attachment to his body, and in his dream he walked through piles of brick dust. *Yoo hoo, that's ash. How about some juice?*

Tara stood dressed, arms folded across her chest, "I have to go." She looked like she had been drinking – squinty and ruddy; last night's pressed shirt rumpled – but she may have been angry or nervous.

"How long have I been... what time is it?"

As he started to climb out, she dropped her arms and pushed him back into bed. "It's early," she whispered.

Allen Ivan Schwartz broke no new ground and did nothing spectacular but made some good money, paid for his son's education, turned the air conditioning up to high on balmy days and the heat higher in February. His first marriage was a failure and his second marriage failed and he moved on.

She came right up to his face, extending a clownish mug.

"You're a fucking asshole. Look at me!"

All too quickly, the tinnitus increased.

"Did you feel that?" he asked.

She held onto his arm as the wave moved through.

Everything shifted but the experience was unlike the earthquake exhibit they had seen at the Natural History Museum – nothing rattled; everything leapt and they, in bed, rode the swell.

When it ended, she went to kiss him but bit his lip instead and the laying on of wax, fiberglass, latex, painted rope, papier Mache, enamel, plaster, weights and woman, otherworldly woman leaned against the wall next to a fiberglass tube, pants and panties at her ankles, arms outstretched, shirt pulled up around her neck, hair chopped short and shaved on the left side revealing a scar of recently plucked off stitches, and she sang too without opening her mouth, "I seem to recognize your face/ Hauntingly familiar/I can't seem to place it." That last piece, the last work of her living career, employed assistants... there are assistants everywhere but not an impression of them on the work.

* * *

"This is not a kosher meal," he said to Chanie who flipped through an art book while sitting on his couch. He offered to pour her a glass of merlot. She accepted.

"Spaghetti and meatballs," he said and she remained in the book.

His mother's copy of *The Fannie Farmer Cookbook* remained open on the counter next to the little oven. Italian tomato sauce on page 298, meatballs on page 170, garlic bread on page 325, and a tossed green salad on page 272.

Chanie sipped her wine and slipped between kind of blue and moving into the underground clearing the background palate and she ate a piece of cheese and he knew that she knew that they were to eat meatballs and he wondered if she would, in fact, eat the meatballs being that he was still unsure of her religious adherence; and then there was a moment before opening the second bottle of wine when he felt more Jewish than she being that he was visibly concerned about his nonKosher cuisine. He watched her slip into a selflessness, an emotionally-realized individual, sensitive and loving, with each sip and each bite of cheese.

He felt like an infidel and wanted to confess his sin.

"Are you ready for a bowl of pasta?"

"Anytime."

"Meatball?"

"Sure, please."

Treyf.

"One or two?"

"One is fine, thank you."

"Parmigiano?"

"Let me taste it first."

"Spoon?"

"No thanks."

"The pasta is al dente."

"That's fine."

"I hate mushy pasta."

"That's fine," and she twirled a few strands around her fork and removed a piece of meatball that had settled in a pool of sauce along the side of the handmade, ceramic bowl – a bowl made by a college girlfriend of his.

She ate the pasta and the meatball and said, "Sure, I'll try some of that cheese," and he passed the bowl with the grated cheese – a different kind of bowl, not handmade, that he found in the kitchen cabinets when he first moved into his garage apartment. Not his own bowl. The house's bowl.

She sprinkled a little cheese and took another bite.

"You're smiling a lot. This is very unlike you," she said and he realized that he had been.

"Should I frown?" he asked. "Feign stoicism?"

"No, just not used to you smiling. You always seem worried, distracted."

"I'm sorry."

"For being happy. That's silly."

"I'm happy you're here."

"I'm glad that I bring you happiness. You deserve it."

He no longer had anything in him that remotely echoed of guilt or sorrow or fear. He wanted to tell her about Tara. He wanted to tell her that he still pined for a lesbian. She moved over on the couch, closer to where he was sitting. "You don't mind, do you," she said – not a query – and she leaned into him, her leg next to his khaki pants – her soft, Jewish leg; and she placed her bowl of pasta on the floor.

His face reflecting in the glasses over her grey eyes, he saw himself and he saw that he was better looking than he last remembered.

I want to vomit.

She pulled him closer without touching him and he could

smell the two bites of pasta on her breath – the hint of garlic, the basil, the wine staining her teeth, and mint, lots of toothpaste mint; and she kissed him, reached deep into his mouth. He was eating mints. His hand touched her unpierced ear, her cold cheek, and her hair, all that beautiful hair, falling ringlets escaping the past.

Where is the humor in all of this?
Step forward, monster. Step forward.

Her demeanor was different. Something was missing from her. He could lament his behavior of the past two nights but he didn't. She stood naked, her back to him. *There have been lots of backs.* He stroked the soft fuzz of her unshaven leg. She put on her panties – simple, white panties – and turned around, tufts of pubic hair poking out.

"I'm going," she said softly. "I should go." She remained topless, the heft of her breasts, her healthy, young breasts, held a heavy confidence.

"It's almost five in the morning," Will protested, "Stay."
Stay.
"I don't think so."

He wanted to ask if he had done something wrong.

"Don't worry," she said to him as she pulled on her sweater, "we're fine."

And all that remained was the tossed about sheets on her side of the bed. She did not leave like she had left before, before he broke every rule in the book, with a kindness in her gait and the promise tomorrow.

She was gone.

"This is not the end," he said to himself.
This is not the end.
I love her.
Who?
Her, god damnit, her.

* * *

"Anya is coming to LA next week," he told her.

"I know," she said.

"I knew you'd know, but I have a little something else to talk about," and he hung up the phone.

Brick buildings like teeth with cavities.

Allen

was the Battalion Maintenance Officer in Vietnam – a job usually commandeered by a Major; but being in wartime and shorthanded the position was issued to him when he left officer's school and accepted a promotion to first lieutenant. When describing his job to his son, six-year-old Will, he referred to it as being the chief Jeep mechanic. His soldiers were an elite group, every one functioning in perfect unison with the other, as they repaired and rebuilt the various vehicles and artillery. Will had this vision of them swooping in out of the swamps like an organized damage control unit, fixing tires in the middle of gun fights, jump-starting tank engines wherever tank engines were. Men who put their lives on the line for machines.

Why can't I be a machine?

* * *

"Dad," Will began, "Dad, Jimmy said I was gay. He said, 'You're gay.'"

"Well, maybe you are."

Carla

was far, far removed from her first bullish appearance,

lipstick, hair in a softer crop, wearing a flower-print dress that swayed, sashayed, and she seemed more daisy or azalea in a vase than white carnation on a lapel. She was the feminine twin of herself. She came up and took Tara's hand in a gentle, romantic manner, "We have a lot to celebrate," and led her to the other end of the bar, miles away from Will's sense of celebration. Tara looked back, forlorn, a listless reluctance to leave the side of one lover for a new one. So, Will followed. He followed her around for two days. He did.

Allen

said, "Okay Bebop, we're almost to the Cape," and Will responded in a deadpan seriousness, antsy from the long drive, "Now all we have to do is get to the Cod."

Dana

was taller than he remembered; taller in high heels than the heels she wore before – heels he couldn't really remember her ever wearing. Back then, she existed in Converse All-Stars, black high tops and white low-tops. She wore boots in winter – hand-me-downs from her wealthily married sister who bought handmade work boots from a cobbler in Oregon – but never wore high heels. Will wondered if she were now, cosmetically longer than he was as she hugged him as if he were a soiled infant – arms out, squinting.

Tara

exhaled relief and waved her hand in a "Come here." He reached out and she pulled him through the social wall of bar patrons. Her hand was still in Carla's hand, and her other hand was in his, a troika of perversion of infinite possibilities.

Tara yanked her hand from Carla's grasp and threw herself at Will with an "I'm sorry" and a kiss.

"I still want to talk to you," he said, toning his angst to *meh*, taken by her display of affection.

"Later. For now, let's just drink."

She picked up the conversation they weren't having, "... and it looks like we're almost finished. I have an edit that I really love, less plodding, more to your tastes. I would really love to show it to you."

A woman in a blue pantsuit muscled between Tara and Will to get to her appletini.

"I don't understand why you want a layman's opinion. I don't know a damn thing about movies."

"You're a broken record. Remember records?"

"Being with you is like being in a tornado of non sequiturs."

"Have a drink," she sang. "Oh, just have a damn drink."

"No, I don't want one. I have to go and get Anya from the airport."

"Stay with me."

Carla returned and leaned into Tara as if she were holding her upright. Her short hair threw a shadow across her forehead making her look as if she was wearing a baseball cap. They both stared at Will with an impunity.

Carla then threw her arm around Tara's shoulders with a mix of intimacy and opinion that put Will on the defensive.

He almost asked, "What's going on here?" but there was no discernible treatise between the three that outlined each other's sexual agenda, and if anything, he wanted to break it off with Tara.

Tara nuzzled into the fold of Carla's arm – a wounded drill-sergeant.

The blue pantsuit wedged past, carrying her drinks, and shrugged an "I understand what you're going through" shrug.

Will

sat across from Chanie and imagined the possibilities: *What if I were younger? What if I were Jewish? What if I were?*

Chanie

met Will at a cheap steakhouse on Lincoln Boulevard -- the kind of place to have a deep conversation while sitting on cracked, beige Naugahyde seats under smoky lights.

Chanie dressed conservatively – all of her sexuality was masked from the neck down except for a length of forearm in her three-quarters sleeves on this warm summer night. Her clothing signified the distance between the two. But he knew what was underneath.

"You look awful," she said.

"I haven't been sleeping."

She reached across the table and touched his hand.

A pie-faced waitress with dyed black hair and a perky, pinched smile asked Chanie if she wanted a drink. She looked at Will's beer and said, "Yes."

"I'm corrupting the youth."

"You know what I'm talking about. I'm not going to fail to express my feelings for you."

"Huh?" he lied.

"That would be interesting. All I know about you is this ridiculous sense of loneliness that you wear like a badge and that lascivious way you look at me when I enter a room," and she pointed to the door.

"I can't win," he said.

"Do you hear yourself? When I first saw you the very first day I walked into your class, I felt bad for you. You weren't much older than me and yet you were more distant, more removed socially than a man fifty years older. You were not a loser but the way you moved, talked, wrote, all of it was infused with a futility wrapped in self-effacing humor... But it was this person, this sad, pathetic person, that I felt a connection to. You can't win because you can't see the person offering you a chance. Not everything comes in the form of something material or verbal. Can't you tell?" Her face flushed and her eyes, so brown they were black, began to tear.

"Can't you tell?" she asked loudly, tears falling, diners pausing, waitresses pivoting.

"What?"

"I really love you and this is your last chance to really love me in return. No words. Action," and with that an explosion, a heave, a choke.

Will's body, rigid and lifeless.

"See," she accused with her hand out for alms. "See?"

She slid out of the booth. All the open faces watched her leave and when the glass door closed, mouths agape and full, eyes burning with insinuation turned to Will, the stinking bum who couldn't see the soap from the dirt.

Will

's new construction, the first to be built with bricks that he made by hand, towered over him like an enormous davening Jew.

Allen

imagined what it must've been like to have needles stuck in

his eyes -- he imagined the pop pop, as pins pierced the film of the surface of his eyes.

His aunt, his adopted mother, often talked about her grandfather, her *Andere Vater*, and once described his fading blue eyes, his glaucoma, and the pain of needles being stuck into his eyes.

"They would hurt so much, but he kept on smiling, never frowning, never complaining... Andere Vater's eyes."

Allen, as a boy, heard, "Underwater eyes."

Ghosts

feed off the imagination – ardent specters of thoughts, head chatter that gets the best of the sleepless, restless patron of intoxicants. Nothing has really changed for Will. His anxiety wasn't commanding his midnight attention, his once and former impending coronary episodes were a failed mission of a recent, unknown past – ghosts knocking at the soul's door to get in, "It's cold out here."

Were there crickets in Auschwitz?

There's a burgundy darkness and everyone is too cold and too hot and often both at the same time...

Marta

moved carefully through the day/night, seeking a momentary reprieve from the bombardment of hate and its many forms – self, external, imposed, transposed, clacking, steaming, frigid, naked, damned and oh so damned.

ABOUT THE AUTHOR

Brian Philip Katz, a poet and experimental filmmaker, wrote and directed the award winning films, Roman Buildings, "The ABC Conjecture," and "Noether." He is the co-director of the Creative Writing Program at CUNY Kingsborough.

Running Wild Press publishes stories that cross genres with great stories and writing. RIZE publishes great genre stories written by people of color and by authors who identify with other marginalized groups. Our team consists of:

Lisa Diane Kastner, Founder and Executive Editor
Mona Bethke, Acquisitions Editor, Editor, RIZE
Benjamin White, Acquisitions Editor, Editor, Running Wild Press
Peter A. Wright, Acquisitions Editor, Editor, Running Wild Press
Rebecca Dimyan, Editor
Andrew DiPrinzio, Editor
Cecilia Kennedy, Editor
Barbara Lockwood, Editor
Cody Sisco, Editor
Chih Wang, Editor
Pulp Art Studios, Cover Design
Standout Books, Interior Design
Polgarus Studios, Interior Design
Nicole Tiskus, Production Manager
Alex Riklin, Production Manager
Alexis August, Production Manager

Learn more about us and our stories at www.runningwildpress.com

Loved these stories and want more? Follow us at www.runningwildpress.com, www.facebook/runningwildpress, on Twitter @lisadkastner @RunWildBooks @RizeRwp

ABOUT RUNNING WILD PRESS